"...on a daily basis, a cowboy goes off into the world of cow-care on horses, four-wheelers and in pickups to deal with animals weighing more or less a thousand pounds. While yon cowboy doesn't aim to get kicked, gored, snake-bit, bucked off or otherwise damaged, stuff happens." Gwen Peterson

Chapter One

Chris Jenkins had been the top-ranked barrel racer on the pro rodeo circuit for three years. In a sport dominated by men riding bulls and bucking broncos, she'd managed to carve out her own fan following, with over five thousand Twitter followers, mostly girls who wanted to emulate her success while riding a beautiful palomino horse with its white mane and tail flying in the wind. As with any online thing, there were also the creeps, and no week went by without some cowboy proposing marriage or posting a highly inappropriate picture of himself. Luckily, she'd never run into any of them in more than passing. Not until today.

In Denver, she'd collected another belt buckle, the rodeo equivalent of a trophy, along with a prize check. After packing up her tack and loading Stoli, her five-year-old gelding, into the trailer, she was ready to climb into her pickup when she felt a hand on her elbow. The middle-aged cowboy standing behind her was drunk, dusty, and sweaty. His smile highlighted his missing

The Last Rodeo

Doug Fletcher mysteries book 12

Dean L. Hovey

Print ISBNs
Amazon Print 9780228624233
LSI Print 9780228624240
B&N Print 9780228624257

BWL Publishing Inc.

Books we love to write ...
Authors around the world.

http://bwlpublishing.ca

Dedication

To Larry and Nancy Mohr

Acknowledgement

As always, there is a group of people who deserve credit for helping mold my manuscripts into an engaging story with a minimum of mistakes. Julie reads the first draft of each book, offering opinions and correcting medical situations and terminology.

Deanna Wilson, my horse and cop resource, read numerous pieces of manuscript, often out of context. By tapping her life experience, I was able to insert critical details that added texture and depth to the story.

Mike Westfall, Clem MacIlravie, and Fran Brozo read manuscripts, offered opinions and corrections, steering me to this final version. Natalie Lund and Anne Flagge proofread manuscripts, catching my numerous typos and other errors.

Many thanks to Jude Pittman of BWL for her editing, guidance, and support.

upper front teeth, exposing the tip of his tongue.

"You wanna grab a beer?" he asked.

Not wanting to alienate a fan, she smiled, but shook her head. "Sorry, I've got to hit the road. I'm competing in the Belle Fourche July 4th rodeo, and I've got a couple days of hard driving to be there on time."

Apparently trying to come up with a pick-up line, the cowboy spit a stream of tobacco juice into the grass. "Well, maybe I'll catch you there. I'm running the gate for the bull riders."

Chris put on her corporate smile, the one featured on her Facebook page. "Maybe."

She climbed into the cab and locked the doors before setting her white Stetson on the passenger seat. After starting the engine, she checked her mirrors and saw the cowboy's reflection staring at her. His smile had become more of a leer, and it raised the hairs on the nape of her neck. She slipped her hand into the console and touched the butt of her Glock pistol.

"I guess you're the reason I got that concealed-carry permit."

* * *

Through the wonder of computer analysis, human resources job title sorting, and the National Park Service Inspector General, it had been determined that Jill and I were being underutilized. Our job description as National Park Service Investigators had bugged out when cross-referenced with our assignment at Padre Island National Seashore. Jill's immediate response to the news that we were about to be reassigned to the NPS Investigative Services Branch, and reporting to a new supervisor was met with a knee-jerk reaction. "Let's retire." After my reassurances that we might find our new assignment interesting, especially the prospect of digging into cold cases, she'd agreed to a six-month trial. In return, I agreed to consider the option of moving to Spearfish, South Dakota where her parents and my mother live, and where we own a pair of horses.

Our parents have never been frail, needy people, but a series of health crises had us on the phone with them too often. Our discussions of medical issues and bodily functions were topics I'd never intended to speak about with anyone other than a doctor. Luckily, Jill is very good with our senior citizen parents. When my mother calls, it's usually to Jill. If the call comes to me, I hand the phone to Jill.

The latest emergency had brought Jill to my office. Closing the door, she plopped into the guest chair. "We're going to South Dakota."

"I told you I hate South Dakota winters, but I've got to tell you, July in Spearfish isn't any more tempting than January. The last time I looked, it was hotter in Rapid City than here in Texas."

"Mom fell again and she's having a bunch of tests. I...we need to be there to help interpret what the doctors tell my dad."

Blowing out a breath, I nodded. "I'll call our new boss and tell him we're taking family leave. You book flights."

I cold-dialed Jack Pardee, his number supplied by my present boss, soon to be my ex-boss, but still best friend. It shocked me when Pardee answered the phone after the first ring. "Doug Fletcher, I've been meaning to call you."

"Hi, boss. I should've called earlier to introduce myself, but...well...I haven't."

"Is Jill there with you?"

"Um, no. That's why I'm calling. Her mother is having a health emergency and we need to fly to the Black Hills to help. I don't know how long we'll be needed, but I'd like to believe it won't be more than a week."

"Actually, that might work out well. American Airlines has a hub here in Salt Lake City. Book your flights and plan for a two-day layover when you connect here on your return trip to Texas. We'll get a chance

7

to meet, and we can discuss some of the cold cases I'd like to reopen."

"Sure," I said, trying to sound more upbeat than I felt. "I'll pass that plan along to Jill."

"Give me the dates when you make your reservations. I'll talk to my wife, and we'll grill some steaks and get to know each other a bit." Pardee paused. "I assume you're not vegetarians."

"There are very few things I enjoy more than a medium-rare steak on the grill. Jill grew up on a ranch and I think she ate beef every meal until she went away to college."

The mirth left Jack's voice. "Doug, I've read your files and the two of you sound like very capable investigators. I have no intention of reining you in or trying to control your work. I only ask to be kept aware of what you're working on. I'll do anything I can to break down bureaucratic barriers and make your jobs easier."

"I appreciate that. Be aware that I'm a cynical cop who doesn't like to write reports."

After a laugh, Jack responded. "Matt warned me about the reports and that your expense vouchers often had questionable items, like a hundred bales of hay in payment for guide services."

"That one was on Jill."

"In all seriousness, Doug, I'm looking forward to working with you. Good investigators are worth their weight in gold. Everything I've heard about you and Jill makes me think that we're going to hit it off."

I hung up the phone and stared at it. "I hope you still feel that way after our first case."

Chapter Two

The Texas townhouse air conditioner was humming, sucking the late June heat and moisture from the air. Although still early morning, the forecast called for afternoon temperatures climbing into the 90s, with unbearable humidity. I sat at my laptop, scrolling through the pages of open US Park Service investigations while Jill, my wife and investigations partner, changed from her t-shirt pajamas into what had become her summer uniform, a tan polo and olive-green shorts, the color of NPS uniforms. I'd pointed out that investigators were allowed, and possibly encouraged to wear civilian clothes. Jill responded that she had dozens of serviceable uniforms, all designed to wear like iron, and she preferred wearing the uniforms she owned rather than buying civilian clothing of lesser quality. I knew part of the issue was her frugality. I'd also learned there was nothing to be gained from pointing that out.

I heard Jill's phone ring and ignored it, assuming it was our friend Mandy, offering Jill some ladylike activity that wouldn't interest me. The two of them spent an hour at the gym every day and often played golf early in the mornings Jill was off, before the Port Aransas heat and humidity became unbearable.

Jill walked into the dining room, where I was working. "Guess who called?"

"Mandy is organizing a tea party." Getting *the look,* I offered another guess, "Someone offered you an extended car warranty."

"Since we're flying to South Dakota to deal with my mother's medical issues, your mother wants us to stay for the July 4th Belle Fourche rodeo." Seeing that I was less than enthused, Jill added, "The Black Hills Roundup is one of the biggest regional events of the summer."

"Our new boss sent documentation from hundreds of open Park Service investigations. He asked me…us, to choose one and pick up the investigation."

Pulling a chair next to me, Jill leaned close so she could see my computer screen. "Are there any near Belle Fourche?"

"I don't know South Dakota geography. There's one in Badlands National Park. I assume that's near Spearfish."

Jill slid the computer in front of her and typed in a search for the Black Hills. "Here's a missing person case in Jewel Cave National Monument, south of Mount

Rushmore. And another missing couple in Badlands National Park. That's near Rapid City."

"That's from the 1980s. That case is so cold the employees and witnesses are probably retired or dead."

"Here's a recent one in Little Bighorn Battlefield National Monument. It appears grave robbers dug up a battlefield grave. It just happened, and it doesn't look like there's been any investigation beyond this report."

"Isn't Little Bighorn Battlefield in Montana?"

"Yes, but Belle Fourche is only a few miles from the northeast corner of Wyoming. You can see both Wyoming and Montana from the western Black Hills." Typing in another search generated a route from Belle Fourche to Little Bighorn. "It's just over a three-hour drive. We could easily go to the rodeo, then spend a couple days at Little Bighorn National Monument."

Before I could reply, Jill had punched in a phone number and was walking toward the kitchen.

"Are you calling my mother, your mother, or Uncle Chet?"

With a wave of dismissal, Jill waited for her call to be answered. "Hi, Jack," she said to our new boss, "This is Jill Fletcher. Doug and I were looking through open cases and we'd like to bounce a proposal off you." She went on to explain her plan to combine a visit home with an investigation at Little Bighorn.

I only heard half the conversation, but the tone of Jill's voice made me think her proposal was being well received. She ended the call, smiling. "I'll call your mom. Book flights into Rapid City with a two-week stay."

"Two weeks is a long time if we find out there's nothing to investigate."

"If Mom is okay and the investigation is short-lived, we can spend a lot of time riding..."

My grimace at the proposition of riding horses and spending two weeks with my in-laws garnered a glare from Jill. "Fine. I'll be a good sport, but I suspect there'll be plenty to keep us busy at Little Bighorn for at least ten days."

"You're afraid you'll wet your pants again if you get another spirited horse," Jill said as she walked away, punching numbers into her phone. From the kitchen, I heard her say, "Hi, Ronnie. Doug and I have an investigation that will dovetail perfectly with the Belle Fourche rodeo. Doug's making plane reservations."

Sighing, I pulled up the federal travel website and typed in our city of origin and destination. Within moments I'd booked a two-week trip, a rental car, and a week at a small motel in eastern Montana.

13

.

Our friend Mandy drove us to the Corpus Christi airport. After hugs, we checked our bags through to Rapid City and walked to the TSA checkpoint. The one person in line ahead of us was struggling to get her carry-on bag through the x-ray security screening. An agent inspected our credentials. Instead of waving us past the metal detectors with our firearms, he pulled us aside and nodded toward the woman whose bag was now being unpacked by a TSA agent after exiting the x-ray.

"Do everyone a favor and keep an eye on that woman," the young man with sergeants' stripes said. We hesitated, listening to the woman argue with the TSA agent who was doing the bag inspection. As each item was removed from the carry-on, the passenger's voice rose and became more accusative.

"I don't know what you Nazis hope to find, but there isn't a gun or bomb in my bag."

A female TSA agent appeared and took the passenger's elbow. "Please come with me, ma'am."

"Just a damned minute! I am a tax-paying American citizen. Why don't you search the damned rag heads and wetbacks who are sneaking contraband and weapons of mass destruction into this country!"

"Ma'am, please come with me. We're going to let you cool off for a while."

"Hey! I've got a plane to catch. You can't detain me without due cause."

"Ma'am, you mentioned that there might be a bomb or gun in your case."

"I said there *wasn't* a gun or bomb in my case."

The sergeant guided us past the security point and called for police backup. He put his hand on my back. "This could go south quickly. Could you stay here until I get an armed policeman?" He looked at Jill. "Would you step forward and identify yourself as a federal officer? That might throw some cold water on the situation."

Jill followed the TSA sergeant the few steps to the standoff that was becoming more heated by the moment. Using amazing cop sense, Jill pulled handcuffs from her back pocket and stepped up to the unruly passenger. Holding the handcuffs in front of the woman's face, she said, "Please face away from me while I handcuff you."

The color drained from the woman's face as she stared at the silver handcuffs. "Who are you?"

"I'm a federal officer who is detaining you for being threatening and abusive to these TSA officers."

"You're arresting me for yelling about my rights? That's free speech."

Opening the handcuffs, Jill shook her head. "You can argue that with a judge at tomorrow's arraignment hearing."

"Tomorrow? I have a plane to catch."

"If you want to catch that plane, I suggest that you shut up and comply with the requests of the TSA officers."

I heard the jingling sound of clanging handcuffs as two CCPD officers ran toward the security checkpoint. The woman looked at Jill, then at the two cops who were now a few yards away. She put up her hands. "Fine. I surrender my personal right against illegal search and seizure. Just let me catch my damned plane."

Reaching into the bottom of the woman's carry-on, the TSA agent lifted out three one-liter bottles and set them on the stainless-steel table. The woman looked over. "Hey, be careful with that blue agave mezcal, it costs fifty bucks a bottle!"

The TSA sergeant glanced at me. His look said, *this is the stuff I have to put up with all the time.*

The two CCPD cops stepped into the confrontation, allowing Jill to back away. She looked over her shoulder as a lecture ensued about the illegality of bringing a liquor bottle onto a plane. "I can't believe anyone, in this day and age, doesn't know that you can't bring your own booze onto a plane. There are signs lining the approach to the screening station stating you can't have any liquid container over three ounces in your carry-on."

"There are also signs saying you can't bring booze, guns, explosives, etc. through security. Hell, they have a bin full of pocketknives and shampoo right behind the x-ray machine."

With a smile, Jill leaned close. "Apparently those rules don't apply to tax-paying American citizens."

We bought coffee and a newspaper at a kiosk near our gate. I read the headlines while waiting for our plane to board. Jill took out a pen and started a sudoku puzzle. Announcing that our plane would board in a few minutes, the agent said, "Fletcher, party of two, please approach the podium."

"Put your pen away," I said, picking up my carry-on. "The gate agent wants to speak with us."

I set our boarding passes on the podium and smiled at the middle-aged female agent. "We're the Fletcher party."

Without looking up, she took our boarding passes and started typing into her keyboard. "Your seat assignments have been changed." A printer under the counter rumbled. "Here are your new seats. Please go to the front of the line when we preboard."

Looking at the boarding passes, I saw that we'd been moved a few rows ahead. "Why the change?"

The gate agent looked up. "You're in the exit row. Enjoy the additional leg room."

"Why the change?"

"The flight attendant will brief you when you're seated."

Jill joined me at the door to the jetway. "What's going on?"

"Apparently they think we look like people who could assist the other passengers in an emergency."

Jill looked around at the crowd awaiting the boarding announcement. "There's something more and I'm not sure I'm happy about it."

The jetway door opened and the gate agent scanned our boarding passes. "Please identify yourselves to the flight attendant when you reach the plane."

A young woman met us as we stepped onto the plane. She took the boarding passes and led us to the exit row as the first-class seats started to fill. When we sat, she leaned forward, "One row ahead and across the aisle will be a couple who've caused a commotion on previous flights. They're flagged as potential problems, and their antics have been escalating. Please help me if they pose a problem."

I nodded. "You've got it."

As the flight attendant retreated to assist other passengers, Jill leaned close. "We're not sky marshals."

"No, but we do know how to deal with obnoxious people."

"I don't want to *deal with* jerks. I just want to fly home."

"It'll probably be nothing."

I was proven wrong. Boarding the plane last, there was no overhead storage left for the problematic couple's large carry-on bags. That led to an argument about their bags being gate checked and available for pickup when the plane landed. They finally took their seats, but the couple immediately pushed the attendant call button.

The flight attendants were closing the plane and preparing for the safety briefing. The youngest flight attendant hustled down the aisle and turned off the light. "How can I assist you?"

"When can we get a drink?"

"There'll be beverage service when we reach our cruising altitude. Please buckle your seatbelts and move your seat backs into their full upright position."

"The people up front are drinking."

"They're in first class, and we're collecting their glasses now."

"My wife's diabetic and needs some orange juice."

"I'll bring a can of juice as soon as we're closed up."

The female passenger leaned over. "Make it a screwdriver. If you're bringing orange juice, just pop a shot of vodka into it."

"It'll be plain orange juice, ma'am."

The couple grumbled as the flight attendant retreated. Jill leaned over to me. "I don't believe it."

"After thirty years dealing with jerks in the parks, this surprises you?"

Holding up her hands, Jill leaned back. "I thought we might be dealing with a higher stratum of people on a plane."

As the safety briefing was given, I whispered, "Lower your expectations."

The couple across the aisle were impolite and arrogant, but not verbally or physically abusive, so I didn't intervene. As we departed the plane, I stepped into the galley to speak with the flight attendant. "I would've stepped in if things had escalated."

She nodded. "I saw you watching the show. I appreciate you being ready to assist."

Jill and I hustled to our connecting flight and joined the line already boarding the larger plane bound for Minneapolis. Jill leaned her head on my shoulder. "Maybe we'll be able to sleep on this flight."

* * *

The flights to Minneapolis and Rapid City were smooth and uneventful. Mom and Chet were waiting for us near the luggage claim. Mom hugged and kissed us. Chet shook my hand, then tolerated a hug from Jill that obviously made him uncomfortable.

"We drove Al and Molly's crew cab pickup so there'd be more room for you to sit," Chet said as he led us to the parking lot.

Shaking her head, my mother said, "I told him there wasn't room for four people in the cab of his pickup and that neither Jill nor I was going to sit on Doug's lap for the ride from the airport to Spearfish."

"It's okay, Mom. I've got a rental car."

Chet stopped abruptly. "There's no need for that. Between Rickowskis and us, we've got five vehicles."

"The government is happy to pay for our rental car," I replied.

Chet wrinkled his nose. "I'm not pleased about you using my tax dollars to rent a car when there are perfectly fine vehicles available to you for free."

Feeling Jill's hand on my arm, I cut off my response. "Thanks, we'll cancel the rental car."

Mom insisted I ride in the front seat with Chet while she and Jill took the rear seat. Knowing Chet was a man of few words, I anticipated a long, silent ride. I was surprised when Chet said, "At supper last night, we decided you might be more comfortable in Jill's old bedroom at Rickowskis' ranch. I said that Jill was inheriting my whole spread, including the house, and that you could get used to living there. Molly wouldn't hear anything like that, so it was a short argument."

"Jill's room is fine," I said.

Mom leaned over the backseat. "You remember that they replaced the mattress, so the box spring doesn't squeak anymore when you…"

"I hated that," I said, cutting off her comment. "It squeaked every time I sat down or rolled over."

Chet glanced in the rear-view mirror at Mom, then he smiled. "We heard you kept Al and Molly awake half of one night with your lovemaking."

I opened my mouth to protest, then decided it was best to let the topic drop, or change. "Tell me about the rodeo."

"We've got tickets for all five days of the Black Hills Roundup," Mom said. "It opens tomorrow with the grand parade and mutton busting. It ends with the bull riding finals and fireworks."

"What's mutton busting?"

My question was met with laughter. "It's a kids' bareback event," Jill explained. "They put little kids, pre-cowboys, on sheep and see how long they can stay on."

"Really?"

After chuckling, Chet smiled. "Welcome to cowboy country, Doug."

* * *

Molly and Al met us on their front steps as the sun dipped in the west. Only days after the summer solstice, the South Dakota sun set after 8:30 with twilight lingering until nearly 10 o'clock. We'd been traveling all day and I would've liked nothing more than a shower and a bed, but I smelled pot roast cooking as soon as we stepped out of the pickup. Bedtime at Rickowskis' ranch was many hours away.

Unable to contain her excitement, Molly walked down the steps and limped to us. We'd heard about her falls but didn't understand the lingering effects of her tumbles from the steps. In addition to the limp, Molly looked older and tired. None of those things prevented her from preparing a welcome dinner for her only child and son-in-law.

Burying her head in my neck after kissing my cheek, Molly whispered, "Thanks for coming. We're really worried about Chet…we'll talk after supper."

I steered Chet aside. "We haven't heard about Molly's test results. Do we need to worry?"

"The MRI didn't show anything, so the doctor isn't worried. Molly is convinced she tripped on the front mat and that's what caused her fall. She refuses to discuss any additional testing."

Jill was in discussion with her father and my mother, so I couldn't corner her to determine if she was aware of whatever was going on with Chet. When released from Molly's hug, I turned and saw Chet pulling our luggage out of the pickup with his left hand, his right arm hanging at his side. I trotted to help him, but he had the suitcases on the ground and the tailgate closed before I reached the truck.

He lifted the largest suitcase, then nodded to the other. "You can get the easy one."

"I can take both of them, Chet."

"No, no. I've got this one."

The three women entered the house, leaving Al on the step. He watched Chet and me carry the suitcases across the gravel driveway, then took the large case from Chet when we reached the steps. "I don't suppose I could tempt you with a taste of the good whiskey you gave me for Christmas."

"I'm afraid a beer suits my taste better," I said, shaking his hand as I passed.

"Leaves that much more for Chet and me."

"I'm surprised there's any left," I said.

"I save the good stuff for special occasions, like this. Chet and I finished off his bottle New Year's Eve and we've only had a couple tastes from my bottle since then."

After hanging his hat on a peg behind the door, Chet sat in his usual spot at Rickowskis' dining table. "Al's been pretty protective of that bottle. We had some guys in after we cut the first crop of hay. Al showed off the bottle, bragging that it was a gift from his daughter and son-in-law, then put it back in the cabinet and pulled down a bottle of Old Crow. They boys were mighty disappointed they didn't get a taste of the Gentleman Jack."

"Oh hell," Al said, setting the suitcase in the hallway, "those guys don't know the difference between moonshine and sipping whiskey. They'd probably ask if I had any Coke to mix with it."

The earnest discussion among the three women standing near the stove seemed too serious. Al and Chet were busy sampling the Gentleman Jack whiskey and seemed oblivious to whatever the women were discussing. I got a beer from the refrigerator and stood quietly near the door until Jill looked up. She wiped a tear from her eye, then nodded for me to sit at the table.

Dishes and platters were delivered to the table as Jill set out silverware. A roast that represented a serious portion of some steer's butt was set in front of Al, who sliced it deftly and set half pound slabs on each of our plates, leaving more than half the roast in reserve for seconds.

Discussion centered around the price of feeder calves, the mediocre hay crop, the dry weather, and a neighbor who'd lost his cattle dog in a fight with a badger. Jill and I listened and nodded. Knowing that Molly appreciated people who ate heartily, I dug into my meal with gusto. Jill ate a potato and carrots. She cut up her serving of the roast, although it appeared most of the meat was still attached to the fat she pushed to the side of her plate.

Wiping her mouth, Molly interrupted the conversation. "What inspired you two to come for the rodeo?"

Jill looked shocked by the question. "Ronnie called and suggested that we try to get away for the July 4th celebrations."

Chet's glance at my mother told me he was unaware of that suggestion.

Rather than letting that turn into a discussion, I said, "We've been looking into open Park Service cases, and this is a working trip. There was a grave disturbed on Little Bighorn National Monument and we're planning to spend a couple days in Montana to investigate after the 4th."

"Why would someone dig up an old grave?" Mom asked.

"That's part of the question we're looking into," I replied.

Al ate like he was starving and was quickly done with his second portion of roast. He pushed his plate away and set his napkin on the table. "There's a rumor that Custer's pistol wasn't buried with him. The Native storytellers say it was presented to Crazy Horse after the battle, but there's no evidence that ever happened. When the tribe was disarmed and sent to the reservation, there were no pistols turned over. Now there's all kinds of speculation his gun was either lost on the battlefield, or it was buried with one of the other troopers."

Sliding his plate away, Chet shook his head. "There's no way to know where that old hunk of iron is after a hundred and forty years. Hell, if it's been buried all this time, it's probably no more than a rusty clump of steel. I hear the real treasures out there are the cavalry swords."

Jill waved her fork while she swallowed. "The cavalry wasn't carrying sabers at Little Bighorn. They were traveling light and left all the sabers behind."

"Well, there are a lot of antique dealers who would be very unhappy if that piece of news got spread around. I think every antique shop in the Black Hills has a sword hanging on the wall with a 7th cavalry insignia stamped on the blade. Of course, they all have a big price tag attached to them."

"Anyone ready for a piece of pie?" Molly asked as she stood. "I've got cinnamon ice cream to scoop on top of it."

I looked at the quarter pound of meat and half potato still sitting on my plate. "I'll have to pass."

Al glared at me. "The pie is non-optional. Your only choice is if you want ice cream on it."

Laughing, Chet punched Al's arm. "Leave the boy alone. They've been on planes the whole damned day. He's probably constipated and doesn't have room in his gut. Hell, he hasn't even finished his beef."

Mom caught my eye roll and shook her head, warning me not to respond. Not that I was planning to comment on the state of my guts.

"Yeah," Jill said, standing to help her mother. "Doug was constipated before the trip and he can't poop in the toilets on the plane."

Halfway through a swallow of freshly poured whisky, Chet snorted and choked.

"Damn it, Chet, don't you dare spit out that good whisky!" Al warned.

Chet stomped his foot a couple times, then swallowed. Gasping, he looked at Jill. "You never could pass up a chance to get a dig in, could you?"

"I feel like I'm back in third grade," I said, picking up my plate and gathering the other place settings.

Looking up from the apple pie, Molly's eyes were sparkling. "You remember that we replaced that old squeaky box spring so if the pie makes you feel romantic, no one will be any the wiser."

That comment stopped Jill. "Mom, we are not having the squeaky spring discussion again."

"Of course not, dear." Molly slid a slice of pie onto a plate. "I don't imagine Doug will feel romantic if he's constipated."

As we carried our bags into the bedroom, Jill closed the door and whispered. "Chet had a TIA. It's like a tiny stroke. He's recovering, but Mom and Ronnie are concerned that it was a sign of things to come."

Chapter Three

I'm not sure if it was the sunlight coming through the window or the sounds of breakfast preparation that woke me. Finding Jill's side of the bed empty, I glanced at the red numbers on the alarm clock which showed 5:10. I groaned.

After showering and dressing, I walked to the kitchen where Al was drinking coffee and reading the newspaper. Jill was frying something on the stove while Molly pulled a pan of baking powder biscuits out of the oven. Jill was about to pour something into the frying pan when Molly stopped her. "Don't pour the thickening in too fast and stir like crazy or it'll be lumpy."

"Yes, Mom. I've made sausage gravy before."

"And it was lumpy," Molly countered.

Taking my usual chair at the table, I poured myself a cup of coffee from the carafe and topped off Al's cup. All the places were set, and a trivet had been placed in the center for the pan of sausage gravy Jill was now carrying from the stove. Molly limped over with a bowl piled with steaming baking powder biscuits.

"Molly, I usually eat a bowl of raisin bran cereal for breakfast."

Frowning as she handed me the biscuit bowl, she said, "You'd think that would keep you more regular."

Al chuckled as he folded the paper and took the biscuit bowl from me. "I suspect Doug's irregularity problem was fictional."

"Thank you," I said, scooping gravy with lumps of breakfast sausage over my biscuits.

"Jill told us that she had you on a horse in Arizona." Al said as he scooped gravy.

"We spent a couple days on horseback during our Tuzigoot National Monument investigation."

"How did that go for you?"

I glanced at Jill, who was smirking. "It was a bit of a learning experience, but I got by."

"Jill said one of the horses was a little spirited and scared the piss out of you."

Pretending to ignore the comment, I ate my biscuits and gravy.

"Doug made up for it when he shot the rattlesnake." Jill spread butter on her biscuit, then paused. "Oh, that's right. It was me who shot the rattlesnake. You fell off your horse in the river, right Doug?"

"I jumped off my horse and..." It was obvious that Al and Molly were aware of the whole story, from Jill's perspective. "I got the suspect to admit he killed the victim."

Molly nodded. "Jill said you're a top-notch interrogator."

"She's no slouch herself."

Changing the topic, Jill stood. "We should get going. Belle Fourche is a bit of a drive, and we need to see where we're seated."

Molly grimaced when she tried to lift the cast iron skillet, so I grabbed the handle and carried it to the stove where Jill was loading the leftover biscuits into a storage container. "Your mom couldn't lift the skillet," I whispered.

"She said they were going to let us go into Belle with Ronnie and Chet today. I guess her ankle isn't ready to walk from the parking lot to the stands."

After clearing the table, Jill and I washed and dried the dishes, something Molly had never allowed in previous visits. I was putting the last dishes in the cupboard when my mom and Chet walked in. Molly and Al were in a whispered conversation until the door opened. Al rushed to meet them while Molly remained seated.

"Well," Chet said, keeping his sweat-stained hat on, "I guess it's time for the city boy to see some real cowboys at work."

Jill and I went into our bedroom and closed the door. "I'm really worried about Molly. Something is seriously wrong."

"Mom's having dizzy spells and is short of breath. She's going to see a cardiologist next week," Jill said as she clipped her badge and holster to her belt, then handed my holster to me.

"And Chet has issues, too."

Leaning against the door, Jill nodded. "They're getting old. All four of them look grayer and are moving slower."

"And you feel like you should be here to care for them?"

After blowing out a breath, Jill put her arms around my neck. "I think that day will come, but it's not now."

* * *

The Black Hills Roundup, or BHR as the locals called it, was a bigger deal than I expected. Grandstands surrounded the entire outdoor arena, and the crowd seemed like it might've outnumbered the Belle Fourche population.

After watching the grand parade circle the arena, the announcer asked the mutton busting contestants to approach the gates. Jill stood and pulled my arm. "You must be hungry; it's been two hours since breakfast."

Unable to voice my protest before being pulled away, I followed Jill down the aisle, trying not to step on toes. Jill bounded down the stairs like she was running to a fire, and I threaded my way through the people, apologizing, as I tried to keep up.

Once on the matted grass among a hundred other people, I looked for Jill. I spied her against the back of the grandstand with her phone to her ear. Her furrowed brow told me something was amiss.

"The rush had nothing to do with food," I guessed.

Sliding her phone into her pocket, she drew a breath and blew it out. "Matt says our investigation just got complicated."

I pulled out my phone but saw no messages or missed calls.

"Yeah," Jill said, "he doesn't even try to call you anymore."

"What's complicated?"

"Two rangers walked out to the disturbed Little Bighorn grave to document the damage. Rather than a looted grave, they found a partially buried body."

"I assume we're talking about a fresh body versus the hundred-year-old soldier's remains."

"Yes, a fresh body. They called the coroner to remove the remains. All they were able to determine was that the victim was a woman."

Closing my eyes, I paused. "One of the hundreds of missing Native women?"

"They couldn't say. Bodies deteriorate rapidly this time of year. We'll have to see what the coroner determines." With people starting to crowd our space, Jill nodded toward a fenced area filled with travel and horse trailers.

"What's with all the people camping right here?"

"These are the contestants' living quarters. They stay here, close to their horses."

We walked down an aisle between the trailers, hearing murmured conversations. Ahead of us a young girl was knocking on a trailer's door. She looked at us and fixed her stare on Jill's badge. "Can you help me, ma'am?"

Kneeling, Jill nodded. "What's the matter?"

The girl pointed to Chris Jenkins' name painted on the side of the trailer along with the logos of her half dozen sponsors ranging from HayChix to Wrangler Jeans. "I came to get Miss Jenkins' autograph, but she's not answering the door."

"She's probably registering for the competition or caring for her horses."

Pointing to two palomino horses in a pen behind the trailer, the girl said, "Her horses are here."

That comment about the horses caught Jill's attention but didn't bother me. My only thought was that the girl was much too young to be wandering around the area alone.

She looked dejected. "I guess I'll try again later."

Watching the girl walk back toward the grandstand, I shook my head. "She shouldn't be wandering around here without an adult."

"A lot of ranch people are complacent about the dangers of a city, especially in the middle of the day." Jill turned toward the trailer, cocked her head, and pointed to a brown streak smeared on the door. "Does this look like blood?"

I knocked on the door. "Federal officers. Please open the door." Getting no response, I pulled out my handkerchief and twisted the doorknob. The overpowering stench of blood and feces hit my face, forcing me to turn away and draw a breath.

Jill pushed past me and froze halfway through the door. "Somebody was killed in here. We need to call a local cop."

I dialed 911 and described our location. After ending the call with the dispatcher, I turned to Jill. "You don't suppose this is tied to the body found in a Little Bighorn grave?"

"That's three hours from here." The words were barely out of Jill's mouth when she added. "There are no coincidences in law enforcement."

Looking at the names of all the prestigious corporate sponsors, I asked, "Who is Chris Jenkins?"

"She's the top-earning North American barrel racer."

"Who'd want her dead?"

Waving to a cop at the end of the aisle, Jill said, "About every other barrel racer."

"Do you think she might've been stalked?"

"Every cute rodeo contestant has to beat away lovesick cowboys who want to buy them drinks and bed them."

The cop stopped next to me. "Did you call 911?"

I nodded toward the door. "Put on gloves and check out the inside of this trailer."

After donning purple gloves, the cop pushed the door open and stopped. "Oh Lord, it looks like a slaughterhouse in here." He stepped back and spoke into the mic mounted on his shoulder. "Dispatch, find Chief Arnold and the duty sergeant. I need them at my location."

I offered my hand. "Doug Fletcher, US Park Service Investigation. This is my partner, Jill."

The cop stripped off his purple gloves and shook my hand. He glanced at our badges and looked confused. "What are you two doing here?"

"We'd planned to watch the rodeo until about five minutes ago."

* * *

While the local police inspected the trailer's living quarters, I followed Jill to the rear, where two yellow horses with white manes and tails, shifted nervously in a pen behind the horse portion of the trailer. She spoke softly to them and stroked their necks. The horses stopped shifting their weight and relaxed.

"This is a three-horse trailer and there are only two horses here," Jill said in soft easy cadence.

"So, we've got a missing rider, a missing horse, and a bloody trailer," I summarized.

Easing down the nearest horse's flank while gently stroking his back, Jill examined the hind quarter. "These two are nicely groomed palomino quarter horses with brands. It'll be easy to identify the third horse if we find him."

The men stepped out of the living quarters and stripped off their gloves. The tall, slender police chief spoke in hushed tones to the cop we'd met and a man in western clothes with a badge pinned to his shirt. After a short conversation, the chief approached us. "Something or somebody died in there," the chief said, mopping his brow with a bandana.

"One of Chris Jenkins' horses is missing, too," Jill said, still stroking the neck of the nearest horse.

"I suppose someone as competitive as Chris probably brings three horses to compete. It's possible she's ridden him off."

"That would make her a suspect in whatever happened inside the trailer," I said.

The chief nodded. "That seems unlikely." He cocked his head. "Explain what role you two have in this."

"We were walking among the trailers talking about an investigation we've got at Little Bighorn National Monument. The rangers found a woman's body in a shallow grave," I explained.

Our eyes locked as the chief digested my words. "What are the odds?"

"A million to one," I replied. "Or, if you don't believe in coincidences, it may be a sure thing."

Pulling a cell phone from his pocket, the chief selected a number from the directory and stared at his boots while he waited for an answer. "Connie, call your counterpart over in Big Horn County and ask about the woman's body recovered from the national monument." After listening a moment, he added, "We've got a missing barrel racer from the BHR. Young, fit woman who lost a lot of blood before being removed from her traveling trailer."

I waited until the chief disconnected the call before asking, "Was that your coroner?"

"Yeah, she's got a good head and works well with us. She may call back quickly if she can reach the Big Horn County Coroner."

Handing the chief her card, Jill said, "My cellphone number is there if you want us for anything."

Without looking at the card, the chief locked eyes with me. "I'd appreciate it if you two hung around for a bit." Turning away, the Chief spoke to his detective and two uniformed cops. Then he nodded farther down the aisle of trailers. "What kind of investigations do you two do for the Park Service?"

"It varies," I replied. "We're often looking at cold cases, but we've been involved in a couple murder investigations too."

"Murders in National Parks?"

"It happens," Jill replied. "Not everyone who visits a National Park is a boy scout. We get our share of troublemakers."

"What's your sense of what happened here?"

"I got as far as the door and called 911," I said. "There was a lot of blood, but that's the extent of my opinion."

Chief Arnold looked at Jill's card. "How about you, Investigator Fletcher?"

"The living quarters are attached to a three-horse trailer. There are only two horses here and there isn't any hay in their feed nets. I think someone took a horse. The other horses haven't been fed today, so whatever happened in the living quarters, occurred overnight. I don't see a pickup outside the enclosure capable of hauling this trailer. If there's nobody inside, I'd be looking for a one-ton pickup with dual rear wheels. It probably has logos from Chris Jenkins' sponsors on the doors."

After mulling Jill's comments, the chief looked at me. "Your partner is good."

"Yeah, she only keeps me around to write the reports."

The police chief was taken aback by Jill's quick elbow jab to my ribs.

"My partner, Doug Fletcher, is a smartass. He's a retired St. Paul PD detective who knows nothing about horses or rodeos. I grew up in Spearfish."

Having been outed, I handed the chief one of my cards. "My wife, Jill, has a barrel racing belt buckle mounted on her bedroom wall. She can also shoot a prairie dog in the eye at a quarter mile."

The corner of the chief's mouth twitched before he shook his head. "Our crimes are mostly burglaries and bar fights. We had a murder a couple years ago, but it was part of a domestic dispute. I…ah…would appreciate it if you two hung around and consulted."

"We're officially assigned to investigate whatever happened at Little Bighorn," I replied.

"Who would I contact to make a formal request for your assistance?"

Jill took out her phone and pulled up Jack Pardee's name and phone number in her contacts list. "Here's our boss."

The chief punched Pardee's number into his phone and stood facing us while he waited for an answer. "I hate to go over your heads."

"Chief, I'd prefer to help you with whatever happened here..."

I was cut off before finishing my thought when our boss answered his phone. After a brief conversation with Jack Pardee, the chief handed his phone to me. "Hi Jack."

"I hear you two stepped on a hornet's nest. The police chief seems sincere in his belief that you two would be helpful." Pardee paused. "I'll leave this up to you. If you want to dig into this, you have my permission. If you want to walk away, hand the phone back to the chief and I'll tell him I can't afford to turn you loose right now."

The look in Jill's eyes told me she wanted to be part of this investigation. "We're here and it looks like we can help. With your permission, we'll render assistance."

Pardee chuckled. "I've found that helping our local law enforcement brethren tends to pay dividends. Keep me apprised of your plans."

The chief accepted his phone and took a few steps away while talking to our boss. Jill tugged at my sleeve and leaned close. "I want to be part of this. You talked about how you could follow a car as a cop and sense there was something wrong that needed your attention. Well, I'm tingling because something is very wrong here. Chris Jenkins is talking to me."

"But you don't…"

"Doug, it's like when Junior died. I felt it. I knew he wasn't coming back. I'm getting that now, along with a sense of…" Jill's eyes were filled with determination. "This is something we need to do."

After ending the call, the chief returned. "I think you should look at our crime scene."

Falling in step alongside the chief, Jill said, "Please start a search for Chris' pickup."

"I'll contact the state patrol as soon as I turn you two loose on the trailer."

"We weren't planning to do anything but watch the rodeo today. Can we have booties and gloves?" Jill asked.

"Of course. My guys will fix you up."

* * *

Slaughterhouse was an apt description of the trailer's interior. I took one step inside the door and just scanned the scene. I moved aside when Jill put her hand on my back.

"Holy Hannah," Jill said, swatting at the hundreds of flies buzzing inside the tiny space. "Tell me what I'm looking at."

"Whoever was attacked didn't go down without a fight. Everything that's not nailed down has been knocked around. There's blood splatter on the walls consistent with a knife attack and arterial bleeding."

"So, we're assuming it was Chris who was stabbed."

"Not stabbed. She was slashed repeatedly. There's blood splatter sprayed in at least four directions. The streak streaming down the wall was left when a major artery was cut."

"Someone must've heard her screaming."

"Sadly, the first slash might've cut her trachea. There may have been commotion before she bled out, but it's possible she never let out anything but a gurgle."

"Oh God, Doug. Can you tell that from just looking at this scene?"

"There are too many scenes like this etched in my memory."

"Were the victims always women?"

I shook my head. "The worst attacks seemed to be directed against someone they hated. Gay and transexual men took the brunt of the hate crimes."

"There's a bottle of Pendleton's whisky and two lowball glasses on the floor. She must've invited someone in for a drink."

"I doubt she was drinking with her attacker. The cap's still on the bottle. If I had to guess, I'd say she'd had a drink with someone earlier and hadn't washed the glasses. In my experience, the cap stayed off the bottle as long as my buddies or guests were around."

Jill looked at me. "I had the impression you didn't leave many bottles half full back in your drinking days."

"Not toward the end." I paused and knelt, looking at the bottle. "Chris Jenkins probably wasn't a hard drinking cowgirl. Three quarters of this bottle is left. That's only a few drinks poured."

Looking over my shoulder, Jill commented, "Her bed is a mess. I wonder if a romantic encounter got out of control?"

I stood and looked at the bed in the gooseneck. "There's no blood anywhere but in the living area. It all happened here, and based on the blood splatter, I'd say her attacker was extremely angry about something."

"You can tell that?"

"I'm afraid so."

"Hang on," Jill said. "I assumed victims of assaults were always attacked out of anger."

"Not at all. Burglars and people committing crimes of opportunity most often only attack their victims to escape, not to kill or inflict pain. One shot or one stab wound, and they're gone. This was targeted at whoever died here. Someone was very angry with Chris."

Jill stepped around the blood and into the tiny kitchen area. "There is a clean pot with a spoon, and a bowl in the sink. There are cracker wrappers and a soup can in the wastebasket, and the soup residue in the only bowl has attracted flies. She ate supper alone, before all this happened."

"So, she ate supper alone a couple days ago, sipped Pendleton's with a friend, then let someone else in." I stared at the floor. "It appears the victim bled out in front of the couch, where the carpet is soaked."

"Surely someone heard the commotion."

The Belle Fourche police chief stepped in, catching the end of Jill's comment. "My officers are canvassing the trailer residents. Most are by the arena with the rodeo in full swing. We'll knock on doors tonight after the roundup closes down."

"Did anyone hear a scream?" Jill asked.

The Chief shook his head. "We haven't found anyone who heard any unusual noises." He paused. "It's not quiet here in the evening. People are meeting up with old friends from the circuit and some are celebrating wins. It doesn't quiet down until the wee hours of the morning."

Stepping out of the living quarters, I pulled off my gloves and shoe covers. "I assume you have people patrolling the grounds all night."

"Yeah. This week is all-hands-on-deck. I've got all my city officers on 12-hour shifts, all my part-timers are working every day. The county sheriff has every spare deputy helping my officers manage the crowd, and the state patrol pulls in troopers from all over."

"Did you have an officer walking back here during the night?"

"Keith is off shift right now, but he didn't report anything unusual at shift change. I'll talk to him again when we swap over at eight tonight." The chief paused. "What's your take on the crime scene?"

I nodded to Jill. "It appears Chris ate supper alone, had a drink with a friend, who probably left, then was attacked later."

"Chief, I think she let her attacker in and shortly after that, had her throat slashed so she couldn't call for help. There were a few more slashes, representing the blood splatter on the walls, but the first slash probably cut her carotid artery, so the end came quickly."

After staring at his shoes for a second, he nodded. "That's more than I caught. Thanks."

"I assume she towed the trailer with a pickup. Is it parked nearby?" Jill asked.

"It appears to be missing. I've notified the state patrol and they're watching for it."

The chief offered his hand. "I appreciate your input. I'm sorry to have kept you from the festivities so long."

"Oh shit," Jill exclaimed. "Ronnie and Chet probably think we left without them."

We wound through the crowd and climbed the steps into the grandstand. Mom waved to us with a hot dog in her hand. Chet held up a handful of hot dogs wrapped in white wax paper.

Leading Jill past the seated patrons I said, "Looks like hot dogs for lunch."

"Yeah, greasy ground mystery meat with enough preservatives to keep them pink into the next century."

"Think of them as calories to get you through until supper."

"My hot dog might fall out and I'll have to eat the bun with ketchup and mustard."

Mom stood to let Jill past. "I hope you didn't eat lunch while you've been gone. Chet bought hot dogs and beer for all of us."

Chet handed hot dogs to me and smiled. "We were beginning to think you'd gotten lost."

"Not lost, just distracted. Thanks for the hot dog." Chet passed a white wrapped hot dog to Jill. "Be careful when you unwrap it, so the dog doesn't fall out of the bun." The glare I got didn't improve when I handed her a glass of beer. "You'll need this to wash it down."

"You missed all the kids in the mutton busting," Mom said after finishing her hot dog and wiping her fingers on a paper napkin. "I think they're getting set up for junior calf roping."

Leaning close, I whispered, "Are you having fun, Mom?"

"I've never been to a rodeo and Chet's having a great time explaining it all to me. This is…nice." She paused, then added as she patted my leg. "And it's extra nice because you and Jill are here with us."

My phone vibrated and I answered it, sticking a finger in my opposite ear in an attempt to hear over the crowd noise. "Fletcher."

"I heard from the Custer County Coroner. He's transporting the body to Billings for an autopsy and identification. All he can tell at this time is that the woman had been slashed up pretty badly and she's been dead for a few days. The only hint he's got to her identity is a belt buckle from the rodeo nationals that says Chris."

"I suspect our cases just merged," I said.

"Yeah, Fletcher, I was thinking the same thing."

I pushed the phone into my pocket and Jill leaned close. "Who was that?"

"The Montana coroner contacted Chief Arnold. They're taking the body to Billings for an autopsy. The only clue to her identity is a rodeo nationals belt buckle with 'Chris' etched on it."

Jill's fingers dug into my upper arm. "No coincidences, right?"

"Not often," I replied. "Finish your hot dog. We need to make some phone calls."

"Oops, it just slipped out of my hand." The hot dog bounced off the steps and fell under the grandstand.

"I should ticket you for littering."

Jill gave me her most innocent look, then leaned across my legs. "Ronnie, we've got to make some calls about our case. We'll meet you at four o'clock by the pickup."

"You dropped your hot dog."

"Don't worry, Doug will buy me another one."

* * *

Trying to find a quiet spot behind the grandstands was impossible. The crowd roared at the conclusion of every event and people milled around behind the stands talking, eating, drinking, and standing in line for the food and beverage vendors. "This is like trying to make a call at a Minnesota Wild hockey game."

Jill pulled me toward a long row of blue plastic outhouses. "C'mon, it'll be quiet on the other side of the porta-potties."

It was quieter, but the sickly-sweet odor between the blue plastic boxes and the parking lot was extremely unpleasant. Despite the smell, we startled a young couple necking in a hidden alcove between the outhouses and the fence around a dumpster. The teens, who might've been in junior high, blushed when we arrived, then bolted away when they saw our badges and pistols.

Jill chuckled, "I give them credit for determination."

After wrinkling my nose, I pointed to an oak tree beyond the garbage enclosure. "This stink could gag a maggot and I suspect anyone inside an outhouse can hear us if we stand near them."

"What's the plan?" Jill asked.

"You're going to call our boss and update him. I'll call Billings to see if someone in the morgue will tell me anything."

With her fingers flying over the face of her phone, Jill quickly located the website for the Billings hospital. "You call Jack Pardee. I'll call the morgue."

"This is your big chance to talk to our new boss," I said, having lost the argument as soon as Jill touched the hospital phone number.

"People are more willing to talk to me on a cold call than you. Besides, you've already spoken with Pardee." Jill put up her finger when someone answered at the hospital. "Can you connect me with your morgue?"

I found Pardee's number in my phone and touched it. I hoped to leave a brief message, but the call was answered on the third ring. "Hi, Boss. This is Doug Fletcher and I've got an update on our case."

"That was quick. I thought you and Jill were going to spend a couple days at the Black Hills Roundup before checking in at Little Bighorn."

"Like most plans, that fell apart after about two hours."

"Wow. You two don't waste any time."

"We kinda fell into this one by accident. That's not usually how it goes."

"Cases either go really fast or really slow. We solve quite a few within hours while others are open for years. What's your sense of this one?"

"Well, there doesn't appear to be a spouse or significant other, so we've just eliminated the killer in half the cases I've ever investigated. This wasn't a burglar who was surprised. The slashing and blood splatter tell me whoever killed her was angry and was taking it out on the victim."

"Was she sexually assaulted?"

"We'll have to get that information from the medical examiner or pathologist. The scene just doesn't look like a rape. There's something more behind this."

"What evidence have you got?"

"There's a booze bottle and a couple glasses on the floor. The local cops are sending them to the state crime lab for fingerprint analysis. We think the victim had a drink with someone, probably not the killer, earlier in the evening. The victim's pickup is missing as is one of her horses. I just don't think theft was the motive, but I've seen people killed for twenty bucks in a liquor store robbery. The state patrol is looking for the pickup, which could be a getaway vehicle. The missing horse has me stumped."

Jill ended her call and waggled a finger at me.

"Hang on, Jill just ended her call with the Billings hospital." I put the phone on speaker.

"Hi, Jack. I just spoke with the head pathologist in Billings. The victim's body arrived this afternoon. They are doing a post-mortem exam in the morning and will have a report the next day."

"Are you going to wait for the report?"

I looked at Jill. "How far is Billings from Spearfish?"

"I'd guess it's about a five-hour drive."

I blew out a breath. "I think we should attend the post-mortem. We'll call the pathologist to see if he can delay the exam until we get there tomorrow afternoon."

"I like that plan," Pardee said. "I had a sense that you two weren't content to sit around waiting for reports."

After ending the call with Pardee, Jill spoke with the pathologist who was happy to juggle the timing of the autopsy. She looked at me and bit her lip. "So much for our four days at the rodeo."

"I don't feel too bad about this change of plans. My back was sore after fifteen minutes sitting in the grandstand."

"Chet and Ronnie wanted to give you a real out west experience."

"There'll still be Saturday and Sunday."

"I don't believe that, not for one second. You're like a dog on a bone. There'll be a dozen leads you'll want to follow and you're not going to wait until Monday to jump on them."

"You've got to follow the case when you've got a hot trail."

Pushing my shoulder, Jill said, "Let's give Ronnie and Chet the bad news."

Chapter Four

Chet was disappointed. Mom took the news of our one-day diversion well. After supper, she steered me aside, "I've had enough rodeo to last a lifetime. It's noisy and nearly as crowded as the Minnesota State Fair. And my butt is sore."

"Tell Chet you're not interested in going back tomorrow."

Mom sighed. "We might be able to skip tomorrow, but he's really excited about the bronc riding on Saturday. He told me that's where he won the buckles he gave Jill."

"Can you beg off because you had a bad hot dog?"

I got Mom's indignant scowl. "Douglas, that would be..." A second later a sly smile crept across her face. "Now that you mention it, I feel a little queasy already."

* * *

After breakfast, Molly handed me a cooler and a thermos. "Here are roast beef sandwiches, potato chips, and four bottles of water. There's coffee in the thermos"

I pecked her cheek. "I assume there are restaurants between here and Billings."

"Why eat restaurant food when you've got roast beef on homemade bread?"

Al handed Jill a set of keys. "The new pickup is gassed up, and I changed the oil last week. There's air in the spare tire. I put a bottle of oil, a gas can, a siphon hose, and antifreeze behind the seat. Have a safe trip."

We kissed Molly and I shook Al's hand. "You'd think we were leaving in a wagon on the Oregon Trail," I said as I followed Jill across the driveway.

"You were a scout, and their motto is 'be prepared,' right?"

"Sure," I said, climbing into the passenger side of the truck.

"Well, I think the scouts learned that from ranchers. You never know what you're going to encounter, so you prepare for whatever might come up."

"Hey, this is the twenty-first century, not the 1800s. There are truck stops, rest areas, restaurants, and if all else fails, cell phones."

Jill was silent until we got to the county road. "You may or may not have cell phone coverage on much of this route. The restaurants and gas stations may or may not be open. There might not be another vehicle going past every two minutes." Jill paused. "Welcome to the west."

The first town we encountered was Broadus, Montana. Jill turned into the gas station. "We have more than three quarters of a tank. Why are we stopping?"

"You flatlanders don't get *the gas thing.* You always buy gas when you find an open station because you might not find another when you get below half a tank."

"Seriously?"

"I'd like a candy bar and can of diet soda," Jill said as she put the nozzle in the tank.

"Any special kind of candy bar?"

"The kind I finished off before Halloween."

"Honey, you ate all the candy before Halloween."

"There you go," Jill replied. Then she added, "I ate the Snickers bars first."

As I walked away from the pickup I said, "Not the ones I hid in the bedroom."

"You hid candy from me?"

"I thought we should save some for the trick or treaters."

"I bought more!" Jill said as I opened the convenience store door.

And you ate what was leftover the next day, I said to myself.

* * *

I drove the next leg while Jill washed down two Snickers bars with a Diet Coke.

"You know, the Diet Coke doesn't make up for the calories in the Snickers bars."

"You're on thin ice, Fletcher. The man who eats hamburgers and fries shouldn't lecture the person who prefers salads and veggies."

"I'm just pointing out…"

After lunch at a restaurant with a salad bar for Jill and burgers for me, we drove to the hospital. I parked in the Billings Hospital lot and entered through the emergency room, guessing it was closer to the morgue than the lobby. After glancing at us when the doors slid open, the clerk went back to her computer. "You two don't look like you need a doctor," she said, as we approached the reception desk.

"We're here for an autopsy."

"There are double doors to my left. Go to the end of the hallway and take a right. Dr. Henry's office is on the right."

A male voice invited us in when I knocked on the door. "Dr. Henry?" I asked, stepping into the cramped office.

The well-groomed young man wearing green scrubs turned away from his computer and stood. "Ah, you're the Park Service people," he said, offering his hand. He gestured to a pair of guest chairs and sat behind his desk. "You're here about my Jane Doe."

Sliding forward in her chair, Jill hesitated. "We're about ninety percent

58

certain that the victim is Chris Jenkins, who was killed in her trailer parked at the Black Hills Roundup."

Henry nodded. "I've spoken with her parents and I'm awaiting dental records to confirm her identity."

"What can you tell us about her body?" I asked.

"She was delivered to me fully clothed. I removed her clothing and sent it to the Montana State Crime lab, in Missoula. It didn't appear that she'd been sexually assaulted, but I ran a rape kit anyway, just to be thorough."

"How long had she been buried?" I asked.

Henry shrugged. "When did she disappear from Belle Fourche?"

"No one has seen her since she pulled in on Monday," Jill said. "The blood splatter in her trailer had dried by the time we examined it yesterday."

"I'd say death on Monday is consistent with the condition of the victim's body. It's hard to be specific because the daytime temperatures have been brutally hot, and she was past rigor mortis." Henry slid his chair back, "Tell me about the blood splatter."

Jill looked at me. "It appeared the victim had been slashed viciously, at least four times. One of the cuts hit a major artery which spurted blood onto the wall. There was a puddle of blood on the carpeting that looks like she probably bled out there. The Belle Fourche police canvassed the surrounding trailers. No one heard a scream or fight, which makes me think the first slash may have cut her trachea and carotid."

The doctor picked up a pen and scrawled a few notes while balancing the pad on his knee. He looked up. "That's it?"

Jill shrugged. "It appears her last meal was bean and bacon soup, and she may have had a glass of whiskey with someone earlier in the evening."

Henry smiled and set his pad aside. "That may be the most succinct report I've ever heard. Most cops want to throw out all kinds of extraneous, and useless information, followed by their emotional reaction to the murder scene. You two are good."

"What can you tell us, Doctor?" Jill asked.

"I've only done a cursory external examination of the body, pending your arrival. The victim had five deep cuts on her neck and torso, along with defensive wounds on her hands and arms. Your theory about her trachea being cut is spot on. I can't speculate on the sequence of the cuts, but the slash to her neck is very deep. It could've easily cut her trachea, esophagus, jugular vein, and carotid artery.

Whatever made that cut was very sharp and at least ten centimeters long."

Jill drew a breath. I glanced at her and saw her eyes closed. Her lips moved, uttering a silent prayer.

Sensing Jill's reverence, the doctor waited until Jill's eyes opened. "I've blocked out the rest of this afternoon for the post-mortem. Are you two planning to watch?"

Standing, I nodded. "I prefer to hear all your observations, especially the ones that might not be included in the autopsy report."

"I put facts in the report," the doctor said, opening his office door.

"And we'd also like opinions not usually included in the final report."

Dr. Henry led us to a locked, unmarked door. Inside was a small morgue with a single autopsy table. Pointing to a cabinet next to the entry door, he suggested that we wear disposable coveralls, masks, safety glasses and gloves. "There's a sink in the corner," he said as he pulled on rubber gloves.

"We should be good," I said.

Henry looked at Jill. "This is not going to be visually pleasant, and when I open the abdomen, the exhaust fans won't keep up with the stench."

Jill edged closer to the sink as she slid on safety glasses. "Thanks for the warning.

I'm a ranch girl and I've helped deal with dead cattle and deer. I should be fine."

Pulling open a stainless-steel door, the doctor wheeled out a gurney. "How about you, Doug?"

Spotting a bottle of Vicks VapoRub on the counter, I dabbed a bit on my finger and smeared a bit on my upper lip. "Can't be any worse than the floaters we used to fish out of the Mississippi in St. Paul." I handed the Vaporub to Jill and whispered, "Put some on your upper lip and breath through your mouth."

"Really?" She asked, looking skeptical.

"Trust me."

With an assist from Jill and me, Dr. Henry slid the sheet covered corpse onto the autopsy table. He turned on overhead lights and uncovered a tray of knives, saws, and other implements that looked like something from a torture chamber.

He clicked on a recorder, then slid the sheet off Chris Jenkins' naked body. "The victim's skin has turned dark due to degradation during its days in a shallow grave. There are five major slashing cuts on the victim's body, most running from high on her left side slashing downward to her right, indicating a right-handed assailant. The wound to her neck cut through both the carotid artery and jugular veins and undoubtedly caused massive blood loss that led to the victim's death."

While focused on the doctor's comments and probing with his fingers, I lost track of Jill until I heard her depositing her lunch into the sink. I looked up and saw her with both hands braced on the sides of the sink and her head hanging down.

Dr. Henry glanced at Jill, then at me. "I guess your partner, *the ranch girl*, wasn't prepared for the sight and smell of a body that's been in the sun for four days."

"Jill's tough. I think she got a bad broccoli bit off the salad bar."

After wiping her face with a paper towel, Jill glared at me. "I've field dressed a gut-shot deer. This is…worse."

Henry chuckled. "You've never gutted a deer that's laid out in the July sun for four days."

"Nope. We usually leave those for the vultures and coyotes."

"It's going to get worse when I open her abdomen."

Stripping off her gloves, Jill walked toward the door. "I've got to make a couple phone calls."

* * *

I found Jill in Dr. Henry's office staring at the ceiling, her feet up on the second guest chair. Opening her left eye, she turned her head. "Any surprises?"

"The victim died of exsanguination."

"Is there a term for that in English?"

"She bled to death."

Blowing out a breath, Jill sat up and pulled her feet off the second chair. "We drove five hours to hear what we already knew."

"There's more. She fought off her attacker. The doctor took scrapings from under her fingernails and it's likely we have a DNA sample from her attacker." Taking the second chair, I looked at Jill's sallow face. "Are you okay?"

"I'm more embarrassed than anything. I can't believe the smell."

After briefly considering an expanded explanation of the cause of the smell, I decided to move on. "Did you make some calls?"

"I told our boss we had a probable identification of Jane Doe from Little Bighorn. He asked me to pass that information on to the park superintendent, Kate Ryan. She was sad about the woman's death but pleased that we'd identified the victim so quickly. She asked us to stop at her office on the way back to Spearfish."

Checking my watch, I realized it was already midafternoon. "We should get going. I assume the park closes at six o'clock."

Jill stood and said, "Kate told me she'd stay in her office until we arrived." She paused. "Do we need to hang around until the pathologist finishes his report?"

"He'll email it to me in a day or two after he gets test results."

We walked to the parking lot and Jill stopped next to the pickup. "Test results? Is he checking for drugs?"

Unlocking the pickup, I nodded. "He's going to check her alcohol level and look for other drugs."

Jill stepped into the pickup and closed the door. "Date rape drugs?"

"Those and the usual spectrum of narcotics."

"Doug, I don't want to drag Chris' name through the mud. She's a rodeo celebrity."

Driving out of the parking lot, I composed my response. "The victim…"

"Please use her name, Doug. She was a human being."

"Chris had several broken bones. Her recent collarbone break was probably painful."

"Broken bones are an occupational hazard for rodeo people. Breaks and pain are what end most rider's careers."

"Is that what happened to Chet?" I asked.

"Mom had a long talk with Chet while she nursed him back from a broken leg. He retired from the rodeo circuit to manage the ranch for his mother."

"His mother?"

"Chet's father was crushed against the barn by a bull when Chet was a young man. Mom says Chet sowed some wild oats after his father's death. He settled down after a rodeo bronc threw him, breaking his leg."

"I remember seeing the turnoff for Little Bighorn National Monument. It's like an hour drive, right?"

"Something like that. It's not far off the highway."

Chapter Five

The Little Bighorn Battlefield National Monument sign directed us off Highway 212. We drove down a short road past an entry gate and to a parking area.

Stopping next to our pickup, Jill signaled for me to wait. "The visitor center is as austere as the landscape."

I stared at the tan-colored cement block structure. "It's almost devoid of windows."

Although the temperature was nearly 100°F, Jill shivered. "This place always creeps me out."

Looking toward the battlefield memorial I was swept with a feeling of reverence. "C'mon, the superintendent is waiting for us."

After getting directions from the ranger at the gift shop cash register, we walked to the superintendent's office near the rear exit. Kate Ryan stood when I knocked on her door jamb. "You must be Jill and Doug." She shook our hands and closed the door. "I can't say I'm pleased to see you, considering the news you've got."

"I'm literally sickened by the thought of a robust young woman being killed in her own living quarters," Jill said. "I am pleased that we've identified your Jane Doe."

"You said she was killed in Belle Fourche. How did her body get here?"

"Her pickup was stolen from the parking lot near her trailer," I explained. "I assume her assailant took her keys and brought her body here."

"I read that she was a barrel racing star at the Black Hills Roundup," Kate replied. "There are thousands of people around. Surely someone would've noticed her body being carried to a pickup."

"She was there a few days before the actual rodeo, so there weren't any crowds around. Although cowboys can be a hard-partying group, it's pretty quiet around the living quarters early in the morning," Jill said, speaking softly. "We assume that's when she was killed and her body was removed."

"When did your people notice the disturbed grave?" I asked.

"A visitor reported it to us Tuesday morning. To be clear, it wasn't really a grave that was disturbed. The ground near a marker was disturbed. It marked where a soldier died during the battle. The troopers bodies were all moved to a common grave near the battleground memorial." Kate stood and picked up her Smokey Bear hat.

"It'll be easier to explain if we walk out to the monument."

A cement path led up a rise to a gray obelisk overlooking an area enclosed by a black metal fence. Inside the fenced prairie were grave markers that reminded me of a national cemetery.

Pointing to the farthest right corner, Kate said, "The body was found near that most distant marker, the one closest to the road."

Seeing the irregularly placed markers filled me with a deep feeling of sadness. I had the same feeling when I toured the Gettysburg battlefield. I looked across the hallowed ground where hundreds of soldiers and Sioux warriors had died.

"There are hundreds of markers in the distance," I said.

"That's a National Cemetery. As forts closed across the west, the remains of cavalry troopers were reinterred here. After the Spanish American War, it was opened to all veterans."

"What are the red granite markers dispersed around the prairie?" Jill asked.

"Those are the sites where many of the Lakota and Cheyenne fell defending their way of life."

Jill frowned. "I thought there would be more."

"The exact number of Lakota, Cheyenne, Crow, Arapaho, and Arikawa deaths is unknown. Their oral histories say somewhere between forty and a hundred warriors died here. The granite markers are the sites families have identified as the place their ancestors died during the battle. The tribes removed their dead from here and had traditional funeral ceremonies. Those locations are lost to history."

"Where does the road lead?" Jill asked.

"It goes past the National Cemetery to the Reno-Benteen Memorial."

"And beyond that?" I asked.

"There's a walking trail from there, but the road is a dead end."

Jill looked back. "The only vehicle access to the battlefield is through the front gate?"

"Yes, and it's locked overnight."

"Could someone get in on horseback?" I asked.

"Sure. There are wild horses that roam here. There is also unfenced prairie all around here. A horse could come in from any direction."

Jill looked at me. "It's just like Tuzigoot."

Kate looked confused. "Are you talking about Tuzigoot National Monument in Arizona?"

"We had a recent investigation there," Jill explained. "A body was brought in on horseback and dumped in the park."

Kate, whose head barely reached my shoulders, tipped her head back. "You thought her body had been removed from Belle Fourche in her truck."

"Someone also stole a trailer and one of her horses."

Jill raised a finger. "There is also a stock trailer missing from Belle Fourche. I learned that when I spoke with the police chief while you were viewing the autopsy."

After crossing herself, Kate drew a breath. "I saw the victim when the coroner removed her from the ground. That was terrible. I can't imagine watching her autopsy."

"Yeah," Jill agreed. "I wasn't ready for that duty either."

Kate removed her hat and wiped her brow. "Let's go back to my office where it's cooler."

We bought bottled water in the visitor center and returned to Kate's office. She closed the door and sat before taking a big swig of water from the sweating bottle. "What else can I tell or show you?"

"Were there any horseshoe prints near the corner where the body was found?"

Kate froze. "I didn't notice any down there, but I saw that someone had ridden along the road on Tuesday morning."

"Outside or inside the gate?" I asked.

Kate leaned back and wrinkled her nose. "Both, now that you mention it."

"Does anyone patrol the road past the entrance?"

"I've seen a county cruiser go past on the highway with red lights and siren, but the traffic and population out here hardly justify regular patrols."

"Aren't you worried about the security of the grounds?" I asked.

"Doug, our visitors are usually filled with reverence and awe. There's never been a single marker or building vandalized during my tenure here."

I looked at Jill to see if she had any other questions. She shrugged, so I stood and shook the superintendent's hand. "Thanks for your time."

"No, thank you two, for your quick response and identification of the victim. If there's anything else I can do, or any question I can answer, please don't hesitate to contact me."

I paused at her door. "Actually, I'd like to see Custer's grave."

Kate smiled. "You'll have to visit the US Military Academy"

"He's buried at West Point?"

"Not because of the battle here," Kate explained. "He led a cavalry charge at the battle of Gettysburg that broke up a flanking Rebel cavalry force. That single act may have saved the Union forces from being outflanked and defeated. Historians seem to feel Custer was reckless, in part because of his defeat here, but he earned his general's star in the Civil War and there's no disputing his bravery."

I nodded. "General Patton said, 'There's only one way for a professional soldier to die. That's from the last bullet, of the last battle, of the last war.' That's pretty much the way Custer died."

Kate smiled. "Patton had some real gems. He also said, 'Politicians are the lowest form of life on earth.'"

"Thanks, Kate," Jill said as the women shook hands, "We need to be on the road."

"If you get the chance, grab a meal in Lame Deer. The Spoon and Fork Diner has a limited menu, but I've never had a bad meal there. I like their daily salad."

We walked to the pickup. "I vaguely remember seeing Lame Deer, but I might've blinked and missed the diner."

"You might've blinked and missed the whole town."

Instead of exiting the park, I turned onto the road leading to the Reno-Benteen battlefield. "Are we sightseeing?" Jill asked.

"We need to look around the site where the body was buried."

"What do you think we'll see? The rangers who checked the site walked all over the area, then the coroner's people recovered the body."

"You don't know what you don't know until you know it," I replied.

"Where did that come from?" Jill asked as we met a Jeep returning from the other battlefield.

"I once told a medical examiner that a victim had drowned. That was his reply."

"I don't get it."

"His message was that I was making an assumption based on what I knew; that the victim's body had been recovered from the Mississippi River."

"Were you correct?"

"No. The victim didn't have any water in his lungs, so he hadn't drowned. The ME found blunt force trauma to the victim's head that had killed him before his body went into the river."

I edged the pickup off the pavement neared the Custer battlefield. Jill took one step off the pavement and stopped. "I didn't know what I didn't know." Kneeling, she said. "There are horseshoe prints."

"I wonder if the park allows riders inside the gate."

"Doug, these are prints from Chris Jenkins' missing quarter horse."

"Are her initials stamped into the horseshoes?" I asked.

That comment garnered a glare. "The front shoes are fullered, and the rear are rodeo shoes."

"Can you translate that from 'rodeo-ese' into English?"

Jill blew out a breath. "Barrel racers use specialized horseshoes. The front shoes have deep grooves around the outside of the shoe, so the horse gets additional traction when pocketing around the barrels. Because the rear feet often slide when they hit, the farriers use a different type of shoe, a rodeo shoe, that doesn't grip as well. Look at these horseshoe prints. See the deeply grooved prints? Then look at these prints made by a flatter rodeo horseshoe. These have to be from Chris' stolen horse."

"You don't think these were made by one of the local cowboys touring the park on horseback?"

"No, Doug. Pleasure riders use a breakover shoe, like the ones on the horses we rode in Tuzigoot. These prints were made by very unusual shoes, common to barrel racers."

"We don't know that Chris' horse made them," I replied.

"Some old cop told me there are no coincidences in police work."

Straightening up, I arched my back to stretch it. "Are you calling me old?"

With a chuckle, Jill replied, "If the shoe fits…"

We followed the horseshoe prints to the iron fence, where they stopped. Inside the memorial, the unmown native prairie grass had been trampled by people who'd walked from the gate a few yards away. The grass immediately across the fence from the horseshoe prints was matted.

"It appears that the killer threw her body over the fence here before burying it," I said. "There's dried blood on the grass."

Shaking her head, Jill asked, "Why here? Why not dump her body outside of Belle Fourche and not risk getting caught hauling her around?"

"Maybe this is on the way home for the killer. It's just a bit off the highway and if there's no one around, this might have seemed like a good spot."

"On his way home to where?" Jill asked.

"He could easily have driven onto I-90 and gone west."

"Okay, let's say he lives in Billings or Livingstone. Why steal the horse and dump the body here?"

"How much is the horse worth?"

"I suppose the horse might be worth as much as the pickup. Let's say sixty-thousand dollars."

"People have been killed in liquor store robberies for thirty dollars. One hundred thousand dollars is a big payday."

Nodding toward the truck, Jill was deep in thought as we crossed the road. "I don't buy it. No one would kill Chris to steal her horse and pickup. Like you said, the attack was vicious and personal. We're missing something."

I made a three-point turn and drove to the highway. "A jilted lover?"

"I doubt it. Rodeo professionals tend to shun affairs on the road, especially women contestants. There are too many cowboys looking for a one-night stand and everyone on the rodeo circuit knows who's sleeping around and who isn't into partying."

"The buckle bunnies," I said, reflecting on the earlier conversation about girls chasing the cowboys with championship buckles and notoriety.

"Some of the female competitors have reputations. But most, like Chris Jenkins, avoid that scene. She had a reputation for being focused on her riding and not drinking, smoking, doing drugs, or whoring around."

"She had a drink with someone in her living quarters."

"Maybe a female friend. Or, maybe one of her sponsors brought the bottle as a gift. That wasn't cheap whisky."

* * *

A highway sign announced that we were entering the Northern Cheyenne Indian Reservation. A few miles later, we entered Lame Deer. The town wasn't as small as the superintendent had predicted. If I'd blinked when passing Lame Deer, I wouldn't have missed the town. There were signs directing us to a college, school, police station and a number of local businesses. I turned at the main crossroad.

"Hey," Jill said, "the Spoon and Fork restaurant was right there."

"I saw a sign for The Burger Barn."

"Listen, Fletcher. The superintendent recommended the Spoon and Fork and said they serve salads. You'll find something you'll like there. I'm not sure there's anything I'd choose at a place called The Burger Barn."

"Fine," I said, turning into the parking lot of a gas station and convenience store. I parked next to a pump and used my government charge card to prepay for a fill. Jill got out and stretched.

"I checked Yelp. The Spoon and Fork has all five-star reviews. It mentions their great salads."

"If there's nothing on the menu I want, I'll leave you there and get a take-out order from The Burger Barn and eat it with you."

The slate easel next to the restaurant entrance listed a variety of foods. As predicted, the eatery offered soup, salad, sandwich, and dessert options. Seeing a buffalo burger as the sandwich offering, I was satisfied. "I can live with this." We stepped into the small, air-conditioned space. There were only six or seven tables, one of which was occupied.

A middle-aged woman appeared from the kitchen and waved to us. "Sit anywhere. Can I get you a sweet iced tea or soda pop?"

"Diet cola for both of us," I replied.

The woman opened a cooler and brought us two sweating cans of Diet Pepsi. Setting them on the table, she smiled. "I assume you saw the menu when you came in."

"I thought those might be the daily specials," I said, smiling.

"They're the daily specials *and* the menu. We don't get enough traffic through here to justify a big menu with dozens of choices. Today is wild rice soup and hamburger day. We always have a Cobb or chef salad and pie. Today's pie is blueberry."

"I'll have a buffalo burger and fries," I said.

"No fries. How about a bag of chips?"

"Sure," I replied.

"I'll have the chef salad," Jill said. "What are my dressing choices?"

"We've got homemade French dressing or Italian packets."

"The French dressing sounds good."

An older man with a deeply creased face and Native features eyed us as we ordered and opened our soda pop. After a few seconds, he spoke to the woman sitting with him, folded his napkin, and walked to our table. Without invitation, he pulled out a chair and sat down. "We don't get a lot of white cops here."

"The park superintendent at Little Bighorn had high praise for this restaurant."

The man nodded. "Kate's in here a couple times a week. She's a strong woman and a good representative of the Park Service." He paused. "You two are cops. What brings you to Lame Deer?"

Jill gave the man her most disarming smile. "We're investigating the body they recovered at the battlefield."

"That's some bad stuff, desecrating a place like that. I heard some woman had been dumped there."

"She was murdered in Belle Fourche and her body was found at the battlefield. We're trying to identify her murderer."

"You're not Belle Fourche cops."

Jill shook her head. "We're Park Service investigators."

"But you're investigating a Belle Fourche murder."

From the kitchen, I heard my hamburger patty sizzling. "The murder is incidental to our Little Bighorn investigation."

"Huh. I would've thought the murder would take precedence."

"The police in town are checking into that. We're checking on the body left in the battlefield."

"What are you thinking?"

"I think you're either a nosy gossip or a tribal elder who's checking on two cops who showed up unexpectedly."

The man's face remained expressionless. "Maybe I'm both."

"Did you happen to see a dually pickup hauling a horse trailer drive through in the early hours of Tuesday morning?" Jill asked.

"I was probably awake taking a piss because my doctor says my prostate is the size of a grapefruit. But I was more focused on hitting the toilet than looking at the traffic." The man stood and nodded to Jill. "Good luck."

I took out a business card and handed it to the man. "My name's Doug Fletcher. I'd appreciate it if you'd ask around about the pickup and trailer."

Fingering my card, the man studied my face. "You really don't care if it was a white or an Indian who killed that girl and stole the truck."

Jill stood and put out her hand. "I'm Jill Fletcher. My freshman roommate was Lakota. We spent a lot of hours talking, trying to understand each other. I have nothing but respect for your people and the way of life you've chosen. We'll follow this investigation wherever it leads, but I think the only reason the pickup came through here was because the driver was going west."

The man eyed us carefully. "You are married?"

"We are partners in life and work," Jill replied.

Nodding toward the woman he'd left at the table, the man unsnapped his shirt pocket and put my card in it. "I prefer to keep my women separate from my business. They ask too many questions."

"Will you ask about the pickup, please?" Jill asked.

"I'll call your husband if I learn anything. If he's smart, he'll tell you."

The waitress delivered our dinners. She made sure we had napkins and silverware, then looked at the older couple now having a discussion while leaning over the table. "Did Jay give you the fifth degree?"

"He just checked up on us."

"Nothing happens in Lame Deer without Jay's knowledge. He's the snoopiest old man in town."

Jill stabbed her fork into the lettuce. "Then we spoke with the right person. We're hoping to find someone who saw a Chevy dually pickup hauling a trailer through here early Tuesday morning."

"If you gave your number to Jay, I'm sure he'll get back to you."

I pulled out a twenty-dollar bill and handed it to our waitress.

"I haven't totalled your bill yet."

"That's for Jay and his wife's dinner."

The waitress chuckled. "Jay and his girlfriend. His wife died twenty years ago."

* * *

"How was your burger?" Jill asked as I turned the truck onto the highway.

"It was probably the best buffalo burger I've ever eaten. Most of them have been dry, but this one was really good. The bun was homemade."

"Their homemade salad dressing was outstanding. I'd gladly eat there again if we drive back through here at mealtime." Jill paused, then asked, "Do you expect to hear back from Jay?"

"I think he'll call if he learns something."

"Do you think he'd tell us if the driver was a tribal member?"

I shrugged. "My sense is that he thinks we're not wearing blinders, focused on pinning this on a tribal member. I think he'll be truthful. Besides, I doubt the killer was anyone from the reservation. The motive wasn't stealing a pickup, trailer, and horse. There's something else behind this and we haven't scratched the surface yet."

"What's that Sherlock Holmes quote? 'When you've eliminated all the unlikely, sometimes you're left with only the obvious.'"

"Two problems with that: I don't think that's the quote. Sherlock Holmes is a fictional character written by a guy who was injecting himself with cocaine."

"You know, Fletcher, you can be a real Debbie Downer sometimes."

"It's part of the cynical me that you've grown to love."

"Let's be clear—it's not your cynicism that I love. I put up with it, but I don't love it."

"You only want me for my body. Is that it?"

Jill snorted but didn't reply.

"I knew it!"

"Dream on, cowboy."

Chapter Six

My cell phone rang just as Highway 212 crossed into Wyoming. Fumbling to get it out of my pocket before it rolled over to voicemail, I dropped it on the seat and Jill picked it up. She glanced at the screen. "It's from an unknown caller, do you want me to answer it?"

"Sure. It might be someone connected to the case."

While I adjusted the mirrors to keep the setting sun from blinding me, Jill took the call. "Doug Fletcher's phone, this is Jill." She listened for a moment, then switched it to speaker. "Okay, Jay. Doug is turning off the road in Colony, Wyoming. I've switched the phone so Doug can hear you."

"Hi, Jay. I didn't expect to hear back from you so soon."

"You're in luck. One of the truckers stopped in for a burger."

"He saw the dually pickup passing through Lame Deer?"

"Oh, hell no."

After giving Jill an eye roll, I asked, "Then why are you calling?"

"Are you always so impatient, Doug?"

"Go ahead, tell me what's on your mind."

"This trucker came in for a burger and I asked him about your question. He had the buffalo burger and soup. I let him finish that, then talked to him while he ate blueberry pie. That pie was good. You missed out on a real treat when you skipped dessert."

"Next time."

"I forgot to thank you for buying my supper."

"It was my treat."

"Hey, Jill. Are you still there?"

Jill slid the phone closer. "I'm here, Jay."

"Did I mention my film career when I spoke with you two?"

"No. Do you think we could cover that another time? We're anxious to hear about the trucker."

Making a clucking sound, Jay expressed his dissatisfaction with our lack of patience. "I was on the Lone Ranger television show."

"Really?" Jill asked, trying to sound patient while I grimaced.

"Have you seen reruns of that show?"

"It was one of my dad's favorites when I was growing up."

"I hated being called Tonto. You know that means stupid in Spanish."

"Jay Silverheels played Tonto," I said, trying to reconcile the striking, image of the tall man who played Tonto with the short stocky man in Lame Deer.

"That was me."

Jill opened her smartphone and started a search.

"I got even, though. Kemosabe means soggy bush in Navajo. Every time the Lone Ranger called me stupid, I'd call him a soggy bush."

Turning her phone toward me, Jill showed a picture of Jay Silverheels as Tonto. "Jay Silverheels was from the Mohawk tribe, in Ontario, Canada."

"I got around a lot when I was younger."

"The internet says Jay Silverheels died in the 1980s."

Jay chuckled. "Do you believe everything you read on the internet?"

"Can we get back to the discussion of the trucker?" I asked.

"Sure. Like I said, he liked that blueberry pie a lot."

"Did he see the pickup and trailer in Lame Deer?"

"Oh, hell no, he wasn't anywhere near Lame Deer when he saw it."

In exasperation, I leaned my head back and pushed the phone to Jill, who had infinite patience when dealing with our parents and her Uncle Chet.

"What did he tell you, Jay?" Jill asked.

"Is Doug still there? He was the one who gave me the card and asked me to check around."

"He's still here, just…indisposed."

Laughing, Jay said, "He's still trying to get his head around me being famous?"

"Something like that," Jill said, containing her laughter as I beat the steering wheel in frustration.

"The trucker was going through Broadus when an idiot passed him going west. It was a dually pickup covered with advertising stickers."

"Was he pulling a horse trailer?" Jill asked, her excitement evident in her voice.

"Nope, the pickup was pulling a yellow stock trailer, although he said it looked like there was a white horse's tail in the back."

"I think that's the outfit we're looking for. Did he get a look at the driver?"

"Well, that's the strange part. You don't see much of the driver when someone passes you in the dark. And Billy… Did I mention that the driver's name was Billy? He hauls bentonite clay from the local ranches where it's mined. There's a processing plant right there in Colony. They use that bentonite for all kinds of stuff from kitty litter to ladies' makeup."

"The driver, Jay. Did Billy see the driver? What did the driver look like?"

"I was getting to that."

"Please, tell me about the driver."

"Well, I can't tell you much about him. Billy had been driving a long time and it was dark. He said it looked like the driver was a ghost."

Jill frowned and looked at me. "A ghost? What do you mean?"

"Well, that's where it gets really strange. Billy was tired and when that white face looked at him, well, it kind of freaked him out and he almost ran off the road."

I took the phone from Jill's hand and asked, "The driver's face was ghostly white?"

"That's what Billy thought. Now that he'd had some sleep and time to think about it, he's not sure he wasn't hallucinating. There aren't many people who drive around wearing white makeup."

"Ah, no. I can't say I've ever seen anyone in white makeup except a clown at a fair or in a parade."

Jill leaned close. "Could it have been a rodeo clown?"

"Hmm. What would a rodeo clown be doing driving across Montana in the middle of the night?"

"That's a good question, Jay. I suppose it would keep anyone from recognizing him. On the other hand, the truck and trailer were stolen from the Black Hills Roundup, and there are rodeo clowns there."

"I'll tell Billy he didn't see a ghost," Jay said with a laugh. "People have really been giving him a hard time about having visions or drinking while on the job."

"What's Billy's last name?" I asked.

"Billy Beaverheart. He's a good man. Works hard."

"Thanks, Jay," Jill said. "That information may be very helpful."

"I hope so. It'll be like the days when I was helping the Lone Ranger solve crimes."

Wearing a broad smile, Jill leaned close to the phone. "Only this time you may be helping us solve a real crime." She ended the call and handed me the phone. "He's a funny old man."

"He's delusional about being Tonto," I said as I pulled onto the nearly empty highway.

"He's pulling our legs."

"I've just lost ten minutes of my life that I'll never get back," I replied.

"Admit it. You laughed at Jay's ghost story."

"Sure. He's a regular comedian." I readjusted the mirrors to get the setting sun's glare out of my eyes. "How much credence do you put in the story about the ghost or clown driving Chris' pickup?"

"He offered the information about the sponsors' ads without prompting from us. I think someone seeing a man wearing white makeup while passing me in the middle of the night might make me swerve off the road." Jill paused. "The description of the yellow stock trailer with a horse is new. We can ask the Belle Fourche police chief to check on that."

"Would it be more or less likely that someone would report the theft of a stock trailer vs. a horse trailer?"

"The people who bring horses have their specific trailers, often with living quarters attached. The people who provide rodeo stock often bring steers, broncs, and calves, in semis and trailers. I suspect they get parked in a back corner for the duration of the event and the owners might not miss them until they're ready to load up after the rodeo is over."

* * *

The lingering July sunset had faded to total darkness by the time we reached the Spearfish ranch. From the big living room recliner, Al looked over his shoulder. "I thought you government workers had 9 to 5 jobs." He was watching the news with a remote in one hand and a nearly empty glass of liquor in the other hand.

"It was a long day," I said.

"The rodeo finals are tomorrow. I expect you're planning to make use of the expensive tickets Chet bought."

The hint about the unused tickets was unexpected, but a reminder that we'd returned to South Dakota under the guise of attending the Black Hills Roundup. Jill grabbed my arm before I responded, apparently hoping to cut off a comment that might seem ungrateful. "We've got to meet with the police chief, but we should be free after that."

"Well, you should plan on hanging around Belle tomorrow until after fireworks. They put on quite a show after the last event."

"We'll plan on that," Jill said, squeezing my forearm.

"Is there anything in the news?" I asked, changing the topic.

"Same old crap. Washington politicians are trying to agree on a new budget that was due back in February. Chicago had its one hundredth murder. Some tree hugger from Delaware is trying to shut down our wolf hunting season." After pouring down the last of his booze, Al added, "They should set a pack of wolves free in her backyard. She might change her mind after they eat Fluffy and Kitty. Those do-gooders ought to keep their noses out of stuff they don't understand."

"What's the weather forecast?" Jill asked

"A high-pressure front is stuck over us. It'll be just as hot and dry tomorrow as it was today. We could sure use some rain. The problem is this time of year we don't get rain without a thunderstorm. The Black Hills are so dry a lightning strike could burn a thousand acres." Al clicked off the TV and got up. "Molly left some pork roast, potatoes, and roasted carrots in the refrigerator in case you didn't have time for supper. Turn the lights off when you go to bed."

Jill nodded toward the refrigerator as her father walked to his bedroom. "Eat something or Mom will think we're ungrateful."

"You eat something. You're the one who had a salad for supper."

After opening the refrigerator, Jill stared at the plastic containers Molly had left for us. "I'll heat up the leftovers. We'll eat a little, dirty some plates, scrape scraps into the wastebasket, and leave dirty dishes in the sink. Mom will believe that we ate a late supper."

Chuckling, I took plates out of the cupboard and silverware from the drawer. "You're devious."

"I know my mother and food. She takes it very personally if her guests don't eat like every meal is Thanksgiving."

The beeping microwave signaled the end of the warming cycle and Jill delivered a plate of steaming food to the table. I was eating pork and potatoes when I heard the hinges squeak down the hallway.

Molly, dressed in a pink bathrobe shuffled into the kitchen. "Oh good, you found the leftovers." She paused, then looked at Jill. "You're going to heat another plate for yourself, aren't you?"

"Um, sure, Mom. This is Doug's portion."

Molly smiled and patted my shoulder. "You appreciate my cooking. I could hardly ask for a better son-in-law."

Swallowing, I looked at her over my shoulder. "I thought the son-in-law requirements were shooting and riding a horse."

"Those are Al's expectations. You appreciate a good meal and that means a lot to me." She paused and looked at the small portion Jill warmed for herself. "On the other hand, my daughter eats like a bird." Molly turned and walked away.

"Great!" Jill said, sitting down with her half-full plate. "You get an attaboy because Mom didn't realize what's on your plate was supposed to be split between us. I get the 'Jill eats like a bird,' comment."

"Timing is everything."

"I've been thinking about the clown driving Chris Jenkins' pickup."

94

"What about it?"

Jill pushed a potato around in the gravy. "It's strange, yet plausible. No one would recognize a person in clown makeup."

I ate the last bite of pork Jill had warmed and tried to decide if I'd be able to sleep if I ate the last half potato and a pair of carrots. I set my fork on the plate and pushed it away.

"I hope mom doesn't come back and see all the food you're not going to eat."

I took the plate to the wastebasket and scraped the potato and carrots into the bin, then set my dirty plate and silverware in the sink. "Not a problem. If she questions the scraps in the wastebasket, I'll tell her they're your leftovers."

"Hey! I'm already getting grief about eating like a bird."

"Perfect! I look like an appreciative son-in-law and your reputation is intact."

Jill carried her still half-full plate to the back door.

"Where are you going?"

"I'm feeding my leftovers to the cat."

"I didn't know that was an option."

Jill returned with her gravy smeared plate and set it where she'd been seated. "There. Mom will think I ate all my meal and the scraps in the wastebasket will be from you. I'm going to bed."

Jill was halfway to the bedroom when I grabbed her plate and put it in the sink with mine. She heard the clatter and looked into the kitchen from the hallway. "What are you up to?"

"Hmm, it appears your plate is in the sink and the evidence of who did or didn't eat all their meal has been compromised."

"That will cost you."

I walked up to her and pulled Jill into my arms. "I don't think so."

"Stop it," she whispered. "Your badge is sticking me in the ribs."

I untucked her shirttail and nuzzled her neck. "I love you."

"Stop that. Mom could walk out at any moment."

"Then we'd better move to the bedroom."

"You're in trouble, Fletcher. What makes you think I'll be interested in romance?"

I pulled Jill into the bedroom and closed the door. "You're always interested in romance."

"I am not *always interested in romance.* It's late, you've stirred up trouble, and we need to be in Belle early to talk to the police chief."

"Your mother expects two things from us; that we'll eat heartily and that we'll be deeply in love."

"You're in trouble."

"Yeah, but you're drawn to my bad boy side."

I felt a sharp pain in my big toe that made me step back. "You stay on your own side of the bed tonight, or you'll have more than a sore toe."

"But..."

"But nothing. Put your boxers on and face the door until you fall asleep."

Chapter Seven

Jill's body was warm against my back as the smell of frying bacon drifted into the bedroom. I rolled over and put my arm around Jill's torso. "Your mom's frying bacon. Do you want to shower first?"

After stretching, Jill said, "Go ahead. I'll start the coffee and set the table."

I scooted across the hall to the bathroom in my boxers, hoping that my mother-in-law was either looking away or would be unfazed by the site of my boxer shorts and hairy legs. Pounding hot water helped get my brain functioning after the short night. In retrospect, Jill's rebuff of my romantic overture was for the best. As a young cop with rotating shifts and a drinking problem, I was able to function on five or six hours of sleep. Now twenty years past that point of my life, I'm pleased not to wake up with a hangover, and seven or eight hours of sleep is the bare minimum that allows me to function.

The bathroom door opened when I was drying my back, causing me to spin toward the bathtub. "Take it easy cowboy," Jill said. "I've seen your plumbing before."

"You have, but I thought your mom might've been coming in."

"She'd knock," Jill said as she pulled her long flannel nightgown over her head. She slid past me into the bathtub and pulled the curtain. Her panties flew over the curtain rod and landed at my feet as the shower started.

"You know, I've seen your plumbing before, too," I said to the shower curtain.

"I didn't want to arouse you or give you ideas."

I pulled on a fresh pair of boxers and a polo shirt, then slid on a pair of jeans. "Like that's going to happen in your parents' bathroom while your mother is cooking breakfast."

After a snort, Jill said, "Like that's stopped you before." She paused, then added. "By the way, that was *not* an invitation."

"Are we really going to watch the rodeo today?"

"Your tone makes me think that wouldn't be your first choice."

"I'd really like to follow up on the clown."

"Don't you think we can do both?"

As I closed the bathroom door, I said, "I hope not."

Molly eyed me suspiciously as I exited the bathroom. "I know you two are married, but it still feels strange to see you sharing the bedroom and bathroom."

Pouring two cups of coffee, I nodded. "It's good I don't have a daughter. I'd probably shoot the first guy who kissed her."

Molly accepted a cup from me and smiled. "Doug, just because it seems strange to see you two sharing a bed, doesn't mean I'm not happy. I was sure Jill was never going to get married. Before that was a time when I was afraid she was going to marry some long-haired, tree-hugging hippie. Al would've shot a bull rider if he'd caught him in bed with Jill."

A throat clearing sound came from the living room where Al was leafing through the newspaper. "I wasn't too sure about you for a while, you being a city kid and all. But you're not as bad as I'd feared, and your mom is a nice lady."

"I'm not as bad as you'd feared?"

"If only you could ride a horse…"

"I can ride. I choose not to, but I can ride."

"There's being able to keep your butt in the saddle, then there's *riding*. You may get there some day, but not until you lose your fear of the horse."

"I'm not afraid of the horses. I have a deep distrust of them."

Setting the newspaper aside, Al stood. "That's the same thing." He looked at Molly. "I'll have a couple eggs over easy."

"You'll have eggs however I fix them," Molly replied.

Al winked at me and whispered, "And I'll be happy about it."

"Is that a life lesson?" I asked.

"That's the secret to a happy marriage. There are bigger marital issues than how your eggs are cooked."

With a cast iron frying pan in her hand, Molly walked from the stove to the table. She flipped two eggs, waited one second, then lifted them onto Al's plate. "Over easy." She put two on my plate and winked. "Sunny side up."

Jill came out of the bathroom drying her hair. "No eggs for me."

Molly's eye roll was priceless. "Your husband might appreciate a little meat on your bones."

Jill stopped rubbing her hair and smiled at me. "Do I need more meat on my bones, dear?"

The kitchen came to a silent standstill while Al and Molly waited for my answer. "I think you're perfect just as you are, dear."

Al winked at me, and Molly returned to the stove. "How many pancakes do you want, Jill?"

"One is plenty," Jill said as she walked into the bedroom.

Molly slid two huge pancakes onto my plate, then shook her head. "She eats like a bird."

Jill was back before Molly flipped the single pancake onto her plate. "Birds don't eat three strips of bacon, Mom. I'll be just fine," she said, moving two strips of bacon to my plate.

The back door opened, and Chet walked in with my mother, Ronnie, right behind him. "You're still eating breakfast?" Chet asked. "The rooster crowed three hours ago."

Ronnie shook her head as she poured coffee for Chet and herself. "If you've got any batter left, I bet Chet would eat a pancake or two. It's been nearly two hours since he had his raisin bran and prunes."

Chet blushed. "You don't want to be around me if I don't have my prunes."

"What do my cops have planned for the day," Ronnie asked.

"We got a strange tip that the stolen pickup was driven away by a guy in clown makeup," Jill said. "We need to talk to the police chief about that."

"Clown makeup?" Chet asked.

Jill drowned her pancake in maple syrup. "That's the tip we got. It's unlikely someone would make up an observation like that."

"Hmph," Chet said. "That would make it hard to identify the driver."

The simple wisdom of Chet's words struck home. "That may be the answer. The person in makeup may not have been a clown, just someone trying to keep people from recognizing him."

Jill pointed her fork at me. "If the driver was someone recognizable around the rodeo, wearing clown makeup would certainly make it hard to identify him."

"Do I get a cut of the reward money?" Chet asked, mumbling with his mouth full of pancake.

"There's no reward," I said.

"Hmph. I'll call the police chief and suggest that he offer a reward," Chet said, washing down the pancake with a gulp of coffee. "Hold off on sharing that thought about someone wearing clown makeup as a disguise until I have time to suggest the reward."

Clenching his eyes shut, Al shook his head. "That's not how it works, Chet. You can't throw out the thought that the killer might've been wearing makeup and hope to collect the reward. You have to identify a specific person."

"I am identifying a specific person; a guy wearing clown makeup."

Having lived through so many *discussions* between Chet and her father, Jill waited until they'd argued themselves out. "Chet, you have to name the suspect to collect the reward."

Chet dug a rodeo flyer out of his pocket and unfolded it. "Look here," he said, pointing to a list of rodeo contestants and contributors. "Here are the two rodeo clowns. I think it was either Ken Halsey or Rod Crane. Is that good enough?"

Pushing myself back from the table, I nodded. "Chet, if either of those two is the killer, I'll give you a buck."

"I was hoping for maybe five thousand bucks."

I stood and picked up my place setting. "I think the odds of either of those two being the killer in clown makeup is about five thousand to one."

"But you're going to talk to them, aren't you?" Chet asked.

Chuckling, Jill joined me at the sink. "Sure, Uncle Chet. We'll talk to them, but I think Doug is right about the odds."

Chet grinned. "Dang it, I was hoping for at least some bragging rights if not a cash reward."

Molly hustled to the sink and elbowed us aside. "I'll do the dishes. You two need to catch a clown."

"We'll be home by six," I called over my shoulder as we went out of the door.

* * *

As she buckled her seatbelt, Jill grinned. "You shouldn't lie to my mother."

"What did I lie about?"

"Being home by six."

"Let's call it an aspirational goal. I'd like to be home by six, but realistically, we're working, and the case will dictate our schedule."

"Like I said, you lied."

Jill's phone rang before we could continue the conversation. "Hi Jack. Sure, I've got time for an update. We're driving to Belle Fourche and as long as we continue to have cell service I can talk."

The cell service held up and Jill updated our boss on the trip to Little Bighorn, our discussion with the man claiming to have been Tonto on the *Lone Ranger* television show, and a sighting of the man in clown makeup driving the pickup. She listened intently for a minute, then glanced at me. "Our usual plan is to support the local law enforcement community unless we're on Park Service property." Not happy with whatever she was hearing, Jill put the phone on speaker. "Hang on, Jack. I'll let Doug address that suggestion."

"Hi, Doug. I just told Jill that you two should take the lead on investigating the body found at Little Bighorn National Monument. She was found on Park Service property, and frankly, we could use the press coverage."

"That's not the way it works, Jack. The woman was kidnapped from Belle Fourche, her body was transported across Wyoming and Montana. A Montana coroner did the autopsy, and we're relying on resources from at least three other police agencies. If we ever want to work with these folks again, we'll have to be team players and let them take the lead…and the credit if it's solved."

Pardee sighed. "The Investigative Services Branch is an obscure part of the National Park Service. Some positive press would improve our visibility."

"I agree," I said. "I'll tell the newspaper or television people to give you a call when this is solved so you can explain our role."

"Doug, I don't need your smartass remarks."

"With all due respect, if this is how you operate, you'll have our resignations as soon as we can get to a computer."

"No, no, no. I was just trying to help you understand our need for visibility."

"Have you ever been a cop, Jack? I mean, a real cop who puts his life on the line while doing his job?"

"I'm a trained investigator."

"That's not the same thing. Jill and I are out here. The guns on our hips are not decorative. We may have to put our lives on the line, and the cops we're supporting know that we'll have their backs. We need them to have ours. If I walk in and tell them I'm taking over, we risk putting that delicate relationship on the line. I won't do that. Period."

Jill pulled the phone in front of her. "Have you looked at any of the press conference footage from our previous investigations, Jack?"

"I've read the reports."

"Do an internet search for Fletcher and park service. Watch the videos. We're in the back row but listen to what those local officers say about our role in the investigations."

"Fine. We'll do it your way. But let's be clear, your previous boss let a lot of things slide by. Make sure your reports are clearly written, your expense vouchers have receipts, and your uniforms are spotless if you're in a picture."

I took the phone back. "I don't think we'll have time for a side trip through Salt Lake City on our return trip, Jack. Maybe another time."

After a pause, Jack came back. "Here's the deal, you two. I call the shots. I don't need to hear 'yes sir' but it should be understood that you report to me, and I determine your assignments and role in them. You can either fly here on your way back to Texas, or you'll book a round-trip flight here as soon as you return. I want to see your smiling faces in my office. Understood?"

Jill snatched the phone away before I made a snarky comment. "That's fine, Jack. We'll see you at the end of the investigation. Please understand that the investigation is tense right now and our minds are focused there, and not on being polite rangers talking to the public."

I couldn't hear Jack's response, but Jill listened, then ended the call. She blew out a breath and looked at me. "He needed to hear what you had to say, but you didn't need to…be your usual, cynical self."

"This was our chance to control our work situation. If we'd rolled over and said, yes sir, he would've expected that for the rest of the time we report to him."

"But now he's going to edit every line of our reports and go through our expense accounts with a fine-tooth comb."

"He's a bureaucrat. Jack was going to do those things regardless of what we'd said. His job is to protect his ass and make himself look good to his superiors. Our job is to solve crimes and not piss off our partner agencies in the process. He knows where we stand and it's best to have that on the table from the outset."

The trilling phone interrupted our conversation. "Hi, Matt. What's new in Texas?" Jill switched the phone to speaker.

"What in hell did you say to Jack Pardee? He just called and asked me what kind of impertinent, disrespectful people I'd dumped on him."

Snatching the phone away, Jill turned off the speaker. She explained to Matt what had been said and put context on our impertinence and disrespect, framing it as the ranting of a cynical cop. At the end, she laughed and ended the call.

"What's Matt going to do?"

"He forwarded links of our press conferences to Jack and reminded him that there were letters of commendation from the Secretary of the Interior in our personnel files. Matt asked Jack if the Secretary even knew his name. I guess that was a hot button that ended the call."

We were nearing Belle when the phone trilled again. Jill looked at the caller ID and said, "Jack," before turning the speaker on.

"I think we got off on the wrong foot," Pardee said, the heat gone from his voice. "I understand your situation and your need to rely on other resources for support." He drew a breath. "I've spoken with my boss, and he agrees that it's best to let you have the reins on this investigation. You're more experienced than my other investigators and don't require the guidance they need. That said, I'm behind you on this…but if you burn my butt, I'll have you investigating prairie dog deaths in Jewel Cave National Park. Understood?"

"Thanks for the words of encouragement and support," I said.

"Listen, Doug. I'm unaccustomed to being addressed like that."

"Well, get used to it. If you can't deal with having competent investigators who know how to get results, I'm sure the Secretary of the Interior will be happy to have us report through a different supervisor."

"Just get through this case and we'll sort out a way to live with each other."

"Do we need receipts for the meals we're eating with Jill's parents?"

Jill snatched the phone away and turned off the speaker. "Yes, Jack. He was kidding." After a few more seconds she ended the call.

"Geez, Doug. Don't poke our new boss."

"I don't suffer idiots well."

"Give him a chance. We're an unknown quantity to him. Let's feel our way through this relationship without throwing gas on the flames." Jill turned to me and added, "And if you say, 'yes dear' you'll have a broken rib."

"You're so wise, dear."

Clenching her fists, Jill counted to ten. "Sometimes I wish you'd just swear and get it out of your system."

"I have an extensive vocabulary that is more expressive than a simple four-letter expletive."

"Yeah. Right."

* * *

Belle Fourche Police Chief Arnold was drinking coffee while reading emails. Responding to my knock on his door frame he said, "The door's open."

"We have a lead," Jill said.

The chief's chair spun around so fast that Arnold slopped his coffee. "Sorry, I thought it was Connie with the overnight reports," he said as he dabbed at his pants with a tissue.

"Sorry to startle you," Jill said, sitting in a guest chair.

"What's this lead?"

"We have a witness who saw Chris Jenkins' pickup driving through Broadus on Tuesday morning."

"That's not much of a lead," the chief said. "I assumed her truck was driven to Little Bighorn."

I laughed. "I didn't assume that. Who knows how her body got to the middle of Montana?"

"Aliens didn't transport her there," Arnold countered.

Jill looked around. "Any chance we could get a cup of coffee?"

The chief led us down a hallway to a closet equipped with a sink, refrigerator, microwave, and coffee maker. He threw a dollar bill into a coffee can and took two unmatched cups off a drying rack. "Help yourselves."

"Someone is missing a yellow stock trailer," Jill said as she poured coffee.

"Say what?"

"Chris Jenkins' truck was spotted pulling a yellow stock trailer with a palomino horse in the back."

"The person in Broadus said that?"

"Yeah, he saw a yellow stock trailer with a horse in the back. The horse had a white tail, like the missing palomino, and he also gave us a description of the driver."

Arnold had been leaning against the door frame. He straightened up. "What did he look like?"

"He described the driver's face as ghostly white."

After an eye roll, Arnold stepped back and gestured toward his office. "You had me going there for a while."

"Seriously. A trucker going through Broadus was passed by Chris' truck driven by a guy with a face as white as a ghost."

"Who reported this?"

Jill hesitated, weighing her words. "A guy named Jay who we met in Lame Deer. He came over to our table at the café and introduced himself. He was a Cheyenne

112

elder, and we asked him to keep his ear to the ground for information about someone driving Chris Jenkins' truck on Highway 212."

The police chief leaned forward and picked up a pen. "What's this informant's name?"

"Jay."

The chief wrote Jay on a notepad. "Does Jay have a last name?"

"Um, he claimed to have been Tonto on the *Lone Ranger* TV show, so I suppose his stage name was Silverheels. I'm not sure if he goes by that or not."

Dropping his pen, Chief Arnold closed his eyes and leaned back. "You are shitting me. A guy who claims to have been Tonto on television told you that a truck driver saw a ghost driving Chris Jenkins' pickup through Broadus?"

Jill waited for me to jump in, but I leaned back and crossed my arms. She was already knee-deep in the manure, and I decided not to join her unless she started flailing for help. "Um, yeah." She paused. "The truck driver was Billy Beaverheart. You can look up his phone number."

After running his tongue around the inside of his lips like he'd tasted something unsavory, the chief picked up his pen. "Is that his stage name? What television show was Billy Beaverheart on?"

"I'm serious!" Jill protested.

"How do I contact Tonto?"

Again, Jill looked at me. "We're not sure. He called us from the Spoon and Fork restaurant."

"Is he the owner?"

"I think he's got his own table in the back," Jill replied.

"Come on, guys. I thought you two were serious investigators."

I blew out a breath. "Chris Jenkins' truck was pulling a yellow stock trailer. Can your guys check with the people who provide the rodeo livestock to see if anyone is missing a trailer?"

"Was this a ghostly trailer or a real trailer?" The chief asked.

"It was a real trailer with a palomino in the back."

After tapping his pen on the notepad for a moment, the chief nodded. "I'll have one of my guys check with the stockmen."

"Can you think of any reason someone would have a ghostly white face?" I asked.

Chief Arnold stood. "Not off the top of my head, and to be serious, it's not something I'm going to dwell on while the rodeo is going." He walked to the door, signaling for us to leave. "I'll let you know if someone reports a missing yellow stock trailer."

"Thanks," I said as we exited.

"Hey, Fletcher. Why don't you have the Lone Ranger help? He always bailed Tonto out of pinches."

Shaking her head, Jill replied, "I think it was the other way around. Tonto was the one who showed up at the last second to bail out the Lone Ranger."

* * *

The morning was heating up when we walked out of the police station. I handed Jill the keys.

"Sure, you park in the empty street in front of the police station, and you expect me to find a parking spot at the rodeo."

"I'm unaccustomed to parking a big rig like the pickup. You have a pickup at home, so it'll be no problem for you."

Pulling onto the street, Jill glanced at me. "What do you think about the ghost thing? Is Jay yanking our chains?"

"I think he's reporting what he heard from the trucker. I wonder just what the trucker actually saw?"

"I think we should find the Lone Ranger," I said.

"Not you too," Jill replied. "I got enough of that from the chief."

"You never know. We might need one of the Lone Ranger's silver bullets to kill the ghost."

Jill groaned. "I think silver bullets are for vampires."

"No, you need a wooden stake for vampires. I think silver bullets kill ghosts."

"Can we talk about this seriously?" Jill asked.

"If you have a serious suggestion, I'd be happy to hear it. Otherwise, I think we should check the gun shops for silver bullets."

"You're doing this just to irritate me, aren't you?"

"Is it working?"

Jill pulled to the edge of the street. "Get out. If you're going to be a pain in the ass, you can walk the rest of the way."

I opened the door and stepped out. "Thanks for letting me out close to the grandstand. I think you're going to drive for blocks to find a parking spot for this rig."

"Dammit, Fletcher. Sometimes you really piss me off."

"You're the one who told me to get out here." I closed the door and watched Jill drive off spitting gravel as she accelerated.

I found Mom and Chet in the stands as the bronc riding finals started. Mom looked past me, then cocked her head. "Where's Jill?"

"She's parking the truck."

"You didn't wait for her?"

I took a seat next to Chet. "She dropped me off so I wouldn't have to walk all the way from the remote parking lot."

Chet tipped his head back just far enough to look at me from under the brim of his Stetson. "I haven't been in this relationship thing very long, but that doesn't sound like a good strategy."

"Let's hope she cools off on the walk from the parking lot," I replied.

Mother glared at me. "You do remember that she carries a gun."

"She won't shoot me."

Chet smiled. "Not all shots are meant to kill."

Fifteen minutes later, Jill arrived with a cardboard carry tray holding four coffee cups. Her smile made me uneasy as she handed coffee to Chet and Mom. "Here's yours, dear."

I took a sip and nearly gagged on the intense sweetness. "I like my coffee black without sugar."

Still smiling, Jill replied. "I know."

Chet's belly bounced as he laughed. "Like I said, not all shots are meant to kill."

I dumped my coffee out under the stands and tucked the plastic lid into the empty cup. "I'd like to take a walk back to Chris Jenkins' trailer."

Jill pulled her feet back. "Have a nice walk. Let me know what you see."

"I could use someone to watch my back," I said, waiting for her to stand.

"I sure hope you don't run into any trouble, dear."

Chet chuckled. "As I recall, the last time I slept on Molly and Al's couch, it was a little lumpy."

The guy seated behind me leaned forward. "Could you sit or move on? We're tryin' to see the bronc riding."

"I'm a cop talking to my partner, buddy."

"I ain't your buddy, and I don't care if you're the governor. Either sit or move on."

I stepped past Jill's feet, then felt her hand on my back as I continued down the narrow walkway to the aisle. Out of the stands I turned. "I'm sorry."

Jill placed her hand flat on my chest and pushed. "Move out of the crowd before continuing your apology."

I had no further apology, but decided it was best to move on while I contemplated additional words. Nearing the competitors' living quarters, I stopped. "I was being a jerk. I'm sorry."

"That's it?"

"What more is there to say?" I asked as a young woman dressed in an embroidered shirt and white hat approached.

The woman slowed and put her hand on my arm. "Flowers work for my boyfriend."

The woman's words broke the tension and Jill smiled. "I don't want flowers, but I do want you to be serious sometimes."

"I'm frequently serious."

"I asked you a serious question, and you gave a smartass answer."

My mind raced back to our discussion in the truck. "You mean about the silver bullets?"

"No. About why someone would wear white makeup."

"I don't have an answer. That's why we got into the discussion." I had a sudden flash and stepped away. "Miss!"

The woman turned. "What? Do you need the name of the florist?"

I jogged a few steps to catch up with her. "Were you here Monday night?"

"Yeah, I got here last Sunday for the preliminary qualifications."

"Did you see or hear anything unusual that night?"

"I crashed early because I had morning races."

She turned away and took a few steps toward an entrance I hadn't seen. "One more question, is this the gate you always use to enter the arena?"

"Yeah, this is the contestants' entrance."

Jill caught up with me. "I can hear the gears turning in your head."

"The local cops went from trailer to trailer, interviewing the contestants. Chief Arnold said it was a hit or miss effort, depending on who happened to be around when they went through."

"So?"

"Let's talk to the contestants as they enter and leave the arena. We should be able to catch all of them at some point during the day."

"We can do that," Jill said, "but a bunch of contestants were eliminated in preliminary rounds so they may be gone."

"Let's try for a couple of hours. You approach the women and I'll talk to the cowboys."

Jill's eyes lit up. "I think the cowboys might prefer talking to me."

"And the women might think I'm a creep trying to buy them a drink."

"Pin your badge to your shirt. They'll at least stop and talk to you." Jill paused and her dimples appeared. "Who knows, maybe you'll meet a couple badge bunnies who want to buy *you* a drink."

That comment froze me. "Let's approach them together."

* * *

There was a rush of contestants right after we'd decided to do joint interviews, so we split up, interviewing whoever went

120

through our side of the entrance. No one had seen or heard anything unusual Monday night, although it became clear that a number of the contestants' memories had been clouded by alcohol or some other substance that evening. It also seemed that parties were somewhat spontaneous, and that people, male and female, had wandered among a number of trailers over the nights leading to the rodeo opening.

I ended a conversation with one of the male competitors, a guy in his thirties who walked like someone twice his age. He hadn't seen anything and admitted that he was dosing himself with painkillers and had fallen asleep early every night.

Breaking away from him, I approached a raven-haired woman in a black-sequined outfit. "Excuse me, were you in the living quarters Monday night?"

With a practiced smile that didn't extend to her eyes, she reminded me of a beauty queen who could wave to the crowd without moving her upper arm. "I was." Her answer was curt, and she immediately stepped away.

"Ma'am, we're hoping someone saw something unusual around the living quarters on Monday night."

"Sorry," she replied. She took a step, then stopped and turned back toward me. "Is that the night Chris Jenkins disappeared?"

"It is. We're trying to identify someone who might've entered or left her trailer, or who might've seen someone out of place near the living quarters."

"You know, it was kind of strange, but Chris' door opened as I was walking past. I saw a flash of someone's face, then he pulled the door shut when he realized I was there."

"Was it someone you recognized or could identify?"

"I only saw a flash, but...frankly it spooked me."

"The face spooked you?"

"Yeah, if I didn't know better, I'd say he was wearing white clown makeup."

Chapter Eight

A roar rose from the grandstand as something exciting happened in the arena. When the noise slowly abated Jill grabbed my arm. "Do you hear that?"

Unsure of what I was listening for, I turned my head from side to side. A young woman was yelling from somewhere among the competitors' trailers. Her pleas were muffled by the noise of the crowd, but desperation was evident in her voice. I pointed to my left and yelled to Jill, "Go that way. I'll go right."

The trailers were an assortment of styles and sizes, most being horse trailers with living quarters in the front. Others were popular brands of camping trailers. All were arranged in neat rows.

Cutting between trailers and looking down the rows, the girl's yells became louder and were accompanied by a banging sound, like she was pounding on a trailer's door. In the fourth alleyway I spotted a young teen. Her white hat was in her left hand as she pounded on the door of a rusty, older trailer with her right.

123

"Amber! Come out of there!" She sobbed.

Farther down the aisle, Jill ran toward me as I dashed toward the girl.

Oblivious to my approach, the girl dropped her hat and pounded on the trailer's door with both hands. "Let her out you bastard, she's only fifteen!"

Breathless, I reached the girl and touched her arm. "What's wrong?"

The girl turned to me just as Jill arrived behind us. "My friend is in there with that slimy bull rider. He's going to..." The girl turned to the trailer and pounded her fists on the door. "The cops are here. Let her go!"

Shuffling sounds and curses came from inside the trailer as Jill took the girl's hand. "Tell me what happened."

"My friend has a mouse tattoo that peeks over her jeans, here," the girl said, pointing near the belt buckle on her hip-hugging jeans. "That...bull rider said he'd like to see the rest of the mouse back in his trailer." The girl started sobbing. "Amber's not a buckle bunny. She didn't want to screw that guy. She just wanted to show him her tattoo."

I rattled the locked doorknob and looked at the girl. "How old is Amber?"

"She's fifteen."

I pounded on the door. "Police! Open the door!" Jill punched 911 into her phone and led the girl a step away from the door. I considered breaking the door, but it was two steps above the ground and opened outward. Without a battering ram, there was no way I was going to break it open. "Open the door. The girl is underage, and you'll be arrested for rape!"

The sounds of a struggle came through the thin walls of the trailer. "You're goddamned jailbait! You said you were eighteen!"

"Get off me! I only wanted to show you my tattoo! Help!"

Jill drew her Glock, her face red with rage. "I'll blow the knob off."

"And you'll kill someone inside. No." I pounded on the door again. "Police. Open the door or I'll break it down."

A crash came from somewhere inside the trailer, followed by the sound of running feet. The doorknob rattled, then the lock released. I pulled on the door and a young girl, dressed only in thong panties fell into my arms."

"Piper," the naked girl slurred. "Gawd, he was going to…"

"Amber!" the outside girl yelled, pushing past Jill.

Unsure of the reception I'd get from whoever was inside, I drew my pistol and stepped into the trailer's combination living room/dining area. The filthy floor was littered with beer cans and clothing. Two pairs of cowboy boots; one pair male and one pair female, were jumbled under the small table. At least six beer cans littered the tabletop that was splattered with spilled beer. Outside the door I heard the sound of vomiting and Piper's sobbing.

A sound to my left caused me to raise my gun. A naked man stumbled out of the bedroom, trying to pull on a pair of jeans bunched around his right calf. He hopped down the hallway trying to get his other foot into the jeans. It was evident that his intentions had not been innocent. He cursed as his zipper pulled across his erection.

He'd been oblivious to me until he looked up after snapping his jeans. "Who the hell are you?"

Lowering my gun because he had nowhere to hide a weapon, I took in the situation. The man, perhaps in his thirties, was barely more than five feet tall. His hair was dark and the hair of his head, arms, and chest was sweaty and matted. Two prominent pink scars jumped out at me. One ran the length of his left upper arm and another curved over his left shoulder.

Outside, I heard footsteps and the sound of an urgent conversation between Jill and a man. A second later, a Belle Fourche cop stepped into the trailer. "Jimmy Conroy, what the hell have you done this time?"

126

"It was that prick-teasing bitch's fault. She told me she was seventeen…eighteen."

The cop, whose name tag read Hooper, surveyed the beer cans on the table. "Regardless of what you had planned for the bedroom, the legal drinking age is twenty-one, Jimmy."

"Yeah, well, she was asking for it."

Hooper looked at Conroy's bulging crotch. "It appears you were ready to give it to her." He paused. "Or did we arrive after the act?"

Conroy seemed to have a buzz from the beer. Amber, with a towel draped over her naked top, wasn't accustomed to drinking alcohol and continued to retch outside the trailer.

"I never stuck her," Conroy said. "We were just…cuddling."

Hooper removed a pair of handcuffs from his belt. "Turn around, Jimmy. We'll see what the girl and forensic people say about what happened."

Raising his hands and backing down the hallway, Conroy said, "You can't arrest me! I'm in the bull-riding finals this afternoon!" He turned and ran down the short hallway with Hooper on his heels.

Following the men down the hallway, I watched the two of them wrestling on the bed. Hooper rolled Jimmy onto his stomach, but the wiry bull rider fought like a tiger. Conroy was about to bite the cop when I grabbed his left arm and twisted it until it popped.

"Goddamn you! That's my bad shoulder!"

"You're resisting arrest. I had to use reasonable force to assist Officer Hooper."

Pulling Conroy's arms behind his back, Hooper searched the tangled sheets for his handcuffs. I pulled them out of a stained fold of linen and handed them to him.

"Thanks," he said, clipping the cuffs on Conroy's wrists as the bull rider swore at me. "Who the hell are you anyway?"

"Fletcher, from the Park Service."

Hooper, his uniform sweaty and wrinkled from the struggle, pulled Conroy to his feet.

"This isn't a park," Conroy sneered.

I shook my head. "We happened to be in the area and heard the girl yelling for help."

Hooper looked at me, then studied the badge I'd pinned to my shirt while we were interviewing people. "That's no park ranger badge and I've never seen a park ranger carrying a gun."

"My partner and I are Park Service investigators assisting with Chris Jenkins' murder. We were interviewing competitors by the arena entrance when we heard the commotion."

Hooper looked at the messy bed and shook his head. "For the sake of that little girl outside, I hope you got here in the nick of time."

Conroy struggled against the handcuffs. "I wasn't going to do anything she wasn't asking for. Did you see that outfit she was wearing?"

I blew out a breath, biting my tongue. "It sounded like she was saying *no* when we arrived."

Glaring at me, Conroy said, "As far as I'm concerned, she said *yes* as soon as she walked into the trailer, and then again when we opened the first can of beer."

Hooper pushed him toward the door, reciting the Miranda warning as they passed me.

Jill was kneeling next to Amber and Piper when I stepped out of the dark trailer into the sunlight. A number of contestants had gathered around them, and someone had given Amber a shirt to cover her torso. Bruises were starting to blossom on the girl's thighs and one of her cheeks was swollen. Activity farther down the aisle between the trailers caught my attention as two paramedics jogged toward us.

Bending down, I whispered to Jill, "She needs to go with the paramedics. The hospital needs to treat her and run a rape kit."

Overhearing us, Amber wailed, "No! My mom will kill me."

Piper nodded. "Her mom is a really strict Baptist. She doesn't know we came to the rodeo. She'd kill Amber if she saw her outfit and knew she'd gone into a bull rider's trailer."

Squeezing Amber's shoulders, Jill whispered, "I've been in trouble with my mom, too. But she only yelled at me because she loved me and cared what happened to me. She'll be relieved that you're safe." Jill nodded to the paramedics who bent down, then they helped Amber to her feet.

Chief Arnold appeared from the crowd and took me aside. "Hooper called in and said some park service cop stopped a rape attempt. What's going on?"

The explanation went on for several minutes with him nodded and sighing. At the end, he shook his head. "I dread shit like this. Between the rodeo and the Strugis bike rally week, we make more arrests than during the entire rest of the year."

Sadie Getchell, a woman I'd been interviewing at the contestant's gate, walked up to us and whispered, "You should bag that bull rider's sheets. Based on the noises I've heard coming from his trailer, you might find DNA samples from a half-dozen women...and not all of them were moaning with ecstasy."

"I don't suppose you could identify any of them?" Arnold asked.

"Nope. I keep to myself and put earplugs in when I go to sleep."

"Chief," I said, "Ms. Getchell saw someone coming out of Chris Jenkins' trailer the night of her murder."

Perking up, the chief asked, "Can you identify him?"

Getchell looked at me, then shook her head. "Nope."

"Tell the chief why," I urged.

"He was wearing white clown makeup."

The chief's look was priceless. "You're joking?"

"Nope. White face, like a rodeo clown. I saw him for a fraction of a second. As soon as he realized he'd been seen, he ducked back into the trailer."

"Did you tell that to any of my cops?"

"No one except this ranger has asked me about Monday night."

The chief took Sadie, wrote down her name and contact information, then noted her observations. I returned to Jill, who looked hot and tired.

"Men are filthy animals," she said, glaring at me.

I led her to the trailer, and we stepped inside. Jill looked at the mess and shook her head. "You're only reinforcing the male stereotype by showing me this."

"We should find the girl's clothes and bring them to the hospital. Her boots are under the table."

Jill went to the bedroom and returned with hip-hugging jeans and a crop top barely long enough to cover the girl's small breasts. She held up the clothes. "I'm sure Amber thought she was being flirtatious, but nothing she'd experienced had prepared her for an encounter with that bull rider."

"Piper said she was going to show the bull rider her tattoo."

After blowing out a breath, Jill leaned close. "The legal age to get a tattoo in South Dakota is eighteen, unless you have parental permission. Piper wrote and signed a permission slip, and Amber got a mouse tattoo in Sturgis during the bike rally."

"Did you see the tattoo?" I asked.

"It was...provocative. It was a mouse placed so it appeared he was peeking over the waistband of her hip-hugging jeans. The rest of the mouse's body was...um…below her waistband."

"What the hell?"

Nodding, Jill added. "The tattoo artist got an eyeful when he did the mouse's bottom and tail."

I closed my eyes and pinched the bridge of my nose. "Did we get here in time to stop…?"

"Amber wouldn't say. She's going to need some counseling either way."

"Piper said Amber's mom was strict."

"And Amber is a rebellious teen."

Clenching my eyes shut, I said, "I wonder how rebellious?"

Even after barely more than a year of marriage Jill could read my mind. "Don't go there, Doug. It's not our problem. Just pick up Amber's boots and socks."

* * *

We got a plastic shopping bag for Amber's clothing from a woman in one of the nearby trailers and walked to the pickup in silence. Jill handed me the keys but didn't let go of the fob. "This is so messed up."

After pulling her into a hug I whispered, "Yes, it is. Sadly, things like this happen every day."

She clenched me tight. "But I don't want to know about them, and I certainly don't want to witness the aftermath." She released me. "The nearest hospital is Spearfish. You know the way."

The rodeo parking lot was a maze of cars and people walking without paying attention to the traffic. I turned onto the street and drove to the highway. I'd just turned south when I realized Mom and Chet had no idea what happened to us, or that we wouldn't be returning. "Call Mom and let her know what's going on."

Jill pulled her phone out of her pocket and punched in Mom's number. After a few seconds she left a message. "I don't think they can hear the phone over the crowd noise. I'll text her and hope she checks for messages when they get out of the stands."

"You'd better tell her we won't be back."

"Why won't we come back after we drop off Amber's clothes?"

"We'll have to make formal statements at the police station, and we'll have to find a computer to enter an incident report in the Park Service database."

Sighing, Jill stared at her phone. "I'd better call Jack to let him know what's happened."

"Do whatever you have to, but don't put me on speaker. I don't want to talk to him."

Jill punched in a number and held the phone to her ear while it rang. "What if he wants to talk to you?"

"I'm driving and it's against regulations to talk on the phone while operating a motor vehicle."

Before Jill could tell me to pull over, the call was answered. "Hi Jack. We were involved in an incident in Belle Fourche…" She spent several minutes recounting the events at the rodeo grounds, then explaining our plans to deliver clothes to the victim. There were several "Uh huhs," and an occasional, "no," but I was never invited into the conversation.

"Tell him about the clown in Chris Jenkins' trailer," I whispered.

Jill smiled, held out the phone, and activated the speaker. "Doug got a lead on our investigation." She held the phone near my mouth.

"I interviewed a woman who saw a rodeo clown exiting Chris Jenkins' trailer. He saw my witness and quickly backed into the trailer and closed the door."

"Come on, Doug. First you and Jill tell me that a ghost stole the victim's pickup and now you've found a witness who saw a clown at the site of the murder." Jack paused. "This is starting to sound like the plot of an Abbot and Costello comedy. I suppose next you'll find a witness who's sure the Invisible Man is the killer."

"I'm personally betting on Frankenstein."

Jill pulled the phone away and turned off the speaker. "Doug's being a smartass. It's something he's good at."

With a smug look on her face, Jill listened to Jack for a few more moments before ending the call.

"Did Jack have any words of wisdom?"

"He wants you to summarize the investigation in an update report. I think he wants to use it as evidence that you're insane and should be hospitalized."

"Do I get to pick the hospital, or is there somewhere they send all of the insane Park Service investigators and FBI agents?"

"Can you be serious for ten minutes?"

"I'm not sure. Are you going to time me?"

"Doug, just shut up and listen to me." Jill waited for a snarky response. Not getting it, she went on. "Jack's not a fan of sarcasm, and he's not sure if you're joking or serious when we call."

"Perfect! You can be the one to talk to him all the time."

With a withering glare, Jill hunched down in the seat and jammed her phone in her pocket. "Listen, our *team* would work better if you didn't…"

"If I weren't so cynical?"

"Yes! Exactly!" She paused. "You got along fine with Matt when he was your boss. Why can't you extend the same courtesy to Jack? Give him a chance."

"Matt let us run our investigations without interference. Jack wants to steer the bus."

"That's because he doesn't know and trust us yet. Give him some time."

"Honey, we're senior investigators with a track record of success. He should realize that we're capable of deciding how to investigate. We're on scene, and he's a thousand miles away. He can't react to changing information and we can't call him

136

every hour with an update or ask for his input on what to do next."

"Okay. I don't think he wants that level of control, but he does want to know what we're doing and why. He doesn't want to be blindsided by a call from a reporter or his bosses." Jill paused. "And he doesn't appreciate your sarcastic answers to his questions. He wants the same respect he's got for you...us."

"I didn't make up the ghost and clown stories."

"I know that, and so does he. It just sounded...illogical that we'd stumble into an investigation with such improbable suspects."

"Fine. I'll play nice."

"Here's the turn to the hospital."

I steered around the corner, then glanced at Jill. "I would've missed the giant blue sign with the H on it if you hadn't pointed it out to me."

"Dammit, Fletcher, I thought you were going to cut the sarcasm."

"That's with our boss. I don't have that agreement with you."

"If you ever expect to experience romance again, you're going to start behaving."

I let Jill's comment hang until I was parked outside the emergency room. She picked up the bag of clothing and we walked to the entrance. "I think you enjoy romance as much as I do."

I opened the door, but Jill stopped, checking to see if anyone could hear us. "I love you dearly, but I find my caring husband much more endearing than my cynical partner."

"Message received," I said as I followed her to the reception desk.

After a brief conversation with the receptionist, who was reluctant to divulge the names of anyone in the ER, Jill convinced her that we were the arresting officers in an assault case and needed to interview the victim. The receptionist spoke to someone on the phone, then directed us to meet the nurse outside room four.

A serious-looking middle-aged nurse in blue scrubs met us in the hallway. "I see your badges. Can I look at your credentials?"

Both Jill and I handed her our Park Service ID cards featuring our titles and pictures. N. Olson, R.N. compared the pictures to our faces, then returned the laminated cards.

"Your victim is with her mother." The nurse paused. "The doctor has examined her, much to the mother's dismay, and they've refused to allow him to do a rape kit or pelvic exam. The mother is adamant that her daughter is a virgin and there's no need for any of 'that stuff.'"

Jill looked at me for direction.

"Do you have the victim's underwear?"

Nurse Olson's eyes sparkled. She leaned close and whispered. "Her panties are in a plastic bag with the shirt she was wearing when she came in. There's another bag with the sheets from the gurney."

Jill turned so she was facing away from the open exam room door, and whispered, "Is she acting like a rape victim?"

The nurse blew out a breath. "She's been assaulted. She'll have a black eye and there are bruises on her arms and legs. But I'd only be guessing if I said she's had intercourse."

I nodded. "It's irrelevant if Amber's mother wouldn't let the doctor examine her. I assume she won't let Amber testify at a trial either."

"Mom says nothing happened. So, nothing happened." Olson looked at the open door. "Maybe you can convince the mom that you need her cooperation, but my sense is that Amber will be a virgin when she gets married, at least in her mother's mind."

Holding up the bag of clothes, Jill said, "Mom may not be as convinced of that after she sees what Amber was wearing at the rodeo."

Olson smiled and gestured for us to go into the exam room.

We stopped outside a drape drawn to shield the patient from people passing in the hallway and asked permission to come in. A slender woman wearing a mid-calf length dress swept out from behind the curtain and pulled it closed behind herself. "Who are you?"

"We're the officers who rescued your daughter from the rodeo trailer," I said.

"I don't know what you're talking about," the woman snapped.

Jill bowed her head and lowered her voice. "Amber was being assaulted by a cowboy inside a trailer at the Belle Fourche Rodeo. We heard Amber's friend yelling and pounding on the trailer door, and we came running."

"Why did you take her clothes off?"

Jill glanced at me, then back at Amber's mother. "Amber came out of the trailer wearing only her panties. A nearby woman gave her a shirt to wear and I held her head while she threw up the beer the cowboy had been giving her."

The woman was indignant. "I don't believe you."

Deciding it was best not to mention the man's naked state, I said, "The cowboy is under arrest for giving Amber beer. I assume we'll find Amber's fingerprints on the beer cans. We suspect his plan was to get her drunk and to take advantage of her.

Based on her bruises, it appears she was fighting him off when we arrived."

Amber's mother crossed her arms and glared at me. "Amber isn't allowed to attend the rodeo. You're making this up."

"Ma'am, she was at the rodeo," I said. "We have at least a dozen witnesses who saw her come out of the cowboy's trailer and watched her puking up beer."

"Why should I believe you?"

Looking the woman in the eye, Jill said, "I've seen Amber's tattoo—all of it."

"That's ridiculous! Amber doesn't have a tattoo."

"I suggest you go back behind the curtain and talk to Amber about the tattoo. It's a mouse on Amber's lower abdomen."

The mother huffed but slid behind the curtain. There were hushed words, then a gasp. "When did you get that?"

A moment later, the woman slid the curtain back and gestured for Jill to enter. She put her hand up in front of my chest. "I'd prefer if Amber were allowed to maintain some semblance of modesty." A second later, the woman melted and fell into my arms sobbing.

I pulled the drape closed so Jill could speak with Amber in privacy, then led the mother into the hallway. "What's your name, ma'am?"

"Sarah." She glanced at the drape hearing snippets of the whispered conversation behind it. "Sorry, I'm Sarah Burns."

"Amber had a tough afternoon. She's going to need some counseling."

"I'll talk to Pastor Martin."

"I think she's going to need someone she doesn't know. Otherwise, she isn't going to open up and resolve the post traumatic stress she'll have."

"I'm sure the pastor will be fine. He's a great listener."

"What's going on with Amber?"

Sarah turned away from me. "I don't know what you mean."

"She's going through something."

"I don't get it. I mean, we pray before meals and at bedtime. She goes to Sunday school and church every week. Where does..."

"She's a teenager, Sarah. Every teen tries to express their individuality."

Sarah wrapped her arms around herself and shivered. "It's my ex-husband's fault. He had an affair and that set Amber off. It gave her all the wrong messages."

Gentle sobbing came from behind the curtain. Jill said softly, "Doug, please come in here."

Sarah followed me past the curtain. Amber was clenched in a hug and Jill's red eyes made me believe our worst fears. "Amber and I think it would be a good idea for a female doctor to examine her."

Sarah shook her head. "No. I don't want…"

Amber looked up from Jill's shoulder. "Mom. He hurt me…inside. I need the doctor."

Sarah froze in place, shaking her head. "No, no, no. This can't happen. I'll call Pastor Martin and we'll pray."

Jill nodded. "You'll need the pastor and a doctor. Amber has physical, spiritual, and emotional scars that will require therapy."

Sarah spun and stalked out of the room, leaving Amber clinging to Jill. "Doug, talk to the nurse and get a female OB/GYN in here ASAP."

"What's…?"

"Go!"

I trotted out of the room and found nurse Olson at a computer. "Amber needs a female doctor ASAP."

"But her mother…"

I pointed to Sarah who stormed out of the ER. "Her mother just deserted her, and Amber needs emergency treatment."

A page went out for Dr. Wasson, and nurse Olson punched numbers into a phone. "What's your partner's name?"

"Jill Fletcher. Why?"

"I know a family law judge who could assign temporary custodial rights for a child whose mother can't be reached."

The nurse turned away from me, apparently connected to the number she'd dialed. She had a hushed discussion, then waited for a moment before nodding, thanking the person on the phone, and hanging up. "Jill Fletcher is Amber's temporary custodian. A fax will be coming through in a few minutes."

I frowned. "How…?"

Smiling, the nurse said, "It's a small town. The judge is my brother-in-law."

A young blonde woman with a stethoscope around her neck rushed into the ER and approached the desk. "You paged me, Naomi?"

The nurse stood and walked with the doctor to room four while speaking in hushed tones. The doctor entered the exam room and Naomi returned to the nursing station. "Dr. Wasson is the best. She has a great bedside manner, and her patients love her."

"Is there somewhere I can get a cup of coffee?"

Naomi directed me to the cafeteria and promised to send Jill when she got free. I was sipping my second cup of mediocre coffee when Jill walked into the cafeteria. She waved to me, then bought herself a cup of coffee.

"What's up?"

Jill sipped her coffee and leaned close. "That sonofabitch is going down. Amber is going to be messed up for the rest of her

144

life. All she really wanted was an autograph and a bit of adventure."

I pushed my lukewarm coffee away. "Shit."

Jill tipped her head back and stared at the ceiling. "How did we get here? I mean, we were looking for a killer and a stolen horse. How did we end up in the middle of a sexual assault case?"

I reached out and squeezed Jill's hand. "Because we're caring people, we step in where we're needed. Sometimes it's dealing with a drunken plane passenger, and this time it's rescuing a messed-up teenager. It's all part of the job."

"Yeah, well sometimes this job really sucks."

Unable or unwilling to cry, I laughed.

Jill pulled her hand away. "It's not funny, Doug."

"I'm sorry, it's just that you've taken another trip to Cynical Island. Welcome to my island condo."

"That's it, isn't it? That's why you look for the bad in everyone and sit with your back to the wall when we're in a restaurant."

"You've known that for almost two years, yet you keep me around."

"I was happy sitting in my apartment eating microwaved dinners while watching Hallmark movies until you came along."

"No, you really weren't."

After a sigh, Jill took my hand. "No, I really wasn't. And now you've turned me into an adrenaline junkie. I actually enjoy feeling my heart pounding in my chest."

"Well, the other side of that coin is holding the hand of a teenage rape victim while she cries about her lost virginity."

"About that…Amber wasn't a virgin."

"No way! She's only fifteen."

"She had sex with an older student in the backseat of a car during a high school football game."

"Finish your coffee. We need to give Chief Arnold our statements."

"I thought we'd go back to the ranch and… Oh crap. My phone was vibrating while the doctor examined Amber. I bet Ronnie returned my call or texted me."

I stood and walked to the parking lot while Jill read her text messages.

* * *

Having seen us park outside the police station, Chief Arnold met us at the security door. I handed him the two plastic bags from the hospital. "The victim's underwear is in one bag and the other contains the sheets from the ambulance. I assume there's DNA evidence on all of them."

Chief Arnold nodded. "I'll log them into evidence and send them to the state crime lab."

146

Jill drew a breath, steeling herself for what she had to say. "Amber was sexually assaulted by Conroy in the trailer. Doctor Wasson at the Spearfish hospital did a pelvic exam and ran a rape kit. You'll want to interview her."

"You'll want to get a search warrant for Conroy's trailer and send his sheets in for testing, too," I said.

After giving the bags to one of his officers, Arnold nodded toward the hallway. "Let's get coffee then we'll record your interview."

Instead of a stark interview room, the Chief led us to his office. After closing the door, he took out a small recorder, activated it, stated the time and who was in the room, then slid the machine to the middle of his desk. "Jill, why don't you tell us what you saw when you arrived at Conroy's trailer."

Two hours later, we'd both recounted our memories of the events twice, and the chief switched off the recorder. "I think that's it. I'll have the county attorney listen to these. He can contact you if he's got any questions."

We stood and the chief shook our hands. "Thanks for jumping into this. If you hadn't been there, Conroy would've gotten away with this rape and gone on to repeat it."

Jill wrinkled her nose as if she'd just smelled something dead. "I need a shower to rinse this whole experience off me."

Arnold chuckled. "If I didn't have another four or five hours of this stupidity, I'd suggest we go to the bar for a stiff drink."

Grabbing my hand as we walked out of the building, Jill said, "I feel emotionally drained."

I'd only turned the first corner when Jill's phone rang. After a few brief responses, she ended the call and stared at the phone. "Ronnie and Chet want to treat us to supper at the steakhouse on Highway 212."

"No."

"It wasn't an offer I could refuse," she said.

"Shit. I just want to fall into bed and sleep for twelve hours."

"Too late. They were turning into the parking lot when Ronnie called. They'll have a table by the time we get there."

Chapter Nine

Molly Rickowski's breakfast was as large as ever. Chet and my mom showed up just as Molly dished up pancakes, scrambled eggs, and set out a platter of fried bacon. Al wanted all the details about the assault on the teen. In an effort to not divulge lurid and confidential details, I shared a brief, sanitized version of the day. We were out the door by eight, but not without a thermos of coffee and a bag holding two fresh cinnamon rolls.

* * *

Belle Fourche traffic was building as people drove to the roundup grounds for the rodeo finals and fireworks. The street in front of the police station was nearly empty and I wondered if Chief Arnold would be in his office, or if he'd been pressed into crowd control duty with all his officers, the sheriff's deputies, and a few highway patrol officers.

The sergeant inside the entry buzzed us through without questioning. "He's still in his office."

Although his uniform was freshly pressed, Chief Arnold looked like he hadn't slept in days. He was reading a report on the computer while running his fingers through his close-cropped hair. Turning toward the sound of our footsteps, he rolled his eyes. "Can whatever you've got wait until tomorrow?"

"Do you always put off murder investigations when you get busy?" I asked as I sat in a guest chair.

Arnold blew out a breath and shook his head. "That hasn't been a problem in the past. No one's been killed during the roundup."

Jill sat in the other chair. "Is there a reward for capturing the killer?"

"What?" Arnold asked as he shut down the computer.

"My uncle thinks he's solved the case and wants to know if there's a reward for identifying the killer."

"Can your uncle identify the killer?"

"Not really identify him—he's sure the ghost the trucker saw is one of the rodeo clowns."

Leaning back in his chair, Arnold considered Jill's revelation. "I guess that's a possibility. Are you planning to interview them?"

"I doubt that the professional rodeo clowns are involved," I said, "but it would be interesting to talk to them about a person in clown makeup being seen at the murder scene and later driving the victim's truck."

The chief's phone interrupted our discussion. He listened and made a few cursory comments. "I've got to run out to the roundup grounds. One of my reserve officers caught a bunch of kids smoking pot under the stands and he wants to arrest them and throw them into jail." Arnold stood. "You two are capable of interviewing the clowns without me, right?"

Rising from our chairs, I nodded. "You're not going to arrest a bunch of kids for a misdemeanor with all that's going on today, are you?"

Motioning for us to leave, the chief shook his head. "We'll ticket whoever supplied the dope and take the others' names. I'm not going to fill my four jail cells with dope smoking kids when I'm expecting at least a couple of fights and some DUIs."

"Good choice," I said. "I used to work at the Minnesota State Fair and there were dozens of minor incidents that we cleared by escorting the perpetrators out of the fairgrounds after issuing a ticket. We saved the jail cells for pickpockets, physical assaults, and gun-toting gangbangers."

"Luckily, we don't have too many of those incidents. But dozens of liquored up cowboys usually leads to some sort of excitement."

* * *

Finding a parking spot for the pickup took longer than I'd expected, leaving us with a fifteen-minute walk to the rodeo grounds. We checked in with Mom and Chet to let them know we had arrived. Chet was already eating a hamburger although it was only an hour since he'd had breakfast at Rickowskis'.

After wiping the ketchup dribbling down his chin, Chet asked, "Am I going to get a reward for solving the murder?"

"There's no reward," Jill said, taking a seat next to Mom, "and you haven't solved the murder."

Chet looked disappointed, but not so much that it stopped him from taking another bite of hamburger.

"If you two are set, Jill and I need to talk to the rodeo clowns."

Chet perked up and gestured with his ketchup-dripping burger. "I told you it was one of the clowns!".

Mom pushed Chet's burger away, so it didn't drip on her. "Please be careful."

With her hand on Mom's shoulder, Jill said, "This will be a non-threatening interview with a couple professional clowns. There won't be any gun play."

"That's what Doug always says, yet you end up in a shootout at the end of every investigation."

Mom's comments caught the attention of several people sitting nearby who turned to look at us. I put up my hands. "It's okay. We're federal law enforcement officers."

We threaded our way down the row, then walked out of the grandstand, against the flow of people coming in for the championship round of competitors.

Walking around the outside of the grandstand, we met Chief Arnold. He and two officers were having an emphatic discussion with a group of teenagers. A reserve officer stood on the outside of the group, with his arms crossed and looking unhappy.

Past the grandstands, we walked through the gate where the competitors entered the arena. The competitors' staging area was a maze of stalls, trailers, and horse paddocks. Recognizing one of the barrel racers from earlier in the week, Jill asked where the rodeo clowns were.

"The bull people are at the farthest end of the stalls. They keep to themselves. The clowns are past them." The woman paused. "Are you the ranger who busted Conroy?"

After Jill glanced at me, I nodded. "That was us."

"Good on you! Conroy was hornier than a bull in a pen full of cows. He's chased every woman in the rodeo circuit. Most were smart enough to avoid someone as messed up as him. I heard that the inside of his trailer looked like a bomb went off."

Not wanting to pursue Conroy's checkered past, I asked, "Where can we find the rodeo clowns?"

"Keep going past the bull pens. Rod and Kenny have trailers down there. You'll know which ones are theirs because of the ads."

"Do clowns have corporate sponsors?" Jill asked.

The woman laughed. "Everyone else's sponsors are horse, trailer, truck, or cattle related. Their sponsors are…" she paused and smiled. "I'll let you be surprised."

"Will we be able to tell which trailers are theirs?" I asked.

"I'll tell you what; if you can't determine which are theirs, you come back here, and I'll buy you a bronco of Pendleton cowboy whisky."

When we were out of earshot I asked, "What's a bronco of cowboy whisky?"

"You've never heard of Pendleton whisky?"

"When I was drinking, I drank Scotch. I don't recall seeing cowboy whisky on the bar's back shelf."

"Pendletons' distillery is a big rodeo sponsor. It's the name for Oregon's Pendleton Roundup. The bottles are sold in horsey quantities. A small bottle is a pony, a larger bottle is a bronco, and a half gallon is a stallion."

"Ah, it's not a Minnesota thing."

"It's a rodeo thing," Jill replied.

"She piqued my curiosity," I said as we continued past the people milling around the pens.

Unlike the competitor's living quarters, the trailers used by the people who brought cattle and bulls to the event weren't combined with horse trailers and were more utilitarian. Jill laughed as we approached the cattle trailers. "I think we've found them," she said.

Parked end to end, two trailers were splashed with bright logos. As predicted, the logos had nothing to do with horses, cattle, western wear, or tack. The right-hand trailer had logos for Jean and Matt's Fun Emporium and a pizza chain restaurant. The other trailer was sponsored by an on-line costume shop and a company which made adult-themed playing cards.

I apparently studied the playing card logo a moment too long. "Are we going to gawk at the women or are we interviewing clowns?"

"I'm a little surprised that logo doesn't cause accidents on the interstate."

"Only among male drivers, and they're a known road hazard anyway. I think testosterone causes deafness, momentary mental lapses, and the inability to use blinkers, maps, or mirrors."

"Hey, I'm a good driver," I said walking to the trailer featuring the images of scantily clad women.

"Get over it, Doug. They're only drawings."

"Yes, but the art is very realistic."

"The artist was probably a smart woman getting money from body shops and companies who sell automotive paint."

My knock was answered by a young man wearing tattered jeans with red bandanas sewn to the waist and pockets. "Can I help you?" he asked, noting our badges and guns.

"We're investigating Chris Jenkins' death. I wonder if you have a second for a couple of questions?"

The man checked his watch, then nodded. "I've got a while before I have to be in the arena. Would you like a cup of coffee?"

The inside of the trailer was the polar opposite of Conroy's rat's nest. "I'm Rod Crane," the man said, extending his hand before gesturing for us to take a seat in a small booth that appeared to double as a bed.

"I'm Doug Fletcher and this is my partner, Jill."

Crane poured coffee and brought three mugs to the table, then sat across from us.

He smiled at Jill. "Only Doug has a last name?"

"My last name is also Fletcher," Jill said, accepting the steaming mug. "We're police and life partners."

"That's a first," Crane said. He paused, pointing at our cups. "I apologize. I only drink my coffee black. I have sugar and milk if you'd like some."

We waved off the offer. "Black is how we prefer it."

"I'm afraid I don't know how I can help you with the investigation of Chris' death. I knew who she was, but we weren't besties or even on a first-name basis."

"Where were you Monday night?" Jill asked.

"Wow! You don't beat around the bush," Crane said, smiling. "Let's see, Monday night I was at my folks' place in Missoula."

I frowned. "You weren't here for the elimination rounds of competition, Rod?"

"Nah, Kenny and I are here for the weekend. I guess you could say we're the premium entertainment."

"Aren't there rodeo clowns during the preliminary rounds?" I asked.

"The stockmen usually use some roustabouts to distract the bulls in the prelims. Kenny and I are here to make the events more finals entertaining for the crowds. The weekenders expect to see rodeo clowns, so here we are."

There was a knock on the door and a sandy-haired cowboy stuck his head in. "We're on in twenty minutes," the man said. His face was made up with large white patches over his eyes and a wide black smile.

"Hey Kenny, these cops are investigating Chris Jenkins' death. They were asking where we were when she was killed." The blond cowboy stepped in. "I'm not sure when that happened, other than it was early in the week." He extended his hand to Jill, who was nearest the door. "I'm Ken Halsey."

"Chris was killed Monday night," Jill said.

Halsey blew out a breath. "I was in Kansas City on Monday and in Ames, Iowa on Tuesday. Why are you checking our alibis?"

"A couple people saw someone in clown makeup come out of Chris' trailer the night she died. A trucker saw a person in white makeup driving her truck west, across Montana."

"White makeup?" Kenny asked.

I looked at Jill, hoping she could expand on the question. "I guess he had a white face. We thought he might be a rodeo clown," she said.

Rod smiled. "Every professional clown has a unique makeup scheme. Emmet Kelly is probably the most famous clown ever, and he was known for his bowler hat, sad white mouth, and dark shadow beard. Anyone who ever saw a picture of him could identify him immediately. Kenny goes for the big white circles over his eyes and oversized black smile. I do a white base layer, then add a sad red smile, and black stars around my eyes, so I look like a cartoon character who's been knocked out. Our makeup designs are trademarked."

"Do you have any details about the clown face that was seen around Chris' trailer?" Kenny asked.

"We weren't smart enough to ask about those details," I said. "That'll be a good follow up question for our witnesses."

Rod frowned. "There weren't any professional clowns around for the preliminaries. You might be dealing with an amateur—someone who just smeared on makeup and didn't really have a theme or style."

Kenny tapped his wrist. "I'm sorry to interrupt, but Rod and I need to get ready for the arena."

After thanking the clowns, Jill and I walked back past the livestock. "That was enlightening," she said. "I've never considered a clown's look a trademark."

"Rod's comments about Emmet Kelly were illustrative. As soon as he mentioned that name, a picture of Kelly's clown face came to mind."

Jill glanced at me, trying to look very innocent. "I guess I'm not old enough to remember him."

"Give me a break," I said. "You're…"

"Be careful, cowboy. I saw you step in a cow pie a while ago and it might taste even worse than the boot leather you stick in your mouth regularly."

"You're so wise and pretty."

"Nice recovery."

"We need to talk to the truck driver who saw the ghost and the woman who saw the clown coming out of Chris' trailer."

Jill walked in silence for a while, digesting what the clowns had told us. "Do you think the truck driver and barrel racer will be able to remember any details? Both of them only saw flashes of the clown or ghost face."

"They were both surprised to see the person in makeup. I suspect Sadie Getchell will be able to pull back details about the clown's hair, mouth, and eyes if we ask specifically about them."

"Feed me lunch before we search for Ms. Getchell. My breakfast is a distant memory."

* * *

The lunch options at the arena were meant to be handheld, and they were virtually all greasy. I had no problem finding

160

a burger and bag of chips. Jill wandered the food truck area for ten minutes before choosing a walking taco, essentially a bag of Dorito chips with taco meat, lettuce, and cheese scooped on top of the chips.

Watching Jill eating tortilla chips, greasy taco meat, and cheese gave me a chuckle.

"What's so funny?" She asked.

"There's lettuce in your walking taco, but it's hardly a salad or low-fat meal."

"The best of the worst options," she replied. "Do you think we'll be able to get any useful information about the clown sighting at Chris Jenkins' trailer?"

"I'm more concerned about finding our barrel racer before she pulls out. Some of the contestants have already hooked up their trailers and are ready to leave."

"We should split up. You watch her trailer, and I'll try to catch her at the contestants' entrance."

"Why do I get to watch the trailer?" I asked.

With a forkful of taco halfway to her mouth, Jill paused. "I think it'd be good to have a real cop around the trailers after yesterday's incident."

"You don't think you could've handled that?" I asked.

Letting out a sigh, Jill weighed her words. "Let's say you were more inclined to

161

arrest the bull rider. I might've found a reason to shoot him."

"You're a good cop. You couldn't have shot an unarmed man."

Jill shook her head. "Incidents like that make my blood boil. I might've baited Conroy into making a threatening move."

Throwing the hamburger wrapper into a waste bin, I put my arm around Jill's shoulders. "You say that, but I don't believe you could pull the trigger."

"Let's not find out," Jill said, crumpling her taco bag and throwing it away.

I steered her away from the crowd. "Let's talk this through before you react in the heat of the moment. As a human, I know what Conroy did was terrible and deserves punishment. As cops, we're sworn to uphold the law and use reason and control beyond that shown by a civilian."

"I know that. But sometimes it feels good to speculate on how satisfying it would be to shoot someone who deserves it."

I spotted Sadie Getchell stalking through the crowd. She looked angry and was nearly trotting away from the arena. "There she is."

Knowing Sadie's destination was her trailer, we skirted around the outside of the crowd and cut through the rows of trailers. Sadie was already inside the trailer, and it sounded like she was having a one-sided argument.

Jill knocked on the door. "Sadie, can we talk?"

The door flew open, and Sadie glared at Jill, red-faced. "What?"

"We have a few follow-up questions about the clown you saw at Chris Jenkins' trailer."

"I already told you," Sadie snapped, "I only caught a glimpse of the guy."

I stepped forward, hoping to break Sadie's foul mood. "Can we have just a few seconds of your time? Please."

Sadie looked past Jill at me, then seemed to deflate. "Um, sure. Come in." She directed us to her breakfast table. "What do you want to know?"

Being perceptive, Jill leaned forward. "Your last ride didn't go well?"

"I cut too tight and knocked over the second barrel." Sadie paused. "Sorry I took it out on you."

"We have some additional questions about the clown you saw," I said as Sadie sat across from us. "Can you describe his face?"

"I told you, it was white."

"What did his lips look like? Were they white too, or were they red or black?"

Sadie stared at me, apparently trying to envision that second she saw the clown. "They were red."

"Did he have any other markings on his face?"

"I don't think so. Just the white face and red mouth."

"He wasn't wearing a red nose, like Bozo the clown?" I asked.

"No."

"Was he wearing a colored wig?"

"He had a cowboy hat on, without a wig."

"You're doing great," Jill said. "Do you remember anything about his clothing?"

"I was so surprised by his face I didn't notice anything else about him."

"Tattoos on his hands or arms?" I asked.

Shrugging, Sadie shook her head. "I didn't notice any."

Jill put Sadie's contact information into her phone, then we thanked her and stood to leave. "Is there anything else you remember about Chris on Monday?" Jill asked. "Did she argue with anyone or was there someone hanging around her trailer?"

Getchell shook her head. "Monday was a crazy day. People were pulling in and parking their trailers, there were preliminary rounds of competition, and it was a little chaotic."

"Thanks," I said as I stepped out of her trailer.

We were about to step away when Getchell said, "This is probably irrelevant, but I saw Chris talking to a farrier over by the stockmen Monday afternoon."

"Was their meeting confrontational?" Jill asked.

"It didn't seem like it. They were just talking."

Once we were out of earshot, Jill asked, "Why did you ask all those irrelevant questions about the clown's red nose and wig?"

"It's an interrogation technique to make sure the person you're interviewing isn't telling you what you want to hear."

"You do that by asking about things you're sure aren't true?"

"I didn't know whether they were true or not, but it made her think, and she convinced me that she was being truthful and not expanding on what she'd actually seen."

"All she remembered was the white face and red lips. Is that enough to go on?"

We threaded our way through the competitors who were readying their trailers for their departure. "If the clowns were right, what she saw was probably an amateur who smeared grease paint on his face like he thought a clown should look."

"I wish she could've remembered more about his clothing," Jill said.

"Back in the '90s, there was a guy holding up convenience stores. He'd walk in completely nude, with a gun and wearing a ski mask. He'd demand that the clerk empty the till. When the witnesses were questioned, they were so shocked by his nudity that no one could describe him. At the third robbery, the clerk told the cops the only detail she remembered was that he hadn't been circumcised."

Hoping to move the discussion away from the robber's physical assets Jill asked, "Was the robber ever caught?"

"An off-duty cop was buying gas at one of the stores and interrupted a robbery. He disarmed the robber and handcuffed him. The robber had just been released from prison and he'd had a discussion with the other convicts about how they'd been caught because someone remembered their cap, or a logo on their shirt. They decided the perfect disguise was nudity and no one would ever be able to remember anything about them. And it worked."

"Wow. If a naked guy walked up to rob or carjack me, I'd be so distracted that I'd have a hard time describing him unless he had a giant Harley Davidson logo tattooed across his chest."

I stopped at the edge of the trailer parking area and dropped a hint. "We need to contact Tonto and get a phone number for the truck driver."

"Good idea, Doug. You can call Lame Deer while you're standing among the trailers."

"I thought…"

Jill turned and walked away. "I know what you thought but it's your turn to make the call."

"But…" I started to protest.

Over her shoulder, Jill said, "I've spoken with our new boss twice now. *You* call Tonto."

I hailed a cowboy walking past Chris Jenkins' trailer. "We're looking for someone who saw a clown near here Monday evening."

With a gesture toward the arena he said, "The clowns park over by the livestock people."

As I entered a search for the Spoon and Fork Restaurant on my phone, a young woman walked down the aisle. "Excuse me, did you see a guy in clown makeup here Monday night?"

"I didn't. Sorry."

I selected the number for the restaurant from their website and after a moment, the phone rang. A young woman answered, sounding cheerful. "Spoon and Fork, where you can eat in or get your meal to go."

"Is Tonto at his table?" I asked.

"Hang on."

The dead air dragged on until I thought the call had been cut off. Finally, Tonto's gravelly voice answered. "Hello, Ranger Fletcher. I'm pleased that you found my answering service."

"We had the impression you were a fixture in the restaurant."

Chuckling, Tonto replied, "The owner likes having me around to greet people and I create an authentic Cheyenne atmosphere for the tourists."

"I'd like to talk to Billy Beaverheart about the man driving Chris Jenkins' pickup."

"Ah, you're intrigued by the ghost."

"We have a witness who saw a man made up like a rodeo clown coming out of Chris' trailer. I'd like to see if Billy's description of the driver matches with the makeup our witness saw."

"I'm surprised to hear a cop asking about characters from children's stories. That's something I'll have to remember."

"How can I contact Billy?"

"He's not here right now. I can have the waitress write down your number. She can ask him to call when he comes through."

"I'd hoped to speak with him today."

"Cops are always in a rush. A good hunter lays a trap and waits patiently." Tonto paused. "I'll give the phone to Trudy so she can write down your number. Then, I'll think about how to contact Billy."

"Thank you."

"I tend to think better when I'm eating. The special is serviceberry pie."

I gave Trudy my phone and VISA numbers. She promised to deliver a slice of pie to Tonto, to help him think. I told her to add a five-dollar tip to the bill.

As I ended the call, a lanky middle-aged cowboy approached. "Excuse me, did you see a man in clown makeup Monday evening?"

With two-days of graying stubble, the man resembled the lead character from the "Longmire" television series. His expression was half frown and half smile, which had me wondering about his take on my question. "A clown?"

"We have a witness who saw a man in clown makeup coming out of Chris Jenkins' trailer the night she was murdered. I'm looking for another witness who might give us a better description of the guy."

Shaking his head, the cowboy stared at me. "A cop asked me that a couple days ago."

"So, you didn't see a clown?" I asked.

"You have a witness who saw a guy in clown makeup...here?"

"Yes, someone saw a man coming out of Chris' trailer and he was made up like a rodeo clown."

"I'll be darned."

The conversation was infuriatingly slow. "You didn't see a clown?"

"Well, there's an old saying I use to cover the times when I've been drinking. 'Sometimes it's better to keep your mouth shut and let people think you're stupid, then to open your mouth and prove it.'"

"I don't understand you."

"Well, I'd had a couple shots of rot gut with Taylor Henry on Monday night. When he ran out of booze, I went to my pickup to get my spare bottle."

The pause dragged on. "And…"

"Well, there was a guy walking around the parking lot with one of those lock fobs. He was pushing the button like he'd forgotten exactly where he'd parked. I was kind of staggering down the row parallel to him when he looked at me. As soon as we locked eyes, he disappeared. At that point, I wasn't sure if he'd been real, or if I was on the verge of seeing pink elephants. So, when the cop asked if I'd seen a clown by the trailers, I said, 'no.'"

"Describe him."

"Well, it was kind of dark, so I didn't get a real good look at him."

"What did you see?"

The cowboy pulled out a bandana and wiped his nose, apparently taking a minute to gather his thoughts. "Well, his face was all white."

"Was he wearing a red clown nose or a fright wig?"

Wrinkling his nose, the cowboy cocked his head. "If that's what your other witness saw, we were looking at different clowns.

The one I saw just had a white face and a tan Stetson."

"Describe his mouth."

"That's the other thing that freaked me out. He had this wide red grin. It raised the hackles on my neck."

"Which way did he go after he saw you?"

"Like I said, he disappeared. Poof!"

"Do you think he might've ducked down behind the trucks?"

"I didn't hang around to find out. I mean, here's this evil looking clown who's staring at me like he's smiling. Then he just disappeared. I hightailed it out of there and locked myself in my living quarters."

"You said he was pushing a key fob. Did you see him do that?"

"I don't think so… No, I saw him looking around when the pickup's horn honked, and lights flashed."

"What kind of pickup?"

"Like I told you, I'd been drinking."

I nodded. "Think about it for a second. Try to visualize the pickup with the flashing lights."

"I think it was a Chevy with dually rear wheels." The cowboy paused, in thought. "Yeah, it was a tan Chevy with advertising all over it."

"Do you remember any of the ads?"

"Aw man, it was dark, and I was drunk."

"Try to picture the truck and signage."

"There was a HayChix logo on the hood."

I took the cowboy's name, Simon Blanchard, and got his Colorado address. "Thank you," I said.

"That clown, he was evil, wasn't he?" Simon asked.

"We think he killed Chris Jenkins, and he was stealing her pickup when you saw him."

"Damn. I was ready to stop drinking after that sight. Maybe I'm not as much of a drunk as I thought I was."

"Having pulled myself out of a bottle at one point in my life, I'd take this event as a sign it was time to leave the cap on the bottle."

"But I do like the taste of Jack Daniels whiskey."

"That's something I deal with every time I get a whiff of an open bottle. On the other hand, my life is so much better without booze."

Simon licked his lips as if he could taste the booze. "I'd sure miss it if I quit."

Chuckling, I folded my notebook and put it in my pocket. "I missed the booze for a while, but I found other, more important aspects of my life."

"Like what?"

"I reconnected with my family and married a really nice woman."

"It's kind of hard to do those things when your family are all drunks and the only women you meet are buckle bunnies or bar flies."

"I hear you. I moved away and quit hanging out in bars."

"Whew! That might take more guts than I've got." Simon put out his hand. "Good on you for getting your life together. I'm just not sure I'm there yet."

My phone rang as we shook hands, ending my philosophical discussion with Simon. "Doug Fletcher."

"Um, you're the ranger who was talking to Tonto?"

"That's me. Is this Billy Beaverheart?"

"Yeah, I got a call from Trudy at the Spoon and Fork. She said you wanted to talk about the ghost I saw."

"Are you somewhere you can talk for a couple of minutes?"

"I'm on my cell phone, driving across I-90. There's no one out here, so go ahead and talk."

"Tell me about your encounter with the guy wearing makeup and driving the Chevy with dual rear wheels."

"It was late, and I was tired. Headlights had been approaching me from behind for miles. When they caught up, the driver passed me, and I got a glimpse of his face in my side mirror."

"When did that happen and where were you?"

"It was Monday night…no it was early Tuesday morning. I was hauling a load of bentonite on Highway 212, near Broadus."

"Tell me about the truck."

"Like you said, it was a Chevy with dualies. He was hauling a yellow stock trailer that had a horse in the back."

"Do you remember anything special about the truck?"

"It was a newer model. There are lots of beat up, rusty old trucks in that area, and this one wasn't even dusty."

"What color was the truck?"

"Whew, it was late at night, and I was tired." Billy paused. "It was light colored. Not white but maybe tan."

"Did you notice any markings on it?"

"Um, yeah, it had some stickers on the side, like ads."

"Describe the driver."

"Like I told Tonto, I thought he was a ghost. His face was eerie white. Not like a white man. I mean it was bright white, like a ghost or something."

"We think he might've been wearing rodeo clown makeup."

"Whew. That'd make more sense than seeing a ghost."

"Do you remember anything else unusual about his appearance like a red nose or wig?"

174

"He didn't have a red nose, but now that you mention it, he has this really weird smile, like the Joker in the Batman movies."

"He didn't have any other facial features or hair that you remember?"

"No, just the white face and scary smile."

"What do you remember about the horse?" Jill asked.

Billy frowned. "It's strange, but it looked like the horse had a white tail."

"Like a palomino?"

"I guess. There aren't many palomino horses around, so it's kind of odd. But the tail looked white to me."

"Is this a good number to call if I have more questions?"

"It's my cell phone and it's always with me."

"Thanks, Billy."

"Thank you for putting my mind at ease. It's easier to accept having seen a rodeo clown than seeing a ghost."

Chapter Ten

After talking to another six or seven people who hadn't seen a rodeo clown on Monday, I meandered through the trailer area to the contestants' arena entrance. Outside the area reserved for the contestants' living quarters, I ran into a crowd of people in line for the food trucks and trailers. The lines were long, and people were using upended plastic barrels as makeshift tables. I could see the sign for the contestant's arena entrance, but I couldn't see Jill over the sea of people crowded ahead of me.

Halfway through the horde of people, I was surrounded by the aroma of a dozen different foods, snippets of conversations, and an occasional roar from the rodeo crowd. I was near sensory overload. People bumped into me, and I found myself holding one hand on my wallet and the other hand on my pistol.

Shouts from the far side of the crowd caused me to quicken my pace, but the swarm of people ahead of me made it impossible to rush toward the voices. As I neared the contestant's entrance, the crowd got thicker as people moved forward, trying to see the cause of the commotion. Hearing Jill shout "Stop!" I ended my polite walk and began pushing people aside without excusing myself.

"Police! Move aside," I said over and over, as I pushed shoulders and stepped on feet.

Nearing the far edge of the crowd, I heard a male voice yell, "Get away, bitch!" Pushing my way through the last ring of people, I spotted Jill and a young man wrestling on the ground.

As the man cocked his arm to punch Jill, I lunged forward and grabbed his fist with both hands. "Take it down a notch, Turbo" I said, twisting the man's arm and pinning him to the ground under my knee.

"Get off me," the man slurred as spittle flew from his lips.

Helping Jill roll the man onto his stomach, I asked, "What's going on?"

"He came out of the arena with his arm over Piper's shoulder."

"Who's Piper?" I asked as the man struggled to get his arms free.

Jill snapped the second handcuff, then leaned back, taking a deep breath. "Piper's the girl who was banging on the bull rider's trailer. Her friend Amber was inside."

I lifted the man's cuffed hands, putting pressure on his shoulders. "God damn, that hurts!"

"Take it easy and I'll let up," I said before turning back to Jill. "Where's Piper?"

Scanning the crowd, Jill spotted Piper near the arena entrance with her arms wrapped around herself. "She's over there. I'll talk to her if you've got this cowboy under control."

Easing the pressure on the guy's shoulders, I said, "I've got this. Go talk to her."

Wiping dust from her jeans and shirt, Jill stood, and walked toward the teen.

"What's your name, cowboy?" I asked.

"Who's asking?"

"Listen, I'm trying to have a polite conversation with you while I sort out the situation. What's your name?"

"Judd."

"Do you have a last name, Judd?"

"Let me loose. I haven't done anything."

"The girl you were with is only fifteen."

"What's your point?" Judd said.

"If you were taking her to your trailer for a good time, you'd be committing statutory rape."

"She looks old enough. Besides, if she's willing, who's going to turn me in?"

"I'm going to hold your arm and we're going to stand up."

Judd was on his knees when the world spun. Air rushed from my lungs and my head was slammed into the dust. Reaching for my gun, I felt a hand wrapped around the butt of my pistol.

"What are you doing to my friend, Judd?" a male voice hissed behind me.

"I'm a cop," I choked out, my words slurred because my mouth was half in the dirt. "Let go of my gun." I reached for the hand that was trying to draw the pistol from my holster.

Wrestling for control of my gun, time moved slowly. I couldn't hear the crowd or shouts around me over the sound of my heart pounding in my ears.

"I'm gonna kill you," the voice said as the man struggled to pull my pistol. I felt his finger repeatedly pull the trigger, but the safety was on and held against my side. His left hand ground my face into the dirt, and I felt his knees pinning my thighs to the ground.

After being yanked onto my side, the man's hand released his grip on my gun. Suddenly free from the man's grip, I rolled onto my back and pulled my pistol. My left eye was nearly blinded by dust, but I swung the Sig around, sighting with my right eye. A man in a blue uniform wrestled with my assailant. "Hold your fire!" the cop yelled.

I jammed the pistol back into the holster just as Jill threw herself on top of the man who was wrestling with the cop. After struggling to gain my balance and clear my eyes, I crawled toward the cop and Jill.

Judd, who was handcuffed, kicked and tried to knee me. Yanking the handcuffs with all my strength, I heard a pop. Judd screamed in pain.

I scanned the crowd to see if anyone else intended to join the fray. A middle-aged man stepped out of the crowd and knelt on Judd's legs. "Are you okay?" He asked me.

Jill got to her knees, her face red from the heat and exertion, her clothes rumpled and dusty. We watched the Belle Fourche cop help the handcuffed second assailant to his feet with the assistance of a couple good Samaritans.

Motion to my left caught my attention as a pair of EMTs jogged toward us. One knelt next to me and put her hand under my chin. My first thought was that her triage skills were lacking because she was attending to me. My second thought was, *oh shit, am I the worst of the injuries?*

"What's your name?" she asked as she unzipped her medical bag.

"Doug Fletcher."

"Do you know where you are, Doug?"

After a moment of thought, I said, "I'm at the Black Hills Roundup."

"Why are you at the rodeo, Doug?"

"I was helping my partner arrest a cowboy."

"I'm flushing your eye, then we'll look at the scrape on your forehead."

"Check my partner. She was getting the worst of the abuse before I arrived."

Instead of looking at Jill, she uncapped a water bottle. "My partner will deal with her if she needs assistance," the woman said before tipping my head back and irrigating my eye. "There, can you see now?"

After blinking a few times, I looked at her face and nodded. "Yeah, I'm fine."

Sirens whined in the distance and a sheriff's deputy appeared. He walked past me, joining Jill and the Belle Fourche cop.

"You're not fine, Doug. You've got a lacerated forehead that I'm going to cover with a gauze pad. Then you're going to take an ambulance ride to the ER."

"Really, I'm fine."

Jill knelt beside us as the EMT taped a pad on my forehead. Jill clucked her tongue. "You need a shower and clean clothes."

"You should talk," I said. "You look like you've been wrestling a pig."

"I was wrestling a bull rider," she replied.

The EMT smiled. "Having worked this rodeo for fifteen years, I've learned there's only one reason to ride a bull—because you want to meet an ER nurse." She leaned

181

back on her haunches. "There you go. Your next stop is the ER."

"Hey! Isn't anyone going to look at my shoulder?" a slurred voice asked.

The EMT moved to Judd, who was still pinned face down by a good Samaritan. She looked at his shoulder, then looked back at me. "He's going to the ER too. His shoulder is going to hurt like hell when the alcohol in his system wears off."

Strong hands gripped my shoulder and squeezed. "Well, Fletcher, you do have a nose for trouble." Chief Arnold said as he knelt, assessing the state of my face and clothing. "I've got to say, the other guy doesn't look worse in this case."

"Really?"

"You and Jill will need to make statements at the station after you get seen in the ER."

"I don't need the ER."

"The EMT thinks you should be checked. I think you should defer to her expertise."

Waving off that thought I asked Chief Arnold, "Do you need our statements today, or will tomorrow be okay?"

"Tomorrow will be better. What started all this?"

Jill stepped forward. "I stopped Judd when I saw him with his arm over a teenage girl's shoulder."

Arnold blew out a breath. "Another one?"

"She's the best friend of the girl we pulled out of the bull rider's trailer." Jill paused. "You'll need to have an officer interview her about Amber's rape. I got the impression that Piper and Amber were playing truth or dare. Amber lost and her penalty was having to show a bull rider her mouse tattoo."

"I suppose alcohol was involved," Arnold said.

"I think that was another of the dares Amber lost."

"Shit. I can't believe those girls are that dumb."

Shaking her head, Jill said, "Naïve and dumb. They thought they were invincible."

"Help me up," I said.

Chapter Eleven

A woman's voice intruded on the fringes of my dream. Not ready to open my eyes, I was irritated that she was talking while I tried to sleep. "Turn that damned thing off," I mumbled.

A different female voice spoke close to my ear. "Take it easy, we'll be at the hospital in a few minutes."

"What?"

"Hang on, Jackie. He's waking up."

I opened my eyes and was blinded by the stark whiteness above and around me. My head throbbed and my face hurt. I tried to touch my nose, but my arm wouldn't move.

"What's the last thing you remember, sir?"

"Chief Arnold was helping me to my feet, then the ground rushed up and smacked me in the face."

Jill's laugh irritated me. "Yeah, it's funny how that ground lifted up to smack you. Must've been an earthquake or something." The tone of her voice changed, and she lifted the phone to her ear. "Yes, he's conscious. He just told me the ground rose up and smacked him."

"Who are you talking to?" I asked.

"Hang on Jack, Doug asked me a question." Jill held the phone aside. "Our boss wanted an update on your condition."

"I'm just fine," I said loudly enough to be heard across the ambulance.

"He's not just fine, Jack. The EMT thinks he's probably got a concussion and he reopened the gash on his forehead where the branch smacked him while he was riding in Tuzigoot."

I closed my eyes. "That was the horse's fault. He was trying to knock me out of the saddle."

"That might be a little overkill, Jack. I don't know that Doug's assault rises to the level of a federal crime." Silent for a moment, Jill switched on the speaker function and held it near my face. "A drunken cowboy tackled him. I expect the ER doctor will look him over and then release him."

Jack's voice sounded tinny and electronic. "Any assault on a Park Service employee is serious. People need to know that there are consequences when they strike a ranger."

"I've had my bell rung a few times," I slurred. "It's not a big deal."

"You will summarize the assault in a report before Monday night. I'll call the US

Attorney for South Dakota and notify him, or her, that they need to investigate the incident as an assault on a federal law enforcement officer. My superiors will support that stance." Jack paused. "Are you clear on this?"

Jill stared at me for a second, then turned off the speaker and pulled the phone close before I could express a contrary opinion Jill said, "We're clear on that. I'll get on the computer tomorrow morning and write an incident report."

I looked at the EMT who seemed to be enjoying the conversation. "Mr. Fletcher, you have a concussion. A doctor needs to determine how severe it is. And your broken nose has to be set so the tip isn't pressed against your left cheek."

"It's bad?"

"You look like some of the cowboys we've hauled in after they were thrown, stepped on, or head-butted by bulls. Yes, it's bad."

"Shit, my mother's going to kill me."

"It's not your mother who's going to kill you." Jill hissed. "You're the one who preaches to me about situational awareness. You weren't paying attention when that cowboy lunged at you."

"I'm sure I had a concussion before that."

"You *did not* have a concussion before that. You were more concerned about the dust on your shirt than the angry cowboys watching us cuff Judd."

"In all fairness, it was pretty dusty."

The EMT chuckled and I felt Jill's fist clench my shirt even tighter. "Like I said, your mother's reaction is the least of your worries."

I felt the ambulance slow, then turn. A moment later I heard the distinctive beeping as it backed into the ER bay.

Two hours later I'd been poked, prodded, x-rayed, and examined by at least three different doctors. I looked at Jill, who appeared to be playing a game on her cell phone. "What has the doctor told you?"

She replied without looking up from her phone. "He said you're an idiot who shouldn't be allowed to carry a weapon."

"Can you be serious?"

Jill lowered her phone and gave me a sad look. "Someone is going to set your nose after the painkillers kick in. That's your only broken bone, although your nose doesn't really have a bone."

"And?"

"Your left cornea is scratched, and you have a minor concussion. You'll have to wear an eye patch for a few days to protect your cornea. They're planning to keep you in the hospital overnight for observation." Jill stood and walked to the bed. She picked up my hand and squeezed it. "This isn't your first concussion, so the doctor is more

187

concerned. He said I need to keep a close eye on you for the next few days. If you start having problems with balance or start slurring your speech, I'm supposed to rush you back to the ER."

"If I start acting stupid, you're supposed to rush me back here?"

Jill ran her tongue around the inside of her lips. "I'm not sure I can stop you from acting stupid. You seem to rush into stupid situations without warning."

"Smartass."

Jill smiled for the first time since the confrontation. "Being a smartass is my new superpower."

Sighing, I asked, "Are Mom and Chet in the waiting room?"

"Yeah, along with my parents. There's a Belle Fourche cop outside the door."

"The chief thinks I need protection?"

"Judd is apparently well-liked and Chief Arnold is concerned that liquored up cowboys may decide to get even."

"As I recall, you're the one who arrested Judd."

"Did I say the cop was protecting you?" Jill asked.

"Oh."

A conversation outside the door caught my attention. One of the male voices sounded familiar, but I couldn't come up with the person's name. A moment later, a smiling cowboy swaggered into the room.

"What the hell are you doing here, Jess?" I asked.

The director of the Rapid City FBI office walked across the room and hugged Jill. "I heard your husband stepped in another cow pie at the Black Hills Roundup." After releasing Jill from his hug, Jess Pond walked to my bedside and grabbed my left hand. "The next time you decide to get beaten up by a drunken cowboy, could you do it in someone else's jurisdiction?"

"Why are you here, Jess?"

"Aside from admiring your pirate eye patch, black eyes, and the cotton stuffed up your nose?"

I gave a dismissive wave.

"Well, the Assistant US Attorney called and asked what I knew about some federal agent who'd been assaulted at the Belle Fourche rodeo. I said that was news to me. Apparently, his boss got a call from some irate Park Service bureaucrat ranting about one of his investigators getting beaten up by a cowboy. He asked me to *look into it.*"

Stepping closer, Jill asked, "Who called?"

"Some guy who rattled off a string of alphabet that the attorney didn't recognize. What is the NPSISB?"

"Well," Jill said, smiling, "we've been assigned to the National Park Service Investigative Services Branch. I assume the call came from our new boss, Jack Pardee."

"Yes! That's the name the attorney threw out. Neither of us had ever heard of him. But, when he mentioned Doug Fletcher, bells and whistles went off in my brain."

Closing my patched left eye, I looked at Jess. "Why did he call you?"

"You know how it goes. It's a slow Sunday, so the attorney figured he'd interrupt my morning coffee and reading of the Sunday newspaper."

"Were you at home reading the newspaper?" I asked.

"Hell no. I was in the office trying to sort out the last hornet's nest you two dropped into my lap. We're still working on the drug and interstate prostitution cases against the biker gang." Jess paused and turned to Jill. "Tell me what brought you to South Dakota and why you got involved in a fight with a drunk."

A nurse rolled a cart into the room, interrupting Jill's response. "The doctor is going to set your nose now. It'd be best if your guests waited outside the room.

Jill picked up a plastic bag that had been supplied by the hospital. "Let's get a cup of coffee in the cafeteria, Jess."

"Where's my Sig?" I asked, suddenly concerned that my service weapon might've been lost during the confrontation and trip to the hospital.

Lifting the bag, Jill said, "The Sig is in here with your badge and clothing."

"You're taking my clothes, too?"

The withering glare froze me. "Yes, I'm taking your clothes, too. In your current drug-induced haze, I'm afraid you'd decide to get dressed and walk out."

"I'm just fine," I replied.

Jess smiled at Jill. "It might be a good idea to handcuff him to the bed, so he doesn't wander off."

"Nah. I'll tell his mother to keep an eye on him. She won't let him out of the room."

I tried to give Jill a dirty look which apparently lost something with a patch over one eye. "You're going to tell on me?"

"Damned straight I am! Ronnie won't take any guff from you."

A doctor walked in pulling on a pair of surgical gloves. "After your guests leave, I'll put some lidocaine in your nose, then we'll straighten it and pack your nostrils to hold it in place until it heals."

While he spoke with Jill and Jess, I watched the nurse draw up a syringe of clear liquid. "That's probably enough to numb a horse," I said.

Smiling, the nurse set the syringe on a metal tray. "Trust me, you'll wish I'd drawn up twice that much tomorrow morning."

"Do I have a choice in this?"

Having overheard our discussion, Jill leaned aside to see past the doctor. "I'm not taking you out of here with your nose flopped against your cheek."

"It's not that bad," I said. Then I looked at the nurse. "It's not that bad, is it?"

With a grin, the nurse said, "You look like you lost a fistfight at the Lost Spur. It's that bad."

Jill and Jess walked out as the doctor inserted the lidocaine filled syringe. I imagine everyone in the ER heard my gasp when he pushed the plunger.

"Don't worry," the doctor said, "I'll wait a few seconds for this to take effect before I do the deep injections."

After catching my breath, I glared at him. "That's not very reassuring."

Using a gloved finger, the doctor pushed on my nose. "You may want to see an ENT about straightening your nasal septum at some point in the future." The movement of my nose caused a grinding sound and deep pain.

About to let loose with a string of expletives, I heard my mother's voice. "What have you done now, Douglas? Is Jill okay?"

"Jill's fine. Thanks for asking, Mom."

"You should wait outside the room until the procedure is over, ma'am," the nurse said, taking Mom's elbow and leading her to the door.

"He's got a patch over his left eye. Was it poked out? Are you going to give him a glass eye?"

"He's got a scratched cornea. The patch is temporary."

"Where's my daughter-in-law?" Mom asked as she exited the room. "If she's as beaten up as my son, he's going to get an earful."

"She's fine, ma'am. She's going to get a coffee with an FBI agent."

Mother stopped at the door and glared at me. "I told you to take care of Jill. If she's injured, there will be hell to pay."

With the lidocaine numbing my nose, lips, and tongue I said, "She's just fine."

The doctor chuckled at my unintelligible mumbling as he prodded my face with his finger. "I think you'd better not give a speech until the lidocaine wears off. No one will understand you."

* * *

In a daze from pain pills and lidocaine, I listened to Mom and Chet talk about my eye patch, my darkening black eyes, and the rodeo. Chet was disappointed that they'd missed the bull-riding finals. Mom seemed more concerned that I'd put Jill into danger than she was about my concussion or injuries. Conversation stopped when Jill and Jess Pond walked in.

Mom popped up from her chair and rushed to Jill, hugging her. "Are you okay, dear?"

"I'm fine," Jill replied. She tried to squirm free of Mom's hug, but my mother was intent on holding her tight to make sure she was really there and uninjured.

Jess walked to my bedside and smiled. "You look like you lost a bar fight."

"You should see the other guy."

"Does he have an eye patch, broken nose, and concussion, too?"

"I think so."

Studying my face, Jess shook his head. "That black under your eyes should fade to green and yellow in a week or so."

"Thanks for the encouragement," I replied.

"Jill says you're looking for a rodeo clown who killed a woman and drove her truck to Montana where he dumped the body."

"Yes."

"You do understand that interstate crimes should be investigated by the FBI, right?"

"We're kind of focused on identifying the clown."

"Uh huh. One of my agents took her kids to the preliminary rounds of the bull riding. I called her while Jill and I were having coffee. She said there was a clown with a white face and wide red grin working the arena Monday. He wasn't there Tuesday."

"I don't suppose she got his name and address."

"No, but I gave my agent Jill's contact information and they're interviewing the guys who hired the cattle people to see if they know the clown's name."

I pushed myself up on my elbows. "Where are my clothes? I'm going along."

Stars flashed in my eyes as I struggled to sit up and hang my feet over the edge of the bed. Jess and Jill grabbed my arms as I wobbled, waiting for the explosion of stars to fade. "You're staying in the hospital overnight. Lay down."

My vision was fading to gray as Jill and Jess eased my shoulders back onto the bed. I tried to protest, but a beeping monitor distracted me. A moment later, a nurse rushed in. "His pulse skyrocketed. What happened?"

"He tried to get out of bed," Jill said.

The gray images started to gain color as I laid back. "Um, I might want to just lay here a bit longer."

Brushing hair off my forehead Jill squeezed my hand. "I've got this. You take it easy for a day or two."

Chapter Twelve

I was examining my hospital lunch when Jill walked in with an auburn-haired, middle-aged woman. Our guest's western attire was offset by an FBI badge and a holster on her hip. The woman with Jill smiled and nodded toward my plate as she approached my hospital bed. "There's an old South Dakota saying that covers most hospital food. 'Always take a good look at your food. It's not important to know what it looks like, but it's critical to know what it was.'" She offered her hand. "I'm Special Agent Sharon Vanderhoff."

"I'm pleased my partner found someone to cover her backside."

After glancing at Jill, who remained silent, Vanderhoff said, "I'm not sure who is covering the other's backside, but it's been a pleasure working with someone who knows her butt from her elbow."

Jill smiled. "In FBI terms, that apparently means I'm competent."

Vanderhoff laughed. "Jill, you're more than competent. You're also a big step up from the interpretive ranger I worked with on a theft from Jewel Cave National Monument. That guy didn't know his butt from his elbow. He described the woman who stole a rock from the cave as, 'Kind of cute in a hippie sort of way.'"

I looked at Jill and smiled. "Like the naked robber, he was focused on cute."

"The naked robber?" Vanderhoff asked.

"There was a naked guy robbing convenience and liquor stores in St. Paul. The best description I got was that he hadn't been circumcised."

Vanderhoff snorted. "That's more than we get out of a lot of witnesses. I just wish I had witnesses who could agree on the color of the assailant's jacket. I swear I had three colorblind witnesses at the last bank robbery I investigated."

I replaced the cover on the hospital entrée smothered with grayish-brown gravy and opened the tiny container of vanilla ice cream. "What have you two been up to?"

"Based on Sharon's information about the Monday bull competition, we've narrowed the field of possible clowns," Jill said as she lifted the lid from my lunch and sniffed it. She made a face and replaced the cover as if the meal contained roadkill.

"Do you have a name?" I asked.

Shaking her head, Sharon pushed a plastic container of green Jell-O closer to me. "You should eat this. Gelatin makes your fingernails strong."

197

"Where did you get that old wives' tale?" I asked as I ate the ice cream.

"I worked in a packing plant while I was in college. We threw the pig skins and heads into a big vat and boiled them to extract the gelatin. The women all raved about how strong their fingernails were after working the gelatin line."

"If you're trying to put me off gelatin, it's not going to work."

Vanderhoff shrugged. "I'm not trying to do anything except enlighten my Park Service colleagues."

"Yeah, right," I replied. "What's your plan for identifying the clown?"

"Nine ranches supplied livestock for the roundup. We got names of their employees and we're comparing them to the NCIC criminal database to see how many have criminal records."

After finishing the ice cream, I picked up the lime Jell-O and scooped up a spoonful. "In my mind, Chris Jenkins' murder wasn't some random crime. There was some reason she was killed. Most killers leave their victims at the scene of the attack. This guy took the time to steal her truck and a stock trailer, then load one of her horses into the trailer. It was risky. That sort of thing takes time and astronomically increases your chance of getting caught. Don't waste your time tracking down pickpockets and shoplifters."

Jill and Vanderhoff glanced at each other. Jill drew a breath. "Well, Captain Obvious, we've also ruled out sex offenders and bank robbers. There are three men who've been arrested for assaults during burglaries. We're going to interview them."

Nodding, Vanderhoff added, "Our challenge is that they all pulled out this morning. One is from Kadoka, South Dakota. The others live in Colorado and Montana."

"Can you identify the clown who was working Monday, but wasn't there Tuesday?"

"All the rodeo organizers could tell us was that he worked for one of the livestock suppliers. We talked to all but two of them, but none of them admitted to having a guy working as a clown on Monday."

"My gut says the killer wants us to believe he lives west of Little Bighorn, in Montana or Idaho. I think that's a red herring, intended to lead us in the wrong direction."

Jill closed her eyes and started tapping her right index finger on the windowsill.

A young woman in dress slacks and a white coat walked in. "I didn't realize you had visitors, I'll come back."

Jill waved her in. "We can go."

"I'm Dr. Harris. I'll update Mr. Fletcher's chart on the computer while you visit."

The FBI agent watched as Harris logged onto the terminal and started typing. Satisfied that she was part of the medical team, Vanderhoff asked, "Why did the killer only steal one of Chris' horses? If he wanted well trained barrel racing horses, why not steal all three?"

"One palomino in a herd might not raise any flags," Jill replied, "but if three showed up all at one time, it might bring too much attention to the thief."

I nodded. "There must be a reason the clown needed a horse."

Deep in thought, Vandorhoff stared out of the window. "Jenkins' pickup was found in Alzada, Montana. That's backtracking from Little Bighorn, which would fit with Doug's comments about trying to make us focus farther west."

"But the livestock trailer was found in a ditch east of Alzada," Jill said. "He must've transferred the horse to a different trailer or a truck there."

A thought flashed through my hazy brain but was gone before I could articulate it. "The horse is the key. You guys should talk to Tonto."

Vanderhoff looked to Jill. "Who's Tonto?"

Not waiting for Jill's response, I replied. "He's a guy we met in a Lame Deer restaurant. He used to be the Lone Ranger's sidekick in the television series."

"The Lone Ranger's sidekick lives in Lame Deer?" Vanderhoff asked.

"Yeah. He sits at a corner table all day. I called him and asked for the phone number of the trucker who saw the clown."

Hiding a smile, Vanderhoff asked, "So, did Tonto have the trucker's phone number?"

"Not off the top of his head. Tonto asked the trucker to call me."

Not sure if I was pulling her leg, Vanderhoff looked at Jill, then back at me. "So, this fictional television character told you about a truck driver who saw a clown driving a stolen pickup across Montana."

Not catching Vanderhoff's sarcasm I replied, "Yeah. I think you guys should ask him why the clown only stole one horse."

Dr. Harris, who'd been making notes in my medical records, was obviously intrigued by our conversation. She stared at the computer but stopped typing.

Vanderhoff shook her head. "Horses are valuable, but you don't kill someone to steal one horse."

"Are any of your NCIC suspects from eastern Montana?" I asked.

"No," Vanderhoff replied. "The one Montana NCIC hit was a guy from Lavina, northeast of Billings."

"Did our killer know the guy from Lavina?" I asked. "Did the clown know we'd search the NCIC database and find the Lavina cowboy?"

Dr. Harris turned her stool and listened, intrigued by our conversation.

"That'd make our clown a lot smarter than the average cowboy," Jill said. "That'd make him a lot smarter than any cowboy I've ever met. My dad says most cowboys are all hat and no cattle."

"Meaning?" I asked.

"They're not rocket scientists. A lot of cowboys never finish high school. They love riding and working cattle, but most aren't clever enough to put together a complicated murder scheme."

"The concussion scrambled my brain. Things keep popping up, but they're gone before I can say them." I touched my forehead and felt the bandage over the scrape, then adjusted the eyepatch so it wasn't digging into my cheek. "What's the motive? Why kill Chris Jenkins? Why steal one of her horses? The clown didn't need to kill her to steal a horse. Was he trying to keep her from competing?"

Vanderhoff looked at Jill and raised her eyebrows. "Jenkins was favored to win the barrel racing competition. Who stood to gain if she was gone? Was the new first or second place rider associated with any of the livestock suppliers?"

"It's something else to check," Jill said. "I suppose the difference in prize money between first and second place was substantial."

"No," I said. "The horse is the key to finding the clown. You guys need to talk to Tonto. He's connected with the truck driver and might come up with the clown's name. Who knows, he might even determine the reason why the clown stole only one horse."

Dr. Harris was now thoroughly intrigued by our conversation, smirking while our brainstorming continued.

"Endorsements!" I said, blurting out a thought before it disappeared. "Is there someone who'll pick up a big endorsement deal if the clown killed Chris?"

Jill shrugged. "I don't know what endorsements are worth."

"Go talk to the other clowns. See how much that guy is paid for having the naked women displayed on his trailer."

Vanderhoff stared at me. "There's a clown with pictures of naked women on his trailer?"

"Yes, the clown's sponsor is an advertising company that prints custom playing cards. I guess you send in pictures of your naked girlfriend, and they print playing cards for you. The clown can explain it."

The FBI agent covered her smile with her hand. "I have a hard time envisioning a clown driving around in a trailer with naked women painted on it."

I swung my legs over the side of the bed. "Dr. Harris, will you get someone in here to release me? I have to track down a clown."

The doctor didn't jump up. "Is this the clown that Tonto, the fictional television character, saw?"

"Tonto didn't see the clown. He knew the truck driver who saw the clown driving the stolen pickup." I sighed. "Please get someone in here to release me."

"Mr. Fletcher, I'm a psychiatrist. The ER doctor asked me to evaluate you before your release. Based on your discussion about Tonto, the clown who stole the truck, and the other clown who you think has naked women on his trailer, I'm going to recommend that we do additional testing."

Jill snorted, which brought on a coughing fit. Vanderhoff just smiled.

"Wait! Jill, explain the case, Tonto, and the clowns." I turned to the doctor. "This is a bona fide murder investigation. A clown killed one of the barrel racers and buried her body at Little Bighorn battlefield. That location was just a red herring, so we'd look too far west."

Dr. Harris stood. "I'm going to order a head CT scan to see if you have a cranial bleed that's causing your confusion."

"I'm not confused!" I protested. "Jill, hand me my clothes, badge, and pistol."

Harris put up her hand. "Oh no. No one is going to give you a pistol until you've stopped having delusions about conversations with fictional television characters. We'll get that CT scan scheduled for this afternoon." The doctor walked toward the door.

"Nooooo! I'm fine. We're just discussing a case and you don't understand…"

The last part of my protest was made to an empty door.

I stood and glared at Jill. "Hand me my clothes. I'm checking myself out."

Standing behind me and apparently getting a view of my gaping hospital gown, Vanderhoff said, "Despite your cute butt, I think there are rules against federal law enforcement officers returning to duty before they're released by a doctor. There might also be something about gun toting feds with eye patches. Which side is your dominant eye; the left or the right?"

After gathering the back of the hospital gown, I turned to Vanderhoff. "My right eye is dominant, so the patch on my left eye is irrelevant. Besides, you guys need me. There are several leads to track down and the two of you won't be able to handle all of them."

"Doug, after your discussion about the clown with the naked women on his trailer, the comments about Tonto relaying information about a clown driving a stolen

205

truck, and the story about the barrel racer being buried at Little Bighorn, you'll be lucky if the psychiatrist doesn't send you to a padded room."

Hearing those comments from Vanderhoff irritated me further. "Jill, call our boss and tell him to override the doctor and return me to active duty."

"Doug, I'll gladly dial the phone for you, but I won't tell our boss you're ready to carry a gun. I think he might have the same reaction as Dr. Harris when you tell him the stories about Tonto, the clowns, and the naked women on the trailer."

The FBI agent nodded. "Yeah, the naked women riding on the clown's trailer is the icing on the cake."

"The naked women weren't riding *on* the clown's trailer. They were part of an advertising logo printed on the side of the clown's trailer."

"Um, that makes it so much clearer. So, this ad encouraged you to have fifty-two women to pose nude. Then, you'd send those pictures in and have a deck of cards custom printed? Or did you need fifty-four models, two of them posing as jokers?"

I sat down and glared at Vanderhoff. "You're mocking me. That's not what I said."

Jill waved her hand in front of me. "That's what the doctor heard. I assume she needs to give you a clean bill of health before you can return to duty." Jill turned to Vanderhoff. "Will you call Jess Pond and ask if he can free up another agent or two to assist with the investigation until Doug is cleared for duty?"

Vanderhoff shook her head. "You can call Jess and explain Tonto, the clowns, and the body buried in Little Bighorn battlefield. I'm not stepping in that cow pie."

Jill's phone buzzed and she stepped toward the door to answer it. She froze, then looked back at me. "Actually, Jack, there was a psychiatrist here a few minutes ago. Based on the conversation the doctor overheard, she's ordered a head CT scan. She won't release Doug for duty until she sees the result of that scan." Jill listened, then stared at me. "He's not taking it very well. We're in the midst of a rapidly evolving investigation and Doug's having a hard time sitting it out."

I put out my hand. "Let me talk to Jack."

"Hang on, Jack. Doug wants to say something."

"Hi Jack. There's been a misunderstanding. The psychiatrist overheard us discussing a contact who calls himself Tonto, and the fact that our murder suspect was wearing clown makeup."

"Fletcher, I don't know you well but I won't approve your return to work until the psychiatrist determines that you're mentally fit."

"But Jack, I'm fine."

"Call me after the psychiatrist releases you."

I handed the phone back to Jill. "Shit."

Jill motioned toward the door and Vanderhoff walked out of the room. "I'll update you this afternoon, after the CT scan."

"Great."

* * *

Jess Pond walked in with a daisy bouquet. "How's the patient?" he asked.

"The patient isn't a happy camper."

Jess set the flowers and his Stetson on a counter next to the closet. "Special Agent Vanderhoff and Park Service Investigator Fletcher are trying to find silver bullets. They're apparently meeting with the Lone Ranger and his sidekick this afternoon and want to feel like they're part of his team."

I glared at Jess with my right eye, but his broad smile was disarming. "What did they tell you?"

"Vanderhoff said you'd given the psychiatrist reason to have you committed to the state hospital."

"I was just…"

After putting up his hand in a stop gesture, Jess nodded. "I know, what you said was taken out of context. But still, it was damned funny. It's not often we get an investigation that involves clowns, naked women in trailers, and the Lone Ranger's sidekick."

"The women are not in the trailer. They're not entirely naked, and they're featured in a logo on the clown's…" I could tell that Jess was yanking my chain.

"Fletcher, there's an old cowboy saying. 'When you find yourself deep in a hole, stop digging.'"

"Is there anything new in the investigation?"

"There are a couple of things. The Assistant US Attorney showed up at the jail to interview the cowboy who jumped you. He'd sobered up and had been released despite the writ filed by the feds to hold him. Apparently, it's standard practice to release drunk cowboys once they've sobered up unless they have to pay for damage to a saloon. The county judge called your assault *a fight between drunks* and let the guy go without a hearing."

"I bet that frosted the US Attorney."

"I was called by the federal magistrate's clerk. They've issued an arrest warrant for the cowboy and asked me to track him down."

"That sounds like something handled by the US Marshal's fugitive task force."

"They thought the cowboy might still be in Belle Fourche, so they asked me to send someone over to make an arrest and deliver him to the federal lockup in Rapid City. The cowboy was hooking up his trailer when my guys arrived. He was surprised that two FBI agents had been dispatched to arrest him for a rodeo fight, but he surrendered without putting up any resistance." A smile spread across Jess' face. "People are usually docile when confronted by a pair of FBI agents, unlike the way they respond to a pair of park rangers."

"What happened to him?"

"The last I heard, a public defender and the Assistant US Attorney are working on a plea deal. The guy who assaulted you is apparently a well-known troublemaker with a long record. He'll have to serve some time in a federal prison, and the federal felony conviction will make it illegal for him to ever own or possess a firearm again."

"I won't have to hang around to testify?"

"No, the pictures of your eye patch, black eyes, scrape. and the notation of your concussion were enough to motivate the public defender and assailant that a trial wouldn't have a positive outcome for them."

"Are Jill and Vanderhoff talking to..." I paused before saying Tonto. "Are they interviewing our contact in Lame Deer?"

"Jill spoke to your friend from the Spoon and Fork. He's passing her phone information to the truck driver. They also discussed why only one palomino was stolen. Your perceptive friend suggested that the killer needed a horse to ride from wherever he dumped the truck and trailer to return to his ranch."

"That's the most rational thing I've heard this week."

Jess nodded. "The victim's pickup was found in Alzada. I had it towed to the South Dakota Crime Lab. They're tearing it apart right now."

"Are there any recoverable fingerprints?"

Chuckling, Jess nodded. "The tech I spoke with said the truck was a target rich environment. It may take them a week just to collect and log all the fingerprints. That's the good news. The bad news is that it appears the pickup was probably dumped somewhere with the keys in it and some teenagers took it joyriding. It's filled with fast food and candy wrappers. The wrappers are covered with fingerprints, as are the truck's interior surfaces and door handles."

"I don't suppose the teens will have fingerprints in the automated fingerprint identification system?"

"It's too early to say. If they're really young and haven't been in scrapes with the law, they won't have prints in AFIS. On the other hand, if even one of them is in the system, we can pin him or her to the theft of the pickup and we may get them to tell us where they found the truck."

"Our murderer was smart. I assume he wiped his prints off the truck before abandoning it. And I bet he knew a place to leave it with the greatest likelihood of being stolen."

Jess shrugged. "Hell, maybe the killer called the joyriders and told them where to find the pickup and keys."

Our conversation was interrupted when my mom and Chet knocked on the doorframe and walked into the hospital room. Mom hesitated when she saw Jess. "Oh, excuse us. We didn't realize you had a visitor."

Jess stood. "Come in. I think Doug and I are through."

Not interested in facing Mom and Chet, I protested, "No, Jess. We need to talk about the plan for questioning the rodeo clowns."

Chet cleared his throat. "They're actually called bullfighters, not clowns."

"Sure. Whatever. You need to get people over to interview the bullfighters before they're gone."

Jess's sly smile told me I'd said the wrong thing. "Sure. I'm personally going to check the trailer with the naked women on it."

"There's a trailer with naked women at the rodeo?" Mom asked. "Is it a bordello or something?"

Jess coughed to cover his laugh. "Something like that." He picked up his Stetson and nodded to Mom and Chet as he left.

"Wait!" I called out, trying to keep from being left alone with Mom and Chet, but Jess was gone.

Chet checked out the leftovers from my lunch. Mom approached my bed, taking my hand while closely inspecting my black eyes and the bloody packing in my nostrils. "Are you okay?"

"I'm fine, Mom."

"If you're fine, why are you still here?"

Chet lifted the lid on my entrée and cocked his head. "Aren't you going to eat this?"

"I couldn't tell what it was, so I passed on it."

Chet found the fork and wiped it with a paper napkin. "It's meat in gravy."

"I couldn't tell which variety of meat it was."

Chet popped a slice of the meat in his mouth. "I think it's pork."

"You aren't certain?"

"It doesn't make much difference to me. I've eaten rattlesnake and racoon. As long as it tastes good, I really don't care."

Mom shuddered. I knew she preferred chicken to most any meat but ate beef at the ranch to be polite. "Why are you still in the hospital?"

Chet didn't wait for my response. "He probably hasn't pooped yet. They always keep me in the hospital until I poop."

"I had a concussion and they're making sure I'm safe to leave."

"Safe from what?" Mom asked.

"Safe is the wrong word. They want to make sure my head injury isn't serious."

"What about your eye? Can they save it?"

"I'm not going to lose my eye. I've got a scratched cornea and they want me to wear the eye patch while it heals."

"You didn't eat the mashed potatoes either," Chet said, poking at them with the fork.

"Help yourself," I replied.

"How bad is your concussion?"

"I don't think it's that bad, Mom. But the doctor ran more tests this afternoon."

"What kind of tests?"

"A CT scan of my brain."

Mom squeezed my hand. "That sounds serious. Where's Jill?"

"She's working on the murder investigation with an FBI agent."

214

"Why aren't you with her?"

I sighed. "They won't give me my clothes, badge, or gun until they've evaluated the CT scan."

Unconcerned about my CT scan, Mom asked. "Do you trust the FBI agent who's with Jill?"

"The FBI has top notch agents who are smart and well trained. Jill will be fine."

Mom protested. "You've said some pretty nasty things about the FBI over the years."

"I've had a problem with some of the bureaucrats, but the agents here, in the Rapid City office, are top notch. Jill's safe with them."

Having eaten my entrée and potatoes, Chet replaced the plate's cover. "So, are they waiting for you to poop? They gave me prunes and that got things moving."

"My bowels are fine, Chet. They're concerned about my head."

Dr. Henry paused at the door. "I'll come back after your guests leave."

"No, please come in, Dr. Henry. This is my mother and her fiancé. Chet is finishing my lunch."

"Perhaps they could give us a minute to review your CT results."

Mom, no shrinking violet, frowned. "I'd like to hear about his brain."

Dr. Henry looked at me. "It's up to you, Mr. Fletcher."

"Let's just get this over with. Did you find a brain inside my skull?"

"There isn't a brain bleed, which was my greatest fear. That doesn't answer the question about your confusion, which leaves me pondering what to do next."

"Doug is confused?" Mom asked.

"He was talking about clowns, the Lone Ranger, and trailers full of naked women earlier." The doctor looked at me. "Are you still seeing clowns?"

"I wasn't seeing clowns. I'm a Park Service investigator and we had witnesses who've seen a man wearing clown makeup at a murder scene."

Chet cocked his head. "It sounds like he's good to go after he takes a shit."

Mom glared at Chet. "Language!"

Chet looked like a scolded child. "Sorry. Can he leave after he poops?"

"What about the Lone Ranger and the trailer full of naked women?" the doctor asked.

"There is no Lone Ranger. We spoke with an elderly man on the Cheyenne reservation who claims he was the Lone Ranger's sidekick, Tonto, on the television show. I'm sure he's not Jay Silverheels, but we're humoring him by calling him Tonto."

"And the trailer of naked women?"

"One of the rodeo clowns is sponsored by a company that custom prints calendars and playing cards. He's got the card

216

company logo painted on the side of his trailer. The logo features images of scantily clad women on playing cards."

"Do you have a headache or double vision?" the doctor asked.

"I doubt I can have double vision while one eye is covered by a damned patch, and I don't have a headache."

Doctor Henry checked my reflexes, then checked for nystagmus by moving her finger left and right in front of my eye. "I don't see any need to keep you in the hospital any longer. You asked about getting your badge and gun back. Are you a cop?"

"I'm a Park Service Ranger. I ticket litterers and scold parents with unruly children."

Mom glared at me. "He's an investigator. He and his partner seem to get into a gunfight during every investigation."

Dr. Henry raised her eyebrows. "Which is it; ticketing litterers or shooting at bad guys?"

"Some of each," I replied.

"You can't return to work until we remove the eyepatch and packing from your nose. That's to make sure your nose is stable. Not getting punched or firing a gun will allow your brain to heal from the concussion. Deal?"

"Fine. I won't carry my gun and I promise not to get involved in any physical confrontations."

The doctor looked at my mom. "Do you trust him to abide by that promise?"

"Oh, hell no. He's got no sense at all. If you let him out of here, he'll be racing off to some stupid confrontation or arrest."

Chet stepped closer to my bed. "I think you need to keep him here until he poops. That'll keep him out of commission for a few days, especially if you don't give him an enema, prunes, or raisin bran."

Mom turned to Chet. "Unlike some people, Douglas has been regular his entire life. Even going back to the days when I changed his diapers…"

"Mom. Please."

"What? I was being honest."

Dr. Henry was struggling to stifle her laughter. "His bowel movements aren't a concern." She turned to me. "I won't allow you to return to active duty until I assess you again in a week."

"I've already explained the clowns, Tonto, and the naked women. You misunderstood me."

"Uh huh," Henry said without conviction as she left the room.

Mom glared at me. "You're not going back to work."

"You're already concerned that Jill's at risk without me watching over her."

"Douglas, you just assured me that the FBI agent with her is competent. Now you're trying to tell me you'd do a better job of looking out for her. Which is it?"

"Jill's perfectly capable of watching out for herself. Compare my injuries to Jill's. We were in the same fight."

"You're not at all reassuring." Mom turned to Chet who was nibbling at some leftover on my lunch tray. "Let's go, Chet. Doug's being a jerk." At the door she added, "I'm going to tell Jill to bring only your pajamas. If you're going to play cop, you'll have to do it in jammies and slippers."

Just in time to catch the end of Mom's rant, Chief Arnold stepped into my hospital room. "Sorry to interrupt," he said.

Waving off the apology, Mom pulled Chet's arm as he tore open a leftover package of saltines that had come with the beef broth. "The doctor said not to give him a gun."

The chief watched Mom and Chet walk past, then looked at me. "I assume that woman was your mother. My wife and mother are the only people who speak to me like that."

"My mother-in-law uses the same tone," I replied.

Chuckling, Chief Arnold closed the door. "At least your mother-in-law speaks to you. Mine gives me the icy glare and silent treatment."

"Is there a line of cops in the hallway waiting for their turn to bug me?"

"Nope, just me," Arnold said, leaning against the door. "We checked the fingerprints on the two glasses from Chris Jenkins' living quarters. One set matches her. The other set is from Robert Fields."

"Is he one of the rodeo clowns?"

"No, he's Chris' manager."

I frowned. "To get a result that quickly, his prints had to be in the AFIS database. Is he a criminal?"

"He was a National Guard company commander in Iraq, so his prints were there from the Army."

"Did you talk to him?"

"Yeah, he's really broken up over Chris' death."

"Do you think he's sincere?"

"I do. He brought a bottle of whiskey to Chris' trailer Monday evening to celebrate her new corporate endorsement. They had a glass, then he left. He was playing poker with some of the stockmen when Chris was murdered. His alibi checks out."

"Does he know a clown who wanted to kill Chris?"

"I didn't ask that specific question, but I did ask if there was anyone unhappy with Chris. He said all the other barrel racers hated Chris' success, but they respected her as a professional. She didn't go out of her way to make friends, preferring to keep her personal and professional lives separate."

"Did she have a husband or boyfriend?"

"Chris had been engaged to a guy in Omaha a few years ago, but she broke it off. Fields said he was an insurance executive who treated Chris royally. She liked that for a while, but when he asked her to quit riding so she could be his trophy wife, she decided she wasn't ready to give up the excitement of the rodeo to become a socialite."

"Do you think the jilted lover is a suspect?" I asked.

"Fields didn't think so. The insurance guy recovered and is now happily married to a former model who's happy to be on his arm at charity functions."

"Did the manager suggest any other suspects?"

"He was a mess and won't be helpful until he gets his head together."

The door rattled, and Arnold pulled it open. A woman from the food services department carried in a tray followed by the aroma of roasted chicken. "Oh good, you finished your lunch," she said, swapping the fresh meal for the tray and plates Chet had picked over. She rolled the tray table to my bedside and smiled. "Is there anything else you need?"

"A burger and fries or pizza would be nice," I replied.

Winking at me, the woman smiled. "There's a pizza place around the corner that will deliver to the break room. If there wasn't a cop watching, I'd let you bribe me to order a pizza for you."

Arnold chuckled as the woman passed with the empty tray. He walked to the bed and lifted the metal lid covering the entrée. "I'd stick with hospital food until you get out. You wouldn't want to irritate the dietician who arranged for this carefully designed meal of skinless chicken breast and overcooked carrots."

"Hand me a spoon and the orange Jell-O."

Clucking his tongue, Arnold unwrapped the silverware. "You know how they make gelatin?"

"Yeah, I got that story earlier. I pretend I don't know about the pigs who gave their lives so I could eat orange-flavored Jell-O."

Arnold picked up the container of vanilla ice cream and peeled off the lid. "They don't even offer flavored ice cream." He used a flat wooden spoon to scoop out a bite.

"Hey! That's my dessert you're eating."

"I'm saving you from the blandness," Arnold replied, eating a second scoop of vanilla ice cream.

"That was going to be the highlight of my meal."

The chief finished off the dessert with the third scoop and set the spoon and empty cup on the tray. "I'll buy you a steak dinner when you get out."

"I'd gladly trade a steak dinner tomorrow for a hamburger today."

"I'll ask one of the patrols to swing by Burger Barn to bring you a meal."

"Thank you. Ask him not to forget ketchup for the fries."

Pausing at the door, Arnold asked, "Is there anything else I can get for you?"

"I'd like my clothes, badge, and pistol."

"I'll leave those to Jill. I have to stay on the good side of the hospital folks."

Chapter Thirteen

After overcoming my aversion to the bland hospital diet, I picked at the chicken and ate the canned carrots. Time had indeed helped with my brain function and the hospital solitude allowed me to reflect on all the conversations and interviews of the previous week. Pieces started falling into place, and things that seemed irrelevant suddenly seemed worthy of attention.

Looking tired, Jill arrived at the hospital around nine o'clock. She hefted the bag of my belongings onto the bed and waved a sheaf of papers at me. "I have your discharge instructions, so we can leave as soon as you get dressed."

I pulled underwear out of the bag and slipped them on under the hospital gown. "What have you done today?"

"Sharon and I…"

"Hang on, who's Sharon?"

"After a while, it became clear that calling each other Special Agent Vanderhoff and Park Service Investigator Fletcher was cumbersome. We're now Sharon and Jill."

"Sounds reasonable," I said, pulling on socks, then jeans.

"Sharon and I drove to Alzada where the stolen truck was found. The gas station had security camera video of the teens parking Chris Jenkins' truck and running. The clerk knew the names of two kids, so we drove to their houses. In Boyes, the first set of parents were protective and denied that their son would be involved in a truck theft. We showed them the video of the kids bailing out of the stolen pickup and they had a sudden change of heart. After assurances we were not there to arrest their son for stealing the truck, they brought the pimply-faced kid down from his bedroom and let us question him. We got the names of all five kids involved, and he told us where they'd found the truck. It was parked on the shoulder of the road near Boyes, with the driver's door open and the motor running. After determining that the driver wasn't nearby, they jumped in and drove it to school, in Broadus. After school, they drove it around until it was nearly out of gas and left it in Alzada."

"What time did they find it?"

"They found it early Tuesday morning, when they were driving to school." Jill said, as she watched me button my shirt. "The second kid was a girl from a ranch outside Albion. Her parents saw our badges and called her name before we'd even

225

introduced ourselves. She panicked when she saw us, and immediately threw all the other kids under the bus. She goes to the Ekalaka High School, so she didn't know where the truck had been found and wasn't involved in the joy ride until Tuesday afternoon."

I tied my shoes and stood. "Great information. I've had time to think about our interviews and there are a couple of things we should follow up on tomorrow." I stepped toward the door, but Jill didn't move. "What?"

Waving the discharge instructions, Jill glared at me. "There is no *we*. You are sitting at the ranch tomorrow, drinking coffee and reading the newspaper. We can discuss what *I'm* doing tomorrow."

"But I've got glaring things that require attention."

"Great. Tell me what they are, and I'll add them to the list of things Sharon and I plan to do."

"I'm fine and time is passing. We need to jump on things."

"Like what?"

"Sadie Getchell said she saw Chris Jenkins talking to a farrier Monday. So, Chris had been over in the livestock area and may have crossed swords with someone there."

"Okay, I can get the farrier's name and follow up. What else?"

"Chief Arnold traced the fingerprints off the second glass from Chris' trailer. The other person was Robbie Fields, Chris' manager. He'd brought a bottle of booze to her trailer to celebrate a new corporate sponsorship. Fields said they had one drink together Monday evening and then he left. I want to do a follow up interview with him to see if we get the same story, and to see if he's thought of anything else."

Jill pressed the nurse call button. "We need to officially check you out."

"I'm checked out and ready to go," I protested.

"Not until we talk to the nurse."

"Fine," I said. Then my eyes went to the bag Jill was holding. "Where are my badge and gun?"

"They're locked in the pickup."

"Great! I'll pin on my badge in the parking lot."

Jill waved the discharge papers at me. "No, you won't. You are released from the hospital, but the discharge instructions specifically state that you are not released for duty until the doctor examines you next week."

A woman in scrubs walked into the room and switched off the call light. "It looks like you're ready to go," she said.

"Is there anything else we need to do before he leaves?" Jill asked.

"There's a bottle of Percocet at the nurse's station. Once you sign for it, you're free to leave."

"I don't need Percocet."

The nurse looked over her half-glasses. "Honey, you'll be happy you have them tonight after you start moving around."

"I can't return to work if I'm on Percocet."

The nurse looked from me to Jill. "You've got a spunky one, dear. My husband would be milking the doctor to get off work for as long as the doctor would authorize."

"It's okay," Jill said. "With or without Percocet, he's not returning to work until after he sees the doctor next week."

Nodding in agreement, the nurse looked at me. "That's what I read in the discharge instructions. Have you looked in the mirror? You'd be scaring people with your black eyes, eye patch, bandaged forehead, and bloody packing in your nose."

I touched the cotton plugs in my nose. "My nose plugs aren't bloody."

"Trust me, honey. If you exert yourself, there'll be blood running from your nose like a faucet. Just go home and take it easy for a week."

I followed Jill out of the hospital. "A week? I can accept that I might need to rest tomorrow, but I'm not taking a week off of work."

228

Jill unlocked the truck and held the door for me. After I buckled my seatbelt, she handed me the white pharmacy bag. "Did you hear anything the doctor or nurses said?"

"I heard them, but I'll be fine tomorrow."

"No, you won't. Your head is going to hurt like hell, and you'll bleed if you exert yourself." Jill started the truck and drove out of the parking lot. "You're going to sit at the ranch and take it easy if I have to hog tie you to a chair and sedate you."

"But..."

"There is no but. I've notified the Park Service of your injury, and you're on short-term medical leave. If you continue to argue with me, I'll call Jack and he'll suspend you."

"But there's so much to do!"

"Sharon and I will be working our way through the list while you sit at home."

"Your list needs prioritization."

"Tell me what you think needs to be dealt with and I'll discuss it with Sharon."

"There may be more than the two of you can get to," I protested.

"Jess Pond promised whatever resources we needed."

"Fine. I'll take tomorrow off, and we can discuss what happens after that."

"Don't you give me 'fine.' I don't need your attitude. I'll chalk it up to the pain, for now. Starting tomorrow, you'll be a model patient or I'll…"

"You'll what?"

"Or I'll make you as miserable as you make me."

"Just leave me with my badge and gun. I'll be fine."

"No! You won't have a badge or gun. That's the one leverage I've got over you and I plan to use it."

I was about to say, fine, when it occurred to me that might not be well received. "All right. I'll sit at the ranch and play cribbage with your father. I demand a daily review of my condition."

Jill cracked a smile. "I'll review your condition daily, but you're not getting your badge and gun back until the doctor releases you."

"You know that not being part of this investigation is going to drive me crazy."

"I'll give your cell phone back to you and I'll update you each step of the way."

Reflexively, I patted my pants pocket. "You took my cell phone too?"

"It was for the best. I didn't want you to call Jack and start ranting about killer clowns, trailers full of naked women, and the Lone Ranger."

"Jess Pond said you and Sharon were shopping for silver bullets, so you'd be ready to partner with the Lone Ranger."

Jill smiled. "Thank you."

"For what?"

"You finally quit arguing and joked with me."

"You'd better leave me a few bucks before you leave tomorrow."

"Why? You're not going anywhere."

"Your dad plays cribbage for a quarter a game and fifty cents a skunk. I think he cheats."

"He uses superior strategy."

"Yeah, somehow his superior strategy results in him having hands full of fives and a crib full of sevens and eights."

"I'm sure he'll take an IOU."

"Great."

* * *

Accustomed to sleeping on my side, I found myself rubbing my nose against the pillow causing jolts of pain. I slept on my back until my snoring became intolerable. After two years, Jill had become accustomed to my usual snoring, but with my nose plugged, the snorts and growls sounded louder to me. About midnight, I drifted to the living room recliner with a quilt and slept fitfully until I surrendered and took a Percocet about one o'clock.

The combination of my aching face and the sound of perking coffee woke me about five. Disoriented by the Percocet and change of location, I panicked and sat up quickly, causing the recliner to thump and making stars dance before my eyes.

Molly Rickowski's voice greeted me from the kitchen. "I wondered if you'd be able to sleep laying down."

After leaning back to make the stars disappear. I blinked my eyes to clear the sleep from them. I lifted my left hand to rub that eye, then remembered the scratched cornea and reasoned it was the cause of the sandpaper feeling.

"Coffee?" Molly asked.

"Yes, give me a second and I'll come to the table."

Al Rickowski's gravelly voice came from behind me. "I was hoping you weren't planning to sit your butt in my reading chair the entire day."

"Shush, Al. Doug's only been in your chair for a while."

"He's been in my chair the whole time I've been awake."

I stood slowly, making sure I was in balance before lifting the quilt from the chair and folding it.

"Leave the quilt, Doug. I'll take care of it after you sit down." A steaming mug of coffee appeared in front of me while I had my eyes closed, hoping to quell the pounding behind my nose. "How bad is the pain?" Molly asked.

"On a scale of one to ten, I'd call it a three."

Sipping my coffee, I looked at Al over the rim of the cup. His head was cocked, and he looked curious. "Were you kicked by a horse?"

"Not a horse. A drunken cowboy tackled me."

"Having been kicked, gored, stomped, and punched, I don't ever recall having two black eyes and a nose that looks like it has a balloon stuffed up it. I expect that pain is more like a six or seven, than a three."

"I don't know. It hurts a lot, but not as bad as when..." I stopped before talking about the car crash I'd been in as a St. Paul cop that had broken several ribs and left me bruised from head to toes.

"Would you prefer something soft, like oatmeal, Doug?" Molly asked.

"After a day of tasteless hospital food, I'd take anything with some flavor to it."

Al nodded. "Biscuits and gravy, dear."

A door opened down the hallway and Jill straggled into the kitchen, pulling a bathrobe around herself. She went to the coffee carafe and poured herself a mug before taking the chair next to me. "I was tempted to pull the plugs out of your nose and stuff them in my ears," she muttered. "Then I considered smothering you with a pillow. I even took out my phone to record your snoring so the court would consider your death a justifiable homicide."

"You could've slept on the couch," Molly said as she slid a pan of biscuits into the oven.

"I was having hot flashes, so I was sleeping in just my panties. It'd be just my luck that Chet and Ronnie would show up early for coffee."

Al clucked his tongue. "Now, now lovebirds. Keep your spats out of the kitchen."

I reached for the bottle of Percocet when I could count my heartbeats by the pounding pain in my face. I popped a pill in my mouth, then scalded my tongue washing it down with hot coffee.

Jill looked at me and rolled her eyes. "And you thought I should give you the badge and gun so you could go out investigating today."

"I…ah…guess that might've been a poor plan."

"Do you remember the list of things you wanted to do today?"

"Um…not off the top of my head."

Al chuckled. "Don't take too many of those pain pills or you'll see leprechauns marching through the kitchen."

"After this crazy investigation, I'd probably see clowns."

Jill jumped in to explain. "We had a witness see a man made up like a clown coming out of the victim's trailer."

"Have you arrested the rodeo clowns?" Al asked.

"Neither of them arrived at the rodeo grounds until Thursday or Friday. The woman was murdered on Monday."

"You're talking about the professional clowns arriving later in the week," Al said as the sound of sizzling sausage came from the stove. "They use roustabouts as the bullfighters during the preliminaries. Some of them wear clown makeup."

Jill stopped with the mug halfway to her mouth. "We checked on the livestock supplier's employees. None of them appeared to be violent killers."

Molly arrived with plates of biscuits swimming in sausage gravy. "I hope this tastes better than the flavorless hospital food."

Jill looked at me. "You can't even smell the sausage, can you?"

I looked at the plate and realized I couldn't sniff because my nostrils were plugged. "No, I can't smell anything."

"How do you know the hospital food was tasteless?" Jill asked. "You can't taste anything but salt and sour with your nose plugged."

I paused, considering her comment. "I think there are taste buds for bitter on the back of my tongue."

Sighing, Jill handed me a fork. "You'd better hope I don't feed you anything rotten for the next week. You'll never taste it."

The sound of truck doors slamming preceded Mom and Chet's arrival. Chet went directly to the cupboard for a plate. Mom sat across from me and studied my face. "Your bruises are worse today, Douglas."

"I'm sure they are. They also hurt more than they did yesterday."

Chet sat down next to Mom and dug into his biscuits and gravy as if he was starving. Mom looked at him, shaking her head. "You just ate raisin bran and prunes."

"Those are just to keep things moving along. This is nourishment." Chet waved his fork at me between bites. "Your face looks like hell. Are you hurt anywhere else?"

Jill held up her coffee cup before I could respond. "It's okay. We weren't going to have children anyway."

I snorted my coffee, which instead of shooting out my nose splashed down my throat, causing a coughing fit. Mom looked shocked and concerned. I looked to Jill, waiting for her to backtrack her statement, but she was happy watching me cough while trying to catch my breath.

"I…wasn't…hurt…*there*…" I wheezed out between coughs.

Al broke into guffaws and even Mom smiled.

Chet nodded. "A horse kicked me there once and mine turned the color of prunes and swelled up like…"

Mom put her hand on his arm. "We don't need to know how much they swelled up."

Chet shrugged and mopped up gravy with his last piece of biscuit.

"What are you doing today, Jill?" Molly asked, hoping to change the topic.

"I'm meeting an FBI agent in Rapid City. We're going to talk with the murder victim's agent. It appears he's the last person to see her alive."

Al frowned. "If he was the last person to see her, why isn't he your main suspect?"

I shook my head and immediately regretted the move as the room appeared to jump around. "Chris Jenkins was his biggest earning star. He's probably going to lose a significant portion of his income without her."

"He's far down the list," Jill said. "We hope he might've known about any friction between Chris and the other competitors."

Chet leaned back from the table. "Cowboys drink and throw punches, but rodeo people are a family and unlikely to kill each other. On the other hand, the rodeo clowns and stock people are a different bunch. They're competitive and surly. The people who own the stock are constantly complaining about how the riders ruin their best horses and bulls."

Chet's comment struck Jill and she became quiet. "I've got to talk to the farrier."

After a nod, Chet said, "Farriers are like women's hairdressers. They hear all the rumors but keep what they hear to themselves. Otherwise, they lose customers and that costs them money."

I put out my hand, as if trying to capture the thought that had raced through without stopping. "The farrier…" I pushed my chair back and stood. "We need to talk to the farrier."

Jill got up and grabbed my arm before I took a step. "*You* aren't talking to anyone but Dad, and you're not doing anything but shuffling cards and moving pegs on a cribbage board."

Al sat up straighter. "Quarter a game. Fifty cents for a skunk."

Chet nodded. "I could get in on some of that action."

"Molly, where's the three-track cribbage board?" Al asked as he stood.

"Look on the closet shelf in Junior's room."

I glanced at Jill, knowing that the mention of Jill's deceased twin brother had been a conversation stopper for three decades. She nodded to her father, who strode down the hallway without hesitation. Our marriage and my mother's arrival had brought enough energy to the ranch to allow Junior's memory to move from an open wound to a scab.

Jill leaned close. "Do you need help getting dressed?"

"I don't think so," I replied. "It's not like I've got a broken arm."

"Have you tried to bend over and put on your socks?"

"Let's go to the bedroom and see how that goes."

Jill closed the bedroom door and watched me sit on the edge of the bed. "Don't even attempt to put on your socks and shoes. I think bending down will cause the blood to rush to your head and make you regret the attempt."

"Hand me a pair of boxers."

I slid off the underwear I'd worn overnight and bent down to pull the boxers over my feet. As predicted, blood rushed to my head, giving me an instant headache. I sat up too quickly and saw stars before the lights seemed to dim.

I felt Jill's hand on my arm. "Lean back slowly so I don't have to pick you off the floor."

Leaning back, colors replaced the gray that had swept over my vision. "You wouldn't have been able to lift me off the floor."

Jill stood with her hands on her hips. "Probably not. I suppose you would've come around once you hit the floor. If not, I would've needed Chet and Dad to get you up."

"Oh, that would've been great. I would've never heard the end of the story about the city kid who passed out trying to pull up his underwear."

After helping with my underwear and pants, Jill wrestled socks onto my feet. "I assume you can handle the shirt yourself."

I chuckled. "I thought I could do the underwear, too."

Jill threw a t-shirt at me. "Try to put that on without hurting yourself. I'm going to shower and dress." She paused at the door. "Try to fall on the bed if you pass out pulling your shirt on."

I was laying on the bed when Jill returned freshly showered with damp hair. "You look professional. Why are you wearing khaki pants and a button-down shirt?"

"I'm trying to not appear underdressed compared to the FBI."

"Call me after you talk to the agent and farrier."

"I don't expect to learn much from either of them," Jill replied, tossing her hair to dry a bit before brushing it.

"That's the way interviews go. You never expect to learn much, but when that one nugget drops, the hours of stumbling around for a clue become worthwhile."

"Okay. Who are you betting will have the nugget; the farrier or the agent?"

"Was Chet right about farriers hearing all the gossip and complaints?"

"I suppose so, but they never repeat any of it."

"You were dealing with them as customers, not cops. The farrier may be more open with you, especially because you're looking for a murderer."

* * *

By noon, I owed Al $4.75 and Chet $2.25. I'd won one game by three pegs, but other than that I'd lost or been skunked every hand. We'd finished three pots of coffee and my hands were shaking from a combination of the caffeine and Percocet.

"I need a bathroom break," I said, pushing my chair back from the table.

"Try not to fall on your way to your wallet," Al joked.

Chet pulled out his wallet and handed Al two one-dollar bills, then dug in his pocket and threw a quarter on the table. "Al's got change for a five now that I've paid him."

I stood slowly, hoping to keep the stars from flashing in my eyes. "All I've got is a twenty," I said, taking a step toward the bathroom.

Al cackled. "Then we'd better keep playing until you lose it all."

"Stop it, Al," Molly said. "Try to be hospitable."

"Doug's family. I don't have to treat him like a guest."

I smiled at the comment. I'd been accepted.

I was washing my hands when my phone rang. I struggled to get it out of my pocket before the ringing rolled over to voicemail.

"Fletcher."

"We just spoke with the farrier. I'm not sure we've got a gold nugget, but there's something fishy going on in eastern Montana."

"Tell me more."

"Hang on while I put the phone on speaker," Jill said.

"Hi, Doug. This is Sharon Vanderhoff, in case you were wondering who was wandering around with your wife."

"Hi, Sharon. Have you found a nugget?"

"The farrier was circumspect. He just let drop that he'd shod a couple horses that had been rebranded while he was working on a Montana ranch."

"I don't know what that means."

"Some operations brand their cattle and horses. If you buy a branded animal, you always ask for a bill of sale so you can prove you've paid for it. Legitimate buyers retain that bill of sale in case anyone ever asks you to prove ownership."

"Okay, I get that. What's rebranding?"

"Well, if you acquire an animal through less than scrupulous means, you might rebrand the animal. If you're really trying to be deceptive, you put your brand right on top of the original brand, so it's obscured or illegible."

"Who's doing that?"

"The farrier wouldn't name the ranch, but he let drop that it's in eastern Montana. He wouldn't say anything beyond that."

"Maybe I'm not thinking clearly, but I fail to see how that could have anything to do with Chris Jenkins' murder."

"If someone is stealing horses and/or rustling cattle, there may be big bucks involved," Jill said. "If Chris heard about that and confronted the rancher about it, she might've put someone's illegal operation at risk."

"We're not talking about millions of dollars, are we?"

Jill cleared her throat. "Some old St. Paul cop told me that store clerks are sometimes shot over $20."

"Okay, I'm choking on my own words. How are you going to find out who's stealing and rebranding livestock, then determine if they killed Jenkins?"

Sharon's voice returned. "We're driving to Robbie Fields' Rapid City house. Armed with the farrier's information, he might have some insight into the rustling operation and how that might be related to Chris Jenkins."

"How much have you lost to Dad?" Jill asked.

"Chet gave him a quarter, so he'd have change for my five-dollar bill."

"Ouch."

"It's painful, but in the greater scheme of things, five bucks is insignificant. And Al's having a wonderful time beating me."

"Do you still think he's cheating?"

"I threw a three in his crib. It was all sevens and eights when he flipped it over."

I heard Sharon laughing in the background. Jill said, "I think the Percocet is affecting your memory."

"Actually, I'm having fun trying to see how he's doing it."

"Is Chet losing too?"

"Chet's losing slower than I am."

"Thanks for entertaining them."

"It's keeping my mind occupied, and it reduces the chances I'll start searching the house for my pistol and badge."

"They're not in the house."

I waited for Sharon to stop laughing. "Last night you said they were in the pickup, then you brought a bag inside when we got to the ranch."

"Yup. I took them out of the pickup, but they're not in the house."

"It'd be cruel if you put them in a horse stall."

"I'm not saying one way or another, but your fear of horses might make a horse stall a safe hiding place."

"I can't believe how mean you've become."

Sharon continued laughing at our banter. "I can't believe you're so bullheaded that you won't follow a doctor's orders to 'stand down.'"

"I think of the discharge instructions as guidelines rather than orders."

"Doug, the doctor said you couldn't return to work until she'd re-evaluated you. Does that sound like a guideline or an order?"

"It sounds like a guideline to me."

Sharon's voice came over the phone. "Doug, violating a doctor's order against returning to work is grounds for dismissal in the FBI. The last time I checked, we were both employed by the federal government and subject to the same rules."

I sighed. "You FBI types are way too 'by the book.' I couldn't work there."

"Let me tell you, Ranger Doug, there's an FBI standing order that says anyone who offers you an FBI job will be posted to Amman, Jordan for the remainder of their career."

"Ouch. Last I heard they'd only be sent to Alaska."

"Either way, hiring you would be a career ending move."

"Luckily, I'm happy in the Park Service where the management is more open-minded."

"We're in Rapid City," Jill said. "I'll call you after we talk to Robbie Fields."

I returned to the kitchen where Chet and Al were sitting with an open bottle of bourbon with silly grins on their faces. "Are you talking to yourself in the bathroom or were you on the cellphone?"

"Which way are each of you betting?"

Mom, who had a glass of sherry, shook her head. "Don't encourage them."

I sat down and looked at the bourbon bottle. "Is that a fresh bottle or have you two already finished half of it?"

"I'm trying to minimize evaporation, so I try not to leave half full bottles sitting on the shelf."

I looked at Mom, who was shaking her head. "Those are their first glasses."

"Would you like a snort?" Al asked.

"I think it wouldn't mix well with the Percocet."

Mom nodded. "I'm glad you've got enough sense to realize that."

Molly retrieved a can of ginger ale from the refrigerator and set it in front of me. "You look a little peaked. The ginger ale might settle your stomach."

Al drank the last swallow of bourbon from his glass, then poured more for Chet and himself. "Did Jill and the FBI woman solve the murder? Is that why they called?"

"A farrier told them he'd worked on a ranch where he'd shod a couple horses that had been rebranded."

Chet froze. "Rebranding livestock is illegal."

"That's what Jill and the FBI woman said, too. The farrier wouldn't tell them who he'd been working for when he saw the rebrands, but mentioned it was somewhere in eastern Montana."

"If he was working for someone who supplied rodeo livestock, that's a pretty small pool of ranch operations."

"We don't know whether Chris heard about the rebranding at the rodeo, or that the people who are rebranding were supplying rodeo livestock. At this point, it's just another nugget of information."

Chet got up and found the rodeo flyer on the side of the refrigerator under a magnet. He smoothed the paper and scanned the front side, then flipped it over and read the back. "The livestock suppliers are listed here," he said, pointing to the bottom right corner. "I know most of these operations and the only one in eastern Montana is McBride's Bar M ranch."

"So, if they were rebranding their stock, what would you do about it?" I asked.

Chet looked at Al, then rubbed the day's growth of stubble on his chin. "Well,

I'd call the livestock inspectors and tell them my suspicions. I suppose they'd go over there and check McBride's brands and ask to see his bills of sale."

"The victim's truck was abandoned near Broadus. Is McBride's ranch within a horseback ride of the highway there?"

Al went to the desk and took out a Montana roadmap. He spread it on the table and set the salt and pepper shakers on the corners to hold them down. "Here's Broadus," he said, pointing to a tiny dot on Highway 212. Where's McBride's ranch, Chet?"

"Seems to me, McBride's spread is here, north of Albion. That'd be an easy ride from Broadus."

My phone chimed and I stood. Al and Chet wanted to hear what was being said, but I was afraid Jill or Sharon might think we were having a private conversation and would be too candid about their meeting with Fields.

"Fletcher," I said as I stepped out the back door.

"I just dropped Sharon off in Rapid City. I should be back at the ranch in twenty minutes or a half hour."

"What did Fields tell you?"

"We're suffering from information overload after talking to the manager. He said Chris Jenkins was having a problem with one of the other riders and they'd had

248

words. He also said she'd been paranoid lately and was sleeping with a Glock under her pillow. I guess some creep had tried to pick her up a couple of times and wasn't taking no for an answer."

"Those could be motives."

"The kicker was something Fields overheard during a poker game. One of the players, named McBride, was kidding about how much easier it was to cover his margins if they made a few midnight additions to their stock. Everyone thought the guy was kidding, but Fields was suspicious about the guy and his operation."

"Did he mention that rustling operation to Chris Jenkins?"

"Fields isn't sure if he told Chris about the rustling. He and Chris discussed many things: her winnings, sponsorships, competitors, and upcoming events. McBride's questionable stock acquisitions may have been among the topics when they were making small talk."

"Chet found McBride's ranch listed as a livestock supplier to the Black Hills Roundup. He said McBride is the only rodeo livestock supplier from eastern Montana."

"That's one more piece of the puzzle."

"We need to find someone who overheard Chris confronting McBride about his illegal activity."

Jill was quiet for a moment. "It'd be even better if someone had seen McBride in clown makeup."

"Of course! If McBride was one of the roustabouts being used as a bullfighter, there might be a bunch of people who saw him in makeup. Tomorrow, we need to track down one or two of the ranchers who provided livestock."

"*We* aren't doing anything. I'll talk to Chief Arnold to see if he knows any of the local ranchers who provided stock for the rodeo. *You* are going to spend the day playing cribbage."

I let out a sigh of exasperation. "I may need a loan to continue playing cribbage with your father."

"Change your strategy. Stop throwing sevens and eights into his crib."

"I'm not throwing sevens in his crib. They just appear there by magic. Poof! 'Oh look, I've got another twenty-four crib with sixes, sevens, and eights.'"

Jill laughed. "Humor him. He's old and won't be around forever."

"I understand that, but I'd rather just buy him a bottle of good whiskey than keep paying for it twenty-five cents at a time."

"There you go! Up the ante to a bottle of booze for whoever wins tomorrow. I'll buy a bottle when I go past the liquor store tonight. It can sit on the table while you're playing."

250

"I don't drink. What's my incentive?" I asked.

"You have my undying love."

"Your love doesn't keep me from seeing stars every time I stand up."

"This too shall pass."

"Sitting here while you're out investigating is driving me nuts."

"I understand that, dear. But it's your only option until the doctor releases you."

"I'm doing better."

"How many Percocet have you taken today?"

"Only three."

"Talk to me about seeing the doctor when you haven't taken a Percocet for two days."

I sighed loudly, to make sure Jill heard it. "Yes, dear."

"You're lucky I'm not sitting beside you, or you'd have a bruised rib."

"I'm already bruised and broken. You wouldn't add to my misery."

"Don't test me, Fletcher. I'll see you in a bit. I'm turning into the liquor store parking lot." Not being a whiskey drinker Jill asked, "What brand does my dad like?"

"We gave him Gentleman Jack for Christmas. It was a big hit."

"Got it."

I ended the call and took a five-dollar bill out of my wallet. Al and Chet lowered the level of bourbon in the bottle by a couple inches since I'd left. I set the money in front of Al and sat down. "We're upping the ante tomorrow."

Al took my five and slid Chet's quarter to me as he grinned. "We're playing for a buck a game tomorrow?"

"Jill's bringing a bottle of bourbon home tonight. Tomorrow's winner gets the booze."

Chet looked concerned. "Ronnie and I were planning a trip to Rapid City tomorrow. But I don't want to miss out on a chance to win a bottle of booze."

Mom was helping Molly prepare supper but overheard our conversation. "We can go into Rapid anytime. Go ahead and play cards tomorrow."

* * *

Jill arrived with a bottle in a brown paper sack. She greeted everyone, set the bottle on the sideboard, pecked me on the cheek, then walked into the bedroom. Al, unable to contain his curiosity about the bottle in the bag, stood and tried to look nonchalant about walking to the sideboard. "What's in the bag?"

I shrugged. "Jill doesn't know anything about booze. She probably bought some rotgut swill for two dollars."

Al pulled the bag open and peeked inside. His eyes went wide, then he smiled at me. "That bottle cost a pretty penny."

"You only get it if you win."

Chet, intrigued by the exchange, stood up and joined Al at the sideboard. Peeling the bag open farther, Chet smiled. "The best of this bet is that I'll get half of that booze whether I win or lose."

Al closed the bag and put it on a shelf. "Don't be so sure about that, Chet. That booze might be too good to share."

Molly, who'd watched the exchange silently, finally chimed in. "You know, Doug might win and take the booze home with him."

Both Al and Chet laughed. Al walked over and put his hand on my shoulder. "There's not much chance of that happening, is there, Doug?"

"Who knows? My luck might take a turn tomorrow."

Chet's belly jiggled like Santa Claus. "Not as long as Al's dealing," he said.

Chapter Fourteen

I'd given up any hope of sleeping in bed, so Molly laid a bedsheet on the recliner and brought out a down comforter. I slept fitfully, taking a pain pill at midnight, which allowed me four hours of uninterrupted rest. I went to the bathroom at four-thirty, then tossed and turned until Molly turned the kitchen lights on an hour later.

"I thought I heard you stirring out here," she said as she measured coffee grounds into the basket.

"I slept a few hours," I said, rising slowly from the chair. "Things are improving," I said. "I didn't see stars when I stood up."

Al was surprised to see me standing in the kitchen. "You're up already?"

"I spent the whole night thinking about how I was going to beat you at cribbage."

Al laughed as he slid on his boots. "You'll have to wait until I get the newspaper and have a cup of coffee." He stepped out of the back door, walking to the mailbox to retrieve the newspaper.

"You didn't have to buy a bottle of booze for him," Molly said as she took down three coffee mugs. "He can afford his own."

I put my arm over her shoulder and hugged her. "I know he can afford it. But I also know he appreciates a special treat, too."

"You know he cheats."

"Of course, I know. How else could he have those huge cribs when I throw cards that don't match what he flips over."

Molly pecked my cheek. "Your Mom raised a good kid, Doug. I tell her that every time you call or visit."

"Thank you. I wasn't sure you and Al were entirely happy about having a city kid for a son-in-law."

"We got over that pretty quickly. I should've known that if Jill ever fell in love, it'd be with someone as special as you."

Jill walked out of the bedroom. She heard the last comment and snorted. "Doug's special?"

Molly took down a fourth mug, then filled them all with steaming coffee. "He's as special as you are, dear."

Gravel crunched in the driveway, so Molly took down two more mugs, expecting Mom and Chet to walk in. We were all surprised when Sharon Vanderhoff knocked, then opened the door.

"I hope I'm not intruding," she said, leaning into the kitchen.

Molly smiled and waved her in. "Heavens no! Everyone's welcome in my kitchen. Do you use cream or sugar in your coffee?"

"I take it black, please."

Al held a chair out for Sharon and Molly delivered a mug of coffee. "Would you eat a couple pancakes?" Molly asked.

Sharon, who was slightly chunky, smiled. "I passed on the Fruit Loops I fed my kids, so a pancake would taste really good." She turned to me and smiled. "You must feel better. You're up and moving already this morning."

"I got a few hours of sleep. That helps."

Sharon studied my face. "I think some of the black around your eyes is starting to fade to purple."

"Ooh," I said. "Progress."

Jill was leaning against the counter, sipping her coffee. She gestured for me to join her. "You might want to put on a pair of pants," she whispered. "Most people don't greet guests wearing only boxer shorts."

"Oh geez," I said. "It's the Percocet."

Pecking my cheek, Jill nodded. "And that's why you're not ready to put on a badge and pistol yet. Do you need help with your jeans?"

"I can do it. I didn't even see stars when I stood up from the recliner."

"Better keep your boxers on," Jill said. "If we hear you fall there will be a group of us helping you get back up."

"You wouldn't…"

"I can't lift up a big beefy man like you all by myself."

"Fine, I'll put on a bathrobe."

"Or you could let your wife help put on your pants."

"Come along."

I sat on the bed while Jill pulled the jeans over my ankles. "What's your plan for today?"

"While you were chatting with my dad, Sharon told me she'd had a call from Chris Jenkins' manager last night. The rustling conversation he overheard was during a poker game with several riders and stockmen. He gave Sharon the names of three other people who probably overheard the revelation. One of the calf ropers is local and was knocked out early in the preliminary rounds. We're hopeful he watched some of the bull riders and might remember if any of the bullfighters wore makeup."

"Local is relative for you ranchers. Are you talking about someone in the Spearfish area, the Black Hills, or somewhere in the Plains?"

"Charlie Rollins lives on the Cheyenne reservation."

"He may be someone Tonto knows," I said as I stood and pulled my pants to my waist.

"I'm sure everyone on the Rez knows Tonto, and most residents probably know each other."

"Say hi to Tonto when you stop for lunch."

Wiping invisible dust off her knees, Jill stood. "If I have any say in the matter, we'll eat in a more…metropolitan area."

"Hey, the food was wholesome, reasonably priced, and tasty."

"I'd prefer an eatery with a slightly more diverse menu than the Spoon and Fork Café offers."

"It'll be your loss, and you won't get to speak with Tonto."

Jill stopped with her hand on the doorknob. "If you want a psych release, you should probably stop talking about Tonto and the Lone Ranger."

"That's what he told us to call him."

Peeling back the dressing on my forehead, Jill said, "Just the same, that's not a particularly…sane reference."

"How does my forehead look?"

"You have a scab on top of the scar."

"Which scar?"

"The scar you got when you forgot to duck when we were chasing the Tuzigoot murder suspect."

"That left a scar?"

After taking a half step back, Jill put her hands on my shoulders. "Do you ever look in a mirror?"

"Every time I shave."

"Don't you look at your forehead?"

"Last time I checked, there weren't any whiskers up there."

Jill unwrapped one of the dressings sent home by the hospital and applied it to my forehead. "You're hopeless."

"At this point in my life, one more scar doesn't make much difference."

"You sound like a damned cowboy."

I grabbed her waist and pulled her close. "Not a cowboy; a cynical cop."

The sound of shuffling cards carried from the living room. Al had the cribbage board set up, there were three steaming mugs of coffee set out for us, and Chet was sitting with his hands clasped at the table.

Al looked up when we walked into the dining area. "I can almost taste that fine Tennessee Whiskey."

I took the empty chair with the coffee mug. "Roll up your sleeves, Al."

"What?"

"If we're playing for high stakes, I want to make sure you're not keeping cards up your sleeves."

Chet started laughing and slapped the table, slopping coffee. "That's a good one!"

Al smiled at me. "Are you accusing me of cheating?"

"No, I'm just keeping you honest."

Sharon's eyes sparkled as she watched the exchange. "Gambling is illegal in South Dakota except in licensed state casinos."

Chet looked over his shoulder at her. "With Doug and Al, it's not gambling. Doug's just slowly contributing to Al's retirement nest egg."

Jill opened the door and motioned for Sharon to follow. Mom, who had been washing dishes, turned toward Jill and wiped her hands. "Can Molly and I come with you two? Sitting here listening to those three coots arguing gets old."

"I think we should check out the new quilt shop in the Rushmore Mall," Molly said.

Mom frowned. "I'm not into quilting."

"Would you rather listen to the old coots play cards?"

Mom set the dish towel on the counter and reached for her purse. "I suppose I could learn to quilt."

Molly picked up her purse and followed Mom to the door. "There are meatloaf sandwiches in the refrigerator when you get hungry."

* * *

My phone buzzed as we wiped up the sandwich crumbs. "How many games are you behind?" Jill asked.

"I've only been skunked twice."

"That's not an answer to my question."

"Well, there are five holes to tally games won. My peg is in the third hole."

"How many games has Dad won?"

"I think he's on his third lap."

Jill held the phone aside and said, "My dad is ahead fifteen games to three."

Sharon laughed in the background.

"What did you learn from Charlie Rollins?"

"Tonto called him a few minutes ago and we're waiting for him at the Spoon and Fork." Sharon said something in the background. "Hang on."

I waited with Chet and Al holding their cards and talking. I suspected they were brewing up some new plan to beat me again.

"Sharon suggested that we put you on speakerphone when Rollins gets here."

"That'd be nice. I'd like to hear what he has to say."

Tonto apparently leaned close to Jill. "Is that you, Doug? You're not letting these women take over the investigation just because a drunk cowboy gave you a black eye, are you?"

"Please turn the speaker on," I said.

"Go ahead," Jill replied.

"Tonto, believe me, if I wasn't handcuffed to this hospital bed, I'd be there."

After a snort, Tonto replied. "You can't feed me lies about being in the hospital. These two women can't keep a secret. They already told me that you're laying around the house losing cribbage games to Jill's dad."

"Somebody has to keep the old coot entertained."

At that, Al looked up. "Which of us are you calling an old coot?"

"Does it matter?" I asked.

Al picked up the cards I'd left on the table and sorted through them, adding one to the crib and replacing it with a different card from Chet's hand. He gave me an evil grin.

"A young guy just walked in and is looking around," Jill said. "Hang on while we catch his attention." A moment later, Jill was back. "I explained who was on the phone and Tonto told Charlie that you were *the real* investigator. I guess that makes Sharon and me your sidekicks."

"Damn straight," Tonto said.

The phone scraped on the table and Jill's voice was farther away. "Charlie, we're investigating Chris Jenkins' death and we hope you may have seen or heard something during the rodeo that will help us find her killer."

Tonto chimed in saying, "Are you going to read him his rights?"

Sharon sighed. "Charlie isn't a suspect, and he's not under arrest. We just want to understand what he saw and heard while he was at the rodeo."

"That's not how the Lone Ranger did it. He always read the bad guys their rights."

"Tonto," I said. "The Lone Ranger never read anyone their rights. The Miranda ruling wasn't made until after the Lone Ranger was off the air."

"What? The Lone Ranger is still on the air. I watched an episode I was in last Saturday. It's the one where I had to sneak up behind the bad guys and…"

"Tonto, can we get on with Charlie's interview?" Sharon asked.

"It's not a woman's place to interrupt a movie star."

I could imagine the reaction Tonto was getting from Jill and Sharon, neither of them being wallflowers. "Tonto, I think you should let the ladies talk to Charlie."

"Fine. But if this conviction gets thrown out because they forgot to read Charlie his rights, I'll be the one laughing."

"Charlie," Jill said. "Do you remember who distracted the bulls during the preliminary rounds?"

"There were a couple guys. Frisco and Rusty took turns."

"Who are Frisco and Rusty?" Sharon asked. "Do you know their last names?"

"Frisco Jones and Rusty McBride."

"Were they wearing clown makeup?" Jill asked.

"Frisco didn't wear any makeup, but Rusty did."

"What pattern did he wear?" Jill asked.

"I don't understand what you mean."

"How did he paint his face? What colors did he use?"

"It wasn't anything special. Rusty just smeared on some white face paint."

"Did he do anything with his nose or lips?" I asked.

"His nose was just white, but he painted on wide red lips."

"Smiling or frowning?" Sharon asked.

"Smiling, as I recall."

"We heard that someone talked about rustling cattle during a poker game and that Chris Jenkins might've heard about that. Do you know anything about that?"

"I really don't know anything about anyone rustling. I mean, that's a big deal and…well…a guy could get killed nosing around something like that."

"Charlie, did you see Chris arguing with Rusty McBride on Monday?"

"I didn't see her say anything to Rusty, but old man McBride was giving her an earful that afternoon. She wasn't buying whatever Rufus was selling because she got right in his face. I thought one of them was going to throw a punch before the old man stalked off."

264

"Did you hear what was said?" I asked.

"Nah, I was getting my horse ready, and they were closer to the livestock pens. I couldn't make out the words, but they were going at it."

Tonto's voice interrupted. "Rufus McBride is a piece of work. He doesn't take crap from anyone. It's probably good that he walked away because I wouldn't put it past Rufus to take a poke at a woman."

"Do you remember any conversations between Rusty McBride and Chris?" Jill asked.

"They had no reason to cross paths. Chris was a barrel racer and McBrides are livestock suppliers. Rusty did some bullfighting, but that wouldn't involve Chris Jenkins."

Sharon asked Charlie to repeat what he'd said, and he talked through his observations again. "Rufus McBride stuck his finger in Chris' face. She batted his hand away, then she walked away shouting over her shoulder."

"What did she shout?"

"She said something about a conversation with the brand inspector."

"Did anyone else see or hear the altercation?" Jill asked.

"Everyone was busy dealing with the rodeo or livestock. I don't remember seeing anyone else."

"What's a brand inspector?" I asked.

"In the old days," Tonto said, "the brand inspector went from ranch to ranch, checking the cattle brands to catch rustlers. Nowadays, they spend most of their time at the cattle auctions checking brands on the arriving cattle and verifying bills of sale."

"Doug, do you have any other questions?" Sharon asked.

"That covers my thoughts and concerns. Thanks."

"Hey, Fletcher," Tonto said. "Remember you owe me a slice of pie for connecting you with Billy Beaverheart."

I laughed. "Jill will pay that debt for me."

"It'd taste sweeter if you paid for the pie in person."

Jill ended the call, and I went back to the cribbage game. I'd had eight points in my card hand when I'd answered the call. When I picked up my cards, none matched. I scooped up the crib, set my cards on top of the deck, then shuffled them. "I'm declaring a misdeal."

Al acted disgusted and threw his cards on the table. Chet grinned at Al. "I told you to leave him at least two points."

The redealt cards were just as bad as the hand I'd thrown in. Al smiled. "It's a shame that you don't have any points."

I set my hand down and leaned forward. "If you're not cheating, how do you know I don't have any points?"

Al pushed his cards to me. "Doug, you don't have a poker face. You're grinning when you've got a hand or frowning when you're holding nothing."

I looked at Chet, who was nodding. "Never play poker. You'd lose your shirt."

My phone rang before I could respond. Jill's name flashed on the caller ID. "We're driving to Rapid City so Sharon can draft a search warrant."

Knowing cell phone conversations weren't secure, I didn't ask for details. "You got a big nugget."

"We hit the mother lode. Sharon spoke with the Assistant US attorney, and he's got a magistrate's clerk waiting for the document."

I closed my eyes and smiled. "Savor the moment. You have to dig a lot of holes to find pay dirt," I said, sticking with the mining metaphors. "When are we executing the search warrant?"

"*We* are not executing the warrant. Jess Pond is making calls to assemble a multi-agency search team. I'll tell you about it tonight."

"You're not going in tonight, are you?"

"Sharon thinks it'll probably happen tomorrow morning if Jess can line up the people he needs."

"I'm coming along."

"You aren't cleared for duty."

"I'll ride along as a civilian if I have to, but I'm coming."

A muffled conversation took place in the background, then Jill came back on the phone. "Sharon says she'll plead your case to Jess, but he's the final arbitrator."

"I'll be there if I have to drive myself."

Another muffled conversation followed before Jill spoke. "Listen, dear. If the doctor and Jess both say no, Sharon says she'll personally handcuff you to a tractor."

"Tell Jess I haven't had a Percocet all day and I'll have the drugs completely out of my system tomorrow."

Jill snorted. "A drug test would still detect the Percocet from last night."

"Just pass along what I said. Okay?"

"Sharon heard you and she's nodding."

Al and Chet were both staring at me when I ended the call. "Jill caught the murderer?"

"She couldn't say over the phone, but they're going to the FBI office to draft a search warrant. That means they've got probable cause to search for evidence of a federal crime."

"That's good?" Chet asked.

"In my experience, an Assistant US Attorney won't take a search warrant to a federal magistrate unless he's ninety-nine percent sure he's going to get a conviction. So yes, that's good."

Al wandered to the sideboard and pulled the booze out of the bag. Cradling the bottle like a baby, he smiled. "Chet, we're drinking the good stuff tonight."

Needing no further encouragement, Chet went to the cupboard and took down two glasses. "You're sure you don't want a taste of this, Doug?"

"No, thanks. I'll just watch you two drink your ill-gotten gains."

Chapter Fifteen

Having reconciled myself to another day of cribbage, I walked Jill to the pickup. "I know that you, Jess, and Sharon will spend the day getting everything ready to execute McBride's search warrant. I'll sit here and play cards again, but when the time comes to do the search, I'm coming along."

"Honey, you have two black eyes, a patched forehead, plugs stuck in your nose, so it sounds like you're talking underwater, and you've had a concussion. You'd be risking another concussion that might be career ending."

I reached out, lifted her chin, and leaned close to kiss her. Our faces were inches apart when she laughed. "I'm sorry. You may be trying to be romantic, but it's hard to look at your eyepatch and two black eyes and be serious."

I leaned back. "No romance tonight?"

"Not unless you put a bag over your head."

"That could happen."

Jill planted the palm of her hand on my chest and gently pushed. "I was kidding. Even a bag wouldn't help. Talk to me again when you look less like Frankenstein's monster."

"I don't have any stitches," I protested as she got in the truck.

"Frankly, stitches might be more attractive than the eye patch, black eyes, and nose plugs."

"Fine," I said, trying to act like I was pouting. "Maybe Al, Chet, and I will drive into Spearfish and pick up some women in a bar." I kidded.

Jill bit her lip to suppress her laughter. "Good luck with that. Two octogenarians and a guy who looks like he was kicked by a mule would be a real catch."

Al and Chet were drinking coffee and arguing about when to cut hay. They looked up and stopped talking. "Well?" Al asked.

"Get out the cribbage board. I'll work on my poker face to see if I do any better."

Al stood. "I think you need a change of pace."

"What do you have planned?" I asked.

"Chet thinks we should go for a horseback ride."

I froze. "I'll play for fifty cents a game if you don't make me ride a horse."

"Make it a buck," Al countered.

"Whatever," I replied, pouring myself a mug of coffee.

Al retrieved the cribbage board and cards. I topped off Chet's coffee as Al asked, "Are you in for a buck a game, Chet?"

Chet smiled. "I wouldn't miss it."

Mom and Molly swept out of the bedroom with paper bags under their arms. "More cribbage?" Molly asked.

"Doug's willing to up the ante today," Al said as he placed pegs in the cribbage board.

"How did you talk him into that?" Mom asked.

"Al threatened to take him horseback riding," Chet said with a grin.

Molly rolled her eyes. "We're going to Chet's to lay out a quilt."

Al froze. "What about our lunch?"

Mom pointed at the refrigerator. "I know it's almost beyond your capabilities, but there's meatloaf in the refrigerator and bread on the counter. You spread butter on the bread, put a piece of meatloaf on top of that, then lay another slice of bread on top of the meatloaf. Have you got that, or do you want me to write out the recipe for you?"

Al frowned. "Doug, has your mother always been this sarcastic?"

I picked up the cards and started shuffling. "That's where I learned it."

Mom patted my head as she walked past. "And I thought you never paid attention to anything I said."

* * *

The cribbage games played out as expected. I was relieved when Jill walked in carrying a red and white striped bag that smelled like fried chicken. Holding up the bag, she announced, "I made supper."

Molly and Mom came in a step behind Jill, with a second bag and a six-pack of beer. "We've got the beverages and dessert."

I swept the partially completed card game aside and pulled the pegs out of the cribbage board.

"Hey," Al protested. "I was three pegs away from double-skunking you!"

"Huh," I said as I put the cards away. "I thought we were tied."

"We weren't tied. I was about to lap you."

"Too late now," I said as I slipped the pegs into a recess in the back of the cribbage board.

Al waved a slip of paper at Jill. "Doug said you'd have to pay his IOU because he doesn't have any bills larger than a ten."

"You lost more than ten dollars?" Jill asked me.

Al got up and handed her the slip. "It's twenty-two dollars as of lunchtime. He hasn't written up the afternoon IOU yet."

Chet laughed while taking plates from the cupboard. "Doug's the unluckiest card player I've ever seen."

"They cheat!" I said, putting the cards and cribbage board away. I stood beside Jill as she removed containers from the bag. "Are you all set for tomorrow?" I whispered.

"Jess was on the phone all day, but he got all the players lined up. The Ekalaka County Sheriff was surprised we had a warrant for McBrides."

"He didn't believe McBrides were rustling cattle?"

"Actually, he was surprised we had enough evidence to get a search warrant. He was sure something fishy was going on at McBride's ranch, but he couldn't put a case together." Jill made sure the others were busy, then whispered. "The sheriff knew McBride had been abusing his wife for years but couldn't get her to file charges. She told the sheriff that her husband would kill her if she ever took him to court or left him."

I pecked Jill's cheek. "Good job, dear."

She glanced at our parents, then leaned close to my ear. "I've been thinking about the romance thing."

"Yeah?"

274

She started laughing before she could answer. "It's not happening. Not even with a bag over your head."

* * *

I watched as Jill climbed out of bed and took fresh clothes out of the suitcase. With clothing in her hand, she stepped toward the door, then realized I was awake. "How do you feel?"

"Did you get the license number of the truck that hit me?"

"It was a drunken cowboy, not a truck."

"I'm sure he looks worse than me."

"Actually, he looks surprisingly good. Unlike you, he was ready for the impact that smashed your head into the ground. And he was drunk so his injuries didn't hurt until the next day."

"Go take your shower. You're depressing me."

After eating two pancakes, two fried eggs, a half pound of sausage, plus two cups of coffee, I pushed my plate away and leaned back in my chair. Jill's dad nodded toward the stove where Molly was staring at me wearing a grin. "You made Mom happy," Al said. "She likes to cook for people who appreciate food."

I nodded to Molly as she came to take my plate. "I hope you had enough to carry you over until lunch."

275

"Molly, I'm in danger of popping my shirt buttons if I have another bite." That comment made Molly smile even wider, displaying dimples that showed me the origin of Jill's. They were the dimples that never failed to melt my heart.

Picking up her plate, Jill carried it to the wastebasket under the sink. She scraped off a half pancake and some sausage. Molly clucked her tongue. "You are never going to put meat on your bones, Jill."

Jill's mind was elsewhere, her intense concentration making her miss Molly's comment. She returned to the table and topped off her coffee, then pushed the carafe to me. "There has to be a way of identifying the guy in clown make-up."

"Other than the vague description of a clown wearing jeans, boots, and a Stetson, we've got nothing. To be perfectly honest, that description fits about half the men in four or five states and at least two Canadian provinces."

"I know. But still..." Jill said, her frustration showing. "I think we can narrow that down to the men who were in early for the rodeo; the competitors, the stockmen, and the vendors."

Al shook his head. "I don't think you can rule out the entire male population of Belle Fourche."

Jill turned her head, not wanting to accept the reality of the potential suspect pool. "There has to be something we're missing."

"The Belle Fourche police have interviewed all the cowboys and vendors. They're satisfied that none of them had a motive to kill Chris," I said.

"The Belle Fourche police found a sex offender sleeping in his pickup," Jill said.

"Chief Arnold said the killer probably ate breakfast in town Tuesday morning after the murder. There's no way he had time to kill the victim, steal her pickup, drive to Little Bighorn, and return."

"But still..."

"We'd be wasting time."

"What else have we got to do?" Jill asked.

"How did her pickup end up in Alzada, Montana with an empty gas tank?"

Jill slapped her hand on the table, startling the rest of us. "That's it! The gas thing!"

"What gas thing?" I asked.

"The killer stole her big-assed one-ton diesel pickup. It can't get more than ten miles-per-gallon. Even with a monster tank, that truck isn't going from Belle to Little Bighorn, then back to Alzada without filling up somewhere. And, if the killer was someone local, they'd be looking for a station with diesel fuel every time they got down to half a tank, knowing that the next station might be closed." Jill turned to her father. "Do you have a Montana roadmap in your pickup?"

"Sure," Al replied. "I think there's a Wyoming map in there too."

Al looked at me as Jill raced out the door. "What's she up to?"

"I think we'll be calling every truck stop in Southeastern Montana to see if they have video of a one-ton pickup hauling a yellow stock trailer in the early hours of Tuesday morning."

In less than two minutes, Jill was back, spreading a map on the table. "There probably aren't more than half a dozen stations with diesel fuel along here," she said, tracing her finger along Highway 212. She took out her cellphone and entered a search. A moment later, she set her phone on the table. Seven red teardrops dotted the route.

"I'll start calling these stations to see if they have security video."

Pulling out my phone I looked at my call history. "I'll call the Carter County sheriff to ask if he's willing to have a deputy retrieve the videos."

"These stations that sell diesel are spread all over. See if he's got a buddy in the Montana State Patrol."

Five minutes later, I was speaking with Major Kevin Epply, the MSP southeast region commander. I explained our investigation and our interest in finding security video from the stations selling diesel fuel.

"It sounds like you're grasping at straws, Fletcher."

"We are, Major. We're sure the killer drove the pickup from South Dakota to Little Bighorn. We're not sure of the route from there, but the victim's truck was found in Alzada."

Jill nudged me and set a notepad on the table. "Major, my partner, Jill, has more information. I'm putting you on speaker."

"Major, there are only a handful of places the killer could've filled up with diesel between Belle Fourche and Little Bighorn. The truck is a one-ton Chevy dually, covered with decals from the victim's sponsors. If we can find a station where the killer filled up, we may be able to get a picture of his face, and possibly a name if he used a credit card late Monday night or early Tuesday morning."

"Do you have a list of the stations?"

Jill read the list of seven service stations she'd identified, and she'd confirmed that they all had security video.

"I'm sure my troopers know which stations sell diesel. I'll have them check the security video this morning and get back to me." Epply paused. "I have one condition."

"What's that, Major?"

"If we identify this guy, my people will be with you when you make the arrest."

Jill pulled the phone in front of her. "Major, we would be delighted to have all the law enforcement support we can get when we make an arrest."

"I'll talk to the dispatcher right away. My people should be able to canvass all those stations before noon."

I could almost feel Jill vibrating as I disconnected the call.

"This is it. We'll have a face and name before noon."

"I love your optimism," I said, returning the cell phone to my pocket.

"Come on. We're going to Belle Fourche. I think the police chief will recognize the face or name of the person who bought diesel."

"There's no rush. We're not going to know anything before noon."

"Get your butt out of the chair. We're going to Belle," Jill said, pulling me to my feet.

Al was laughing. "Fletcher, trying to hold Jill back when she's excited is like lassoing a wild bronc—all you can do is hold on to the rope and hope she doesn't drag you over a cactus."

Jill's eyes were sparkling for the first time in days. "Put on your badge."

"Where are my holster and pistol?"

Jill studied my face for a moment. "You're not cleared for duty. You can wear the badge to show you're a cop, but until you get rid of the eyepatch and pass a concussion test, the doctor won't allow you to carry a firearm."

"But…"

My mother stood alongside Jill. "Douglas, listen to your wife."

Chapter Sixteen

We parked in front of the Belle Fourche Police Station, a newer brick faced annex to the century-old courthouse. The different officer was behind a plexiglass barricade. She looked up from her computer when we entered. I held my Park Service credentials up to the glass. I could tell she was intrigued by my eye patch and bruised face, but she kept her thoughts to herself.

"Park Service?"

"Yes. Is the chief in?"

The officer chuckled. "Yeah, he's in his office."

"What's so funny?" I asked.

"He hates when I let gun-toting people through the security door. You're cops, so it's probably okay. The chief's in the first office."

A solenoid buzzed on the steel door to our right and Jill led me through. She knocked on the chief's door, interrupting a discussion with a uniformed officer.

"Perfect timing," Chief Arnold said, waving us in. "This is Officer Casey. He was just telling me about the ravings of a drunken cowboy."

We shook hands with the chief and Officer Casey. "I've been talking to all the rodeo competitors as I catch them around the living quarters. One of the bronc riders hadn't been around, so I've been back to his trailer a few times. I spoke with him this morning before his hangover was gone and asked if he'd seen anyone suspicious around on Monday night. I'm not sure how credible he is, but he claims a rodeo clown walked out of Chris Jenkins' trailer when he came home from the bar."

"You're not sure he's credible?" Jill asked.

"I suspect he sees pink elephants and green aliens when he's been drinking."

"Did he give you any specifics about the clown?" I asked.

Casey chuckled. "He was wearing jeans, boots, and a cowboy hat."

"That's it?" I asked.

"Aside from the white clown makeup and a red mouth."

I looked at Jill. "I suppose that's pretty standard rodeo clown makeup."

Jill shrugged. "Pretty much." She looked at Casey. "Did he mention blood?"

"You know, he said something strange, like the guy had red hands and polka dots on his white shirt. The red hands thing didn't make sense."

Jill raised her eyebrows. "Bloody hands."

"The polka dots might've been blood splatter," the chief said. "What's the bronc rider's name?"

"It was Alan Sullivan. He hasn't had an eight-second ride yet. According to him, he'd been drawing bad rides. I think he's probably too hung over to stay on the horse after the first buck."

Jill looked at me. "Let's talk to him."

Casey chuckled. "Good luck with that. I got four versions of what he saw in a three-minute interview. He's one…" Casey had an F on his lips but looked at Jill. "He's one messed up cowboy."

"What do you think about the blood splatter theory?" I asked Casey.

"I don't know. Sullivan mentioned the polka dotted shirt in all four versions of his story, so it's possible." Casey looked at the chief. "It could be like that guy who tried to hold up the truck stop."

"What happened?" Jill asked.

Chief Arnold shook his head. "Some druggie decided to rob the truck stop during the quiet overnight hours. He pulled a gun on the clerk. There was a rancher in the bathroom and when he saw the holdup, he pulled his pistol and shot the guy."

"Western justice," I said.

Casey jumped in. "I caught the call and when I got there it was a real mess. I mean that druggie was really…" Again, he looked at Jill who grinned. "Really messed up. The

284

rancher got three shots into him before the clerk got off two more shots. There was blood all over, mixed in with broken bags of chips, punctured bottles of energy drinks, bullet-shredded magazines, and all kinds of shit...I mean stuff."

"Lots of blood splatter?" I asked.

"The crime scene guys spent two days swabbing droplets of blood with Q-tips. It was a real mess."

"I take it the 'druggie' didn't survive?" I asked.

"Oh, hell no," the chief replied. "That rancher saved the county a lot of money."

Casey chuckled. "I'm not sure it was the rancher. Do you remember what the pathologist said, Chief? That guy was like Swiss cheese. They couldn't figure out whether it was the rancher or the clerk's shot that killed that guy. Either way, the district attorney wasn't going to charge them, and no jury would convict them if they went to trial. Hell, they should've got medals!"

My phone chimed during Casey's monologue, so I peeked to see who was calling. I stepped into the hallway. "Hello, Major. Did your folks have any luck with the truck stops?"

"I just texted you a picture of a guy who bought diesel in Broadus early Tuesday morning. He was driving the truck you described."

"Thanks," I said, then paused. "Did your people find an abandoned horse trailer Tuesday?"

"They wouldn't tell me. They'd just have it towed."

"Can you check?"

"Hang on." I heard computer keys clicking. "No horse trailers, but they had a rusty stock trailer pulled out of the ditch."

"Where?"

"Near Alzada, on Highway 212. Trooper Conway had it towed."

"Who was the owner?"

"It didn't have license plates."

"Is someone checking on the serial number?"

After a chuckle, the major replied. "We supplied that information to the state crime lab."

"I assume you laughed because it's not going to be a priority for them."

"Fletcher, finding the owner of a rusted-out stock trailer abandoned on the road is a lower priority than... Actually, I can't think of anything lower priority than that."

I got the name of the company that towed the trailer and thanked the trooper. "I'm sorry," I said, returning to Arnold's office. "I should have a picture of the guy who filled the victim's pickup early Tuesday morning."

In an uncharacteristic moment of excitement, Jill did a fist pump. "Yes!"

I pulled up the picture and held it out to Chief Arnold. "Do you recognize this guy?"

He shook his head, then passed the phone to Casey who smiled and said, "That's Rufus McBride's kid."

Chief Arnold smiled. "I love it when a case comes together."

Chapter Seventeen

Ekalaka Montana was small, as was the county courthouse. The sheriff's department and jail occupied the back half of the first floor behind the one courtroom and county offices. The sheriff's personal office wasn't intended for a meeting of eight people, so we stood, arrayed around the sheriff's desk.

Hank Bostik, the Butte County sheriff, pulled the two guest chairs from the corner and set them next to Jill and Sharon. "Ladies, please take the chairs."

After briefly bristling at the suggestion, Jill read the sheriff's sincerity. "Thank you. It's nice to know there are still gentlemen." She looked up at me, smiling, like somehow the sheriff's gesture and her response contained a message. Sharon nodded her thanks.

Footsteps on the tile preceded the arrival of the Ekalaka Sheriff. Ray Poppen hesitated at the door and let out a whistle. "I haven't seen this many cops in one room since I went to the sheriffs' convention in 1998." A path opened and Ray threaded his way past the other officers. Once behind his desk, the sheriff's gaze locked on Jill and Sharon, the only women in the room. He smiled, then glanced at Jill's badge and pistol. "I think introductions are in order. Please say your name and agency. I'd like this lady to start."

Jill gave her name and identified herself as a Park Service Investigator. Sharon Vanderhoff introduced herself as the FBI liaison. The rest of us, the Butte County Sheriff, a South Dakota DCI livestock crimes investigator, the Montana District 16 Brand Inspector, a Montana State Trooper, and I, introduced ourselves. Poppen nodded to each of us, then introduced himself.

"I spoke with Ms. Vanderhoff last night, and she explained the investigation and suspicion that Rufus McBride has been rustling South Dakota cattle and raising them on his ranch outside Albion. The cattle brands should make that investigation straight forward. I'm confused about why there are more cops here than cattle that have been rustled."

Vanderhoff leaned forward and spoke. "A woman was killed at the Black Hills Roundup. We believe she overheard McBride's son talking about the rustling operation and was killed to silence her."

Poppen leaned back in his chair. "Well, that's a pretty strong accusation. I hope you've got evidence to back it up."

The Carver County Sheriff cleared his throat. "We've got a witness who overheard Rusty talking about the rustling operation, and a different witness who heard the victim confront the murderer, and who encouraged the victim to contact the police about the rustling allegation. We have Rusty McBride's fingerprints inside the victim's abandoned pickup and the trailer he used to steal her horse. I suspect we'll find the victim's palomino horse on McBride's ranch with the rustled cattle."

"Aw shit," Poppen muttered. "I suppose we need to find Rusty and start checking brands on McBride's ranch. I don't suppose anyone brought a horse to work the cattle."

"I've got two horses in a trailer," said the South Dakota brand inspector.

The Montana trooper nodded. "I've got a side-by-side ATV.

"Does anyone beside the South Dakota livestock inspector know how to ride a horse?"

"I was raised on a Spearfish ranch," Jill replied. "I've been riding since my feet reached the stirrups. I also know how to shoot."

The shooting comment brought a round of chuckles from the men, who were all carrying sidearms.

Poppen stood. "Well, let's get this parade on the road. You two with trailers, hang back. I'll go in first, so we don't spook whoever is around the house. After I make sure things are under control, I'll radio for the rest of you to follow."

"Can I ride with you, Sheriff?" I asked.

The sheriff looked at my eye patch with suspicion. "You're a Park Service Ranger?"

"I'm a retired detective working as a Park Service Investigator."

"I'd prefer having a two-eyed deputy covering my back," Poppen replied.

"With all due respect, have any of your deputies ever fired their weapons at anything but a deer that's been hit by a car?"

Poppen paused, the comment apparently ringing true. "You've had to shoot someone?"

"Both my partner and I have fired our weapons in the line of duty, Sheriff."

Jill cleared her throat. "My one-eyed partner is still under the supervision of a doctor and shouldn't be part of an entry team."

Looking at Jill, Poppen nodded and said, "You ride with me, Ms. Fletcher. We're trying to put these people at ease, and you look a lot less like an angry cop than any of the rest of these cowboys."

"I'd be happy to cover your back, Sheriff," Jill said, rising from the chair.

The South Dakota sheriff slapped Poppen on the back as he passed. "Taking Jill is an excellent choice. I know her folks, and I suspect Ms. Fetcher could shoot out a prairie dog's eye at a hundred yards with a rifle or pistol."

Poppen stopped outside the office door until Jill walked through. He fell in step beside her with me trailing them. "You got some pretty high praise back there. But I invest in actions, not words."

"Sheriff, I don't intend to offer your widow an apology."

"You're pretty cocky, Jill."

I stepped close to them. "Jill put thirteen rounds into a running suspect who was firing a rifle at his pursuers. I couldn't do that, could you?"

Poppen stopped and looked at Jill. "Devils Tower, Crook County, Wyoming."

Jill glared at me. "Sheriff, I'm not proud of killing that man. I had to watch his widow hold him while he bled out."

"The Crook County sheriff and I have coffee once a month. He bragged about you."

"I appreciate his praise, but there's no glory in killing a person."

Poppen put his hand on Jill's shoulder. "Just the same, I know that you'll have my back."

* * *

292

I rode with Hank Bostik, the Butte County Sheriff, second in the parade of vehicles driving down the dusty road to Albion. We stopped outside a white building with a sign identifying it as the Albion School. Aside from a weather-beaten barn a quarter mile away, there wasn't another building in sight.

Poppen stopped and walked back to us. "McBride's ranch is the first place on the left. If we drive any closer, anyone outside will see the dust plume from all these vehicles."

I leaned across the console. "How far away is the turn?"

"It's about two miles from here, give or take."

"It'll take us five minutes to get there. Most gunfights don't last that long."

Poppen turned so he could look me in the eye. "First of all, I don't intend to do anything but talk politely to the McBrides and ask permission to inspect their cattle. Secondly, you told me I've got the best backup riding with me."

"I don't want either of your lives on the line," I said.

"Neither do I," Sheriff Poppen replied before slapping the top of Bostik's pickup and walking away.

"I don't like being this far away from the potential action," I said to Sheriff Bostik.

Bostik watched the dust behind Poppen's cruiser, tapping his fingers on the steering wheel. "I think we can sneak closer once the dust plume settles. If I drive slowly, there won't be dust, and we'll look like another dusty pickup driving down the main road. We'll be at the end of the driveway if things go western."

"We'll still be a minute or more away," I protested.

"You're unarmed."

I nodded to the shotgun in the rack behind my head. "I'm a pretty fair shot with a scattergun."

"Unbuckle your seatbelt, grab the shotgun, and be prepared to bail out before the pickup stops rolling."

"The cavalry to the rescue."

Bostik chuckled. "Let's hope we're not repeating Custer's Last Stand."

* * *

McBride's driveway appeared to be a mile long. The ranch consisted of a house, barn, and several outbuildings. Cattle and a few horses fed in the pasture behind the barn, with a larger herd of cattle grazing on a distant hillside. The one palomino horse grazing in the pasture stood out like a neon light among the sorrels and bays. Poppen's cruiser was parked next to the house with the doors open. There were two pickups in

294

the driveway and a huge John Deere tractor was parked outside the barn.

"Something's wrong," I said. "No cop leaves his car doors open if he casually walks up to have a conversation with a homeowner."

Bostik rolled down his window and turned off the air conditioner, allowing a wave of heat into the pickup. "That is odd." He picked up the radio mic and told the rest of the convoy to move ahead. He eased ahead and turned into the driveway as someone ran from the barn toward the house.

"Shit," Bostik said, punching the accelerator. "It's going western."

I picked up the mic. "Officer needs assistance!" We were approaching the barn when the sound of pistol fire came from the house. It was followed by the louder report of a rifle.

Pulling the shotgun to my chest, I grabbed the mic. "Shots fired! Shots fired!"

Bostik jammed the brakes, so we slid to a stop. I jumped out and took one step when the window next to the back door exploded and a bullet passed my shoulder, hitting the frame of the pickup. My dash ended as Bostik and I took cover behind the truck.

The sound of sporadic gunfire reassured me that Sheriff Poppen and Jill were still alive. Unable to sit safely behind the truck while Jill was in danger, I turned to Bostik. "I'm going in."

"What are you thinking?"

"You're going to cover me while I run to the door."

"You're nuts!" Seeing that I wasn't deterred he added, "Grab the rifle from the rack!"

I looked at the military-looking AR-15 on the rack mounted behind the seats. "The shotgun has more stopping power. I'll stick with it." As I turned, another shot crashed through the window, this one hitting the pickup's windshield.

"It's your funeral," Bostik said before he popped up and fired a half dozen shots at the window, breaking out the last of the glass and shredding the lace curtains.

After making sure the shotgun was loaded, I turned to Bostik. "Are you ready?"

Bostik looked at me. "You are nuts."

"I'm wearing a vest."

He rolled his eyes. "Do you have any idea how long it will take an ambulance to get here if you're shot in the leg or shoulder?"

"On three." I counted to three, then dashed for the door as Bostik took slow, careful shots at the window. One struck with a different sound than the others, making me think he'd hit something other than the plastered wall behind the window.

Hesitating with my back against the door jamb, I caught my breath, and steeled myself for whatever was inside the door. Concerned about my lack of depth perception with the eyepatch, I pulled it off. I kicked the screen door that twisted and flew inwards, then stepped into a mudroom. With the shotgun on my hip, I aimed into the open area to my left.

A young woman wearing jeans and a t-shirt lay on the floor in a spreading pool of blood. Her left hand gripped her bleeding abdomen. She blinked at me, then tipped to her right as she lifted her elbow to aim the silver pistol in her hand.

Every cop goes through *shoot/don't shoot* drills during training. Silhouettes depicting armed bad guys, women carrying babies, ministers carrying Bibles, and other images are flashed as you draw your weapon and decide whether the image presents a threat. It's embarrassing to mistake a Bible for a gun, but the exercise makes each cop take a fraction of a second to assess the situation and decide whether to shoot or not.

I didn't shoot.

The woman's eyes were glazed and unfocused. The gun was never aimed at me, and it fell out of her hand. Without immediate medical care, she would die from her wound. Not knowing what was happening in the rest of the house, I couldn't render aid.

"Jill! Are you okay?" I yelled.

"I'm barricaded in a bedroom. Poppen's in the bathroom. There are an armed man and woman in the house."

"The woman's down!" I yelled, pressing my back against the mudroom wall.

A wail emanated from somewhere deeper in the house, followed by a hail of rifle bullets ripping through the plaster next to me. I heard footsteps pound through the house, followed by the sound of a slamming door. Outside the house, I heard the sound of the cavalry coming to rescue us.

Pickup doors slammed and Bostik shouted orders. "Someone ran out the back to the horse shed. Get him!"

Kicking the woman's silver pistol aside, I stepped over her, and took a quick look into the empty living room. Drawing a breath, and with the shotgun up, I stepped into the living room. The well-worn carpeting was littered with spent rifle and pistol shell casings. Bits of stuffing, blown from the sofa and chairs, dotted the floor. The plastered walls had holes high and low. I stepped into a narrow hallway with four doors. Two were closed, and two open.

"I'm in the hallway. You're covered."

I heard the scraping of furniture from the left, followed by Jill's voice. "I'm coming out."

A muffled voice came from the opposite door. "In here." Assuming it was Poppen, I announced that I was coming in, and turned the knob.

The sheriff was in the bathtub with his feet hanging over the near edge. "Are you okay?" I asked, setting the shotgun aside. With Jill at my side, a pistol in her hand, I reached down and pulled aside the shower curtain covering Poppen.

"Where's that damned woman? She shot me!"

I helped him out of the bathtub, pulling on his left arm. His right shoulder was bleeding and the arm hung useless at his side. "She surprised you?"

"Hell, yes! I was all smiles at the door. I reached for the doorknob, and she shot me through the screen."

I looked at Jill who shrugged. "I told him to be careful."

"That's when all hell broke loose?" I asked.

Jill nodded. "Pretty much. I pulled him aside and shot back. I pushed him into the bathtub for cover and held the husband down until you guys showed up."

"Where's that woman?" Poppen ranted. "I want to cuff her myself!"

"I think you'll have to cuff her in heaven, Sheriff," I replied. "She's bleeding out in the mudroom and no ambulance will be here in time to save her."

Gunfire erupted from outside and we all ducked down. It was followed by the sound of hoofbeats. "Aw shit, he's taking off on horseback," Jill said before dashing out the back door.

The brand inspector rushed to unload the horses. The state trooper released the straps holding the 4-wheeler to the trailer and backed it onto the driveway. Jill raced to the second horse and was in the saddle as the Brand inspector spurred his mount. Before I could protest, Jill spurred the second horse and was after the gunman, too.

"Vanderhoff!" I yelled. "Call an ambulance. There's a wounded woman in the house."

"Fletcher!" The trooper yelled at me as he started the 4-wheeler, "you're with me." I raced to the right of the side-by-side seats and sat as he accelerated. "Buckle up. It's going to be a rough ride."

The brand inspector galloped ahead of Jill. I looked behind us as Bostik loaded the gunshot sheriff into the passenger-side of his pickup. I heard Vanderhoff yelling something about the wounded woman, but it was quickly lost in the roar of the 4-wheeler's engine.

"There's an injured woman in the house," I said to the trooper.

He glanced at me as we cleared the last gate out of the nearby paddock. "That

FBI woman just yelled that she didn't make it."

As predicted, I needed the seatbelt. Keeping up with the horses, we followed two ruts across the prairie, the vehicle pitching with each dip and bump. When Jill veered off to the right, the trooper turned so we were off the improvised road, racing across the prairie grass. Low clumps of sagebrush scraped the bottom of the 4-wheeler. The left tire hit a sage clump, throwing me against the seatbelt, then crashing down again when the rear tire hit the same clump. My head throbbed as adrenaline coursed through my system and blood rushed to my broken nose and concussed head.

"I'm going to need a chiropractor after this," I yelled to be heard over the engine.

"If we live through it," the trooper replied with an evil grin.

I found a handle to steady myself, minimizing the pounding. The shotgun slammed against my leg with each hump in the prairie. After five minutes of being tossed around harder than I'd ever experienced on horseback, I turned to the trooper. "We don't have to catch the horses."

"Your partner is on the second horse. Don't you think she'd appreciate us being there when she catches the bad guy?"

"Not if I'm too crippled to get out of this rig."

The trooper, who was maybe twenty-five years old and twenty years my junior, smiled. "This will give you stories for your grandchildren."

"If I live through it."

Ahead of us, the brand inspector's horse raced into the cottonwoods. The brand inspector drew his pistol as he and Jill disappeared over a ridge.

"Something happened," I said. The evolving situation caused the trooper to accelerate like he was afraid he was going to miss the shootout.

Cresting a hill, we found ourselves fifty yards behind the brand inspector who flashed through the edge of junipers and cedars. I looked ahead of him trying to see Jill or the horse they were chasing. The trooper braked as the prairie dipped ahead of us, where the landscape changed from sagebrush prairie to junipers dispersed in front of cottonwood trees. The cottonwoods looked like an oasis in the prairie.

An older Montana state trooper pulled his pickup alongside us and yelled, "What's up?"

Irritated that the trooper wasn't driving ahead to rush into whatever was happening, I said, "My partner and the brand inspector rode in there chasing a shooter!"

The older trooper nodded. "Yup, and they seem to know what they're doing."

I grabbed the young trooper's arm. "Go!"

The 4-wheeler surged ahead, pressing me into the seat as we drove down a steep embankment. We slalomed around junipers until he slowed a few yards from the cottonwoods. "I see denim ahead of us," he said as he turned to follow the edge of the grove.

I saw flashes of the chase through gaps in the trees. The brand inspector was ten yards behind Rusty McBride's horse, both of them at a full gallop. Jill was keeping up, but a dozen yards behind them. We bounced over sagebrush, ruts, and rocks that threw me against the restraining seatbelt. If not for the adrenaline coursing through my veins, the pain caused by the jarring ride would've been unbearable.

Rusty's horse made a terrible sound, half whinny and half scream, as it tumbled. Rusty held on as if he was breaking a bronco, then they disappeared into a puff of dust behind a low clump of junipers. Jill and the brand inspector reined their horses to a stop, and the young trooper turned the ATV into the cottonwoods.

As Jill walked her horse ahead, I could see her lips moving as she spoke to the brand inspector, their words were drowned out by the roar of the ATV engine. We passed the thickest part of the cottonwood grove as the South Dakota brand inspector walked toward Rusty's horse as it thrashed on the ground, making pained sounds. I got an occasional glimpse of Rusty, but the horse's panicked moves distracted me. He was apparently pinned under the horse. Pulling his pistol, the brand inspector took aim. Jill stood next to him with her Glock drawn, but at her side.

"Nooo!" I yelled as the trooper locked the brakes, making the ATV slide to a stop. I was unsure if McBride was preparing to shoot at Jill and the brand inspector, or if they were going to shoot him while he lay pinned under the horse. Neither option was good.

The pistol bucked from the recoil as the brand inspector fired a single shot. Rusty's horse stopped thrashing.

Unbuckling the seatbelt, I struggled to get myself and the shotgun out of the ATV as Jill turned away from the downed horse and rider while slipping her Glock into the holster. Loping ahead, I tried to comprehend what had happened,

Still holding her horse's reins, Jill sat on a fallen cottonwood, staring toward the brand inspector standing next to a small pool surrounded by white alkali left when the water had evaporated. I followed her stare and saw the brand inspector, pistol in hand, standing next to the horse lying on its side. Rusty McBride was trapped under his horse with only his shoulders and head visible.

"What happened?" I asked, kneeling beside Jill as the trooper walked toward the horse and rider with his pistol drawn.

"I think the horse hit a prairie dog hole. It went down on top of the rider." Jill looked up at me. "The horse was suffering so the brand inspector shot him."

"And the rider's dead?"

The South Dakota Brand Inspector overheard my question and nodded. "The horse crushed him when it went down."

The trooper wore the smug smile only young cops have at a death scene. "You got him."

Taking a breath, Jill said, "I feel bad for the horse. It never hurt anyone."

Feeling something tickling my chin, I reached up to pull the annoying thread or spiderweb. Jill saw my hand go up and reacted a second too late to stop me from pulling the bit of gauze dangling from my nose.

"Geez!" I said, letting go of the gauze after giving it a yank. I felt something warm dribbling down my upper lip.

Jill knelt in front of me. "Stuff the gauze back in your nose. You're bleeding."

Disoriented after the banging on the ATV, I looked at the bloody gauze in my hand and said, "Huh?"

Jill looked at her grimy hands and decided not to help. "Hold the gauze to your nostril until I can get something sterile to repack your nose." She looked at the trooper. "Do you have a first aid kit in your ATV?"

"Yeah. What do you need?"

"Gloves and gauze."

Chapter Eighteen

We drove back to Belle Fourche and contacted the police chief. After driving from the station to the rodeo grounds, we stood aside as Chief Arnold informed Rufus McBride of his son and daughter-in-law's deaths. We looked on as the chief clipped handcuffs on McBride. Ranting, the senior McBride demanded to be told who'd shot them, then threatened retribution against the sheriff, Park Service, FBI, South Dakota Brand Inspectors, and any other police agency that came to his mind.

"Rufus, did you hear me? You're under arrest for murder."

"I didn't kill anyone! What the hell are you talking about, Arnold?"

Chief Arnold read McBride his Miranda rights, then led him to the chief's unmarked car. "Your son killed Chris Jenkins. A witness saw you arguing with Chris the day of her murder. If you didn't order the murder, you were an accessory before the fact, which makes you as guilty as your son, who slashed Chris Jenkins' throat."

McBride's bald head turned as red as his face. "You'll never prove that."

Chief Arnold was smiling until he looked my way. "Holy shit, Fletcher. You need to go to the ER."

I turned to Jill who nodded. "Your nose plugs are leaking."

"You didn't think to tell me that before now?" I asked.

Jill put her hand on my upper arm and steered me toward our pickup. "It serves you right. You were supposed to stay home until the doctor released you. Besides, none of your injuries appear to be life threatening."

* * *

After getting a tongue lashing from the ER doctor and the psychiatrist, I spent another night in the hospital. After that, I was told to stay in Rickowski's ranch house until I received a medical release for work.

Starved for information, I walked to the door as soon as I heard Jill pull into the driveway. I met her at the door. "Well?"

She called her mother and father to the kitchen table, and we all sat down. "It took two days to round up and sort all the livestock at the McBride ranch. The inspectors found steers stolen from at least four ranches in Montana, Wyoming, and South Dakota. Chris Jenkins' palomino was in a pasture with half a dozen other horses. Some livestock had the McBride ranch brand; others had a variety of brands or had been rebranded."

Al whistled softly. "They had quite a rustling operation. I'm surprised someone hasn't blown the whistle on them before now."

"The neighbors said the McBride's were prickly, and not into socializing. Visitors were met at the door with a shotgun."

* * *

I followed Jill into the bedroom where she changed from her uniform into jeans and a shirt. "This sucked," she said as she put her badge and gun into a nightstand.

"More than the other investigations?"

"No, they all suck at the end."

"You're just upset because the inspector put down that horse."

"That's part of it, but there's always a letdown when the arrests are made, and we drive away."

"What's going to happen with our parents and Chet when we leave?" I asked, trying to change the subject.

"I suppose they'll continue to grow old and have more health problems."

"Do we need to be here to help them?"

"I think they'll grow old whether we're here or not. I'd prefer not to watch."

"We're flying to Salt Lake City tomorrow to meet our new boss. Are you looking forward to that? His wife is putting on a big spread and he's cooking steaks."

Jill turned to me, still looking sad. "I'd rather be eating shrimp and drinking margaritas with Matt and Mandy."

"We'll do that when we get back to Texas."

"Let's put on our best faces and act like we're happy to meet them."

"I will. I can be a chameleon when required."

"You can be charming," I said, hoping to get a smile.

Jill reached out and touched my cheek. "I sometimes feel like I don't deserve you."

I took her hand and squeezed it. "I'm your other half—the yin to your yang."

"If that's true, Mr. Yin, you'll know that I'm excited about moving into the house by Matt and Mandy when we get back. You'll unpack while Mandy and I cruise the shops in Corpus Christi choosing artwork to hang on the walls."

"Do I get any say in the art?"

Jill cocked her head, considering the question for a beat. "No."

"I'd really like to own a Remington bronze statue."

"There's a shelf in the garage over the workbench. A bronze statue might look nice there."

"Come on," I pleaded. "It's going to cost a couple thousand dollars. It'd be a shame to leave it in the garage."

"You're right. Spend the money on something else."

I sighed. "I like Remington's western paintings, too."

"There's a long, empty wall in the garage. You'll be able to look at it every time you park the truck."

"But they feature horses," I argued.

"And gunfights with Indians. There won't be a western print inside our house. I'm going for a beach feel." Jill paused. "And don't even think about saying, 'yes dear.'"

Chapter Nineteen

The change in air pressure as our plane left the ground caused my head to feel like it was going to explode, so I clenched my eyes shut waiting for the pain to subside. Jill was staring at me when I opened my eyes.

"What?"

"You groaned."

"Not out loud."

"Yes, you groaned out loud."

After a glance out the window, I expected the conversation to be over. "What?"

"Do you want a Percocet?"

"They make my stomach queasy. I'll put up with the pain."

After rubbing my leg, Jill leaned her head on my shoulder. "I don't know what to do about you."

"What's to be done? I'm fine."

"Can you be in pain and be civil to our new boss?"

"I'll stay in the hotel while you meet with him."

"Like hell you will. You'll sit beside me, being the professional you are."

"I want to be a kid. Being a grownup sucks."

A passing flight attendant heard me and paused in the aisle. "Isn't that the truth? But try to keep it together, I've already got one screaming kid in the back."

"I'll work on it," I said as she rushed toward the crying child in the rear of the plane.

"We got an email from Jack," Jill said, moving her finger around the cell phone screen. "There was a fatality at Yosemite. He wants us to look at the reports."

"Yosemite is a big park. They must have half a dozen law enforcement rangers to handle the investigation."

After opening the email, Jill scanned it, then handed the phone to me. "It sounds like they're convinced the guy's fall at Taft Point was an accident."

"Why does Jack want us to look at it?"

Jill handed me the phone and pointed to the top paragraph. I read the email, shaking my head. "Oh shit. Not every death without witnesses is a murder."

"This is a legacy of the Everglades investigation. You solved a…"

I handed the phone back to Jill. "If you expect me to be polite when we meet with our new boss, you'll let me sleep."

Jill patted my leg. "Try not to snore."

My head started to throb when the cabin pressure changed as the plane started the descent into Salt Lake City. Jill was engrossed in the book she'd downloaded on her phone. The plot must've been exciting because her foot was tapping, and she didn't notice when I turned toward her. "I don't suppose we got diverted to Corpus Christi," I said, stretching.

"I think we're passing Great Salt Lake, which probably means we're in Utah, not Texas."

"The nightmare continues."

"Don't irritate me. I can make you more miserable than you already are."

The plane shuddered as the landing gear deployed and the flight attendant began the pre-landing announcement. "I could be more miserable?" I asked as I pulled my seat upright.

Jill was about to make one of her playful threats, but her smile melted away when she looked at my face. "I can't do it. I thought I could threaten to tweak your nose or elbow you in the ribs, but you look like a beaten puppy."

The flight attendant made her pass through, checking tray tables and seat positions. She knelt beside Jill. "You two are the Fletchers, right?"

"We are. What's up?"

"Thank you."

"For what?" Jill asked.

314

"All the crew members are rodeo fans. We heard you solved Chris Jenkins' murder. Thanks."

"It's nice to be part of a successful investigation."

"It looks like your partner was kicked by a horse."

"It was a week of bulls, horses, rodeo clowns, and drunk cowboys. He got on the wrong side of a couple of them."

The flight attendant stood and put her hand on Jill's shoulder. "I was a barrel racer once. I've got a signed Chris Jenkins' poster."

* * *

Still in pain, I sat with my head in my hands while Jill retrieved our luggage from the carousel. "Doug Fletcher?"

I looked up at a trim man wearing a western-cut shirt and khaki pants. His hair was neatly trimmed with graying temples. "Yeah," I said as I stood.

"I'm Jack Pardee," the man said, offering his hand. "Where's your partner?"

I nodded toward the luggage carousel, where Jill was standing with the crowd of people awaiting bags from our flight. "Jill volunteered to get our luggage."

"Sit down. I'll help Jill with your bags."

I watched Jack introduce himself, then felt guilty for leaving Jill with bag retrieval duty. Jack pulled our bags off the carousel and rolled the larger bag to the row of chairs where I was sitting. "My wife is parked in the cell phone parking area. We'll give you a ride to the hotel so you can check in and get cleaned up."

"We can rent a car," I protested.

"There's no need. I'm happy to drive you around and it gives us a chance to talk."

I followed behind Jill and Jack as they walked through the terminal, pulling our roller bags. I couldn't hear what was said, but Jill seemed pleased with the conversation and Jack laughed a couple times. Jack waved to a blue minivan parked at the curb. He loaded our bags in the back as a woman stepped out and introduced herself to Jill. She motioned for me to take the front passenger seat. She and Jill got in the back.

Jack's wife reached between the seats and put her hand on my shoulder. "I'm Carly. I'm really pleased you and Jill were able to fly in to meet us. I'm sure you'd rather be at home recuperating from your injuries."

As much as I wanted to be angry, Carly was sweet, and Jack's smile was genuine. "It's been a long week. I hope we're good company."

Carly leaned back and fastened her seatbelt. "Let's get you to your hotel so you can freshen up. We can talk later about making plans for the evening or just letting you two rest."

* * *

I was sprawled on the bed when Jill walked out of the bathroom, drying her hair. "How badly does your face hurt? Do you need a Percocet?"

"It hurts, but I can probably get by with a couple Tylenol."

Jill dug into her bag and handed me a white bottle. "Tylenol. Take a couple before you shower."

After washing down the Tylenol with water from a plastic cup I asked, "Are we really going to meet Jack and Carly for supper?"

"That's the plan. They offered to meet us in the hotel restaurant if we don't want to spend the evening at their house."

"I'd prefer room service, then falling asleep while you watch television."

Nodding, Jill said, "Let's see how you feel after a shower."

Jill was at the desk talking on her cell phone when I came out of the bathroom in my boxers. She looked up, then said, "He's right here. I'll hand him the phone."

I tried to decline, but Jill jammed the phone in my hand. "Hello."

"Douglas, pull your shit together and act like an adult."

"Mom, I feel like crap, and I just want to rest."

"I raised a polite, considerate son who earned a Boy Scout Eagle award when he was fourteen. Tap into that history and haul your butt to supper with Jill and your boss."

"Mom…"

"Don't make me fly down there!"

Jill stared at me while hearing half of the conversation. She looked worried. Until I smiled. "Fine Mom. I'll be a good son and go out to supper with my wife who looks concerned."

"And Douglas…"

"What Mom?"

"I'm very proud of you."

"I love you too, Mom." I handed the phone to Jill. "Call Jack and tell him dinner at their house will be fun."

Jill raised her eyebrows. "She played the Eagle Scout card, didn't she?"

"That and a few other things."

* * *

Although Jack offered to pick us up at the hotel, I declined, and we took an Uber to their house in the Salt Lake City suburbs. The area was upscale, but not ostentatious. The house had a brick façade on its two-story front, but the open garage doors revealed the blue minivan used to pick us up at the airport, and an older Jeep

318

Cherokee that looked like it had been off-road several times based on the scraped paint and dented fenders.

Carly met us at the door and welcomed us into a tidy entryway with a two-story atrium. Shoes were lined up on a rubber mat next to the door and a beautiful rug protected the oak flooring. "Come in," she said, stepping back and gesturing down a hallway. After experiencing Mandy Mattson's hugs and touches, Carly's polite, but chaste, handshake seemed as cold as those I'd experienced from my mother's stoic Swedish family. My aunts and uncles never hugged us, only shaking hands, while smiling. Even my relatives' smiles seemed as cold as a Minnesota winter.

Jack was in the kitchen, chopping vegetables at a butcher block island. "I'd shake your hand, but you'd smell like onions until tomorrow."

"No problem," I said, standing across the kitchen island from him.

Carly guided Jill to a counter where she was assembling fruit in a cake pan.

They chatted while Jack put the knife in the sink and washed his hands. "As I recall, I offered to grill steaks the first time we spoke. Is that still acceptable?"

"Steaks are great. Jill grew up on a ranch eating the beef they raised, and I've never answered the vegan call."

Jack took a platter of ribeye steaks from the refrigerator and removed the plastic wrap. "I seasoned these this morning, so they should be ready to go." He lifted the tray and nodded to an alcove with a phone. "Please bring the blue folder with you onto the patio."

I glanced at Jill, who was in a light discussion with Carly, both of them smiling.

Jack lifted the lid on the gas grill and pushed the ignitor button. "You're holding the file on the Yosemite hiker who fell. I'd appreciate it if you'd look at it while I put the steaks on the grill."

I sat at a patio table and flipped past the grisly photos of the dead hiker, focusing on pictures taken at the top of the cliff. There were no visible signs of a struggle, just a few footprints in the dust and a cell phone face down near the edge of the precipice. One "selfie" photo showed the hiker's boots near the edge of the cliff.

After considering the photos, I scanned the rangers' and recovery teams' reports. The reports were factual without speculation on events leading to the hiker's death. I was reading the pathologist's report when Jack sat in the chair next to me.

"I never get used to seeing the bloody mess a body becomes after a fall from a cliff."

"I glanced at those pictures, but they rarely tell us much about the cause of the fall."

Jack cocked his head. "What do you mean?"

I paused, staring at the pathologist's report without reading. I wondered if Jack really didn't understand why the photos weren't meaningful, or if I was being tested. "If the victim had been bludgeoned before the fall, all that evidence is lost with the trauma of the impact. The pictures taken at the top of the cliff sometimes show evidence of a struggle, but I don't see any scrape marks or scuffing to indicate the victim had done anything but walk to the edge."

"The picture of the guy's shoes was the last photo in his phone's memory. I wonder if that photo was taken by accident?"

Ignoring that comment, I ran my finger down the edge of the pathologist's report, stopping at his signature. "The person who did the post-mortem exam wasn't a medical examiner?"

"The local coroner had the victim delivered to the nearest hospital where the pathologist conducted the post-mortem examination."

Flipping through the remaining pages of the file, I noted the names of the rangers conducting the investigation. "I don't see a report of a ranger witnessing the autopsy."

"I don't think any of our people were there. The pathologist's report seems thorough."

I flipped back to the pathologist's report and read through his comments about the massive trauma to the body and put my finger on one sentence. "Read this."

Jack read the line and handed the report back to me. "His legs were shattered. That's not unexpected."

Closing the file, I looked at Jack. "The fall was an accident."

"How can you…"

"The femurs were splintered when the victim hit the ground."

"You've lost me."

"If a victim is unconscious when he falls, his body tumbles and most of the time, his legs hit the ground horizontally or diagonally, causing the bones to break into random fragments. People who commit suicide, or slip and fall, twist around to land on their feet. Their feet impact the ground first, causing their femurs to splinter, rather than fragment."

"I find it hard to believe that suicide jumpers twist around like a cat, so they land on their feet."

"A medical examiner explained it to me early in my career. Even though a jumper makes a conscious, albeit irrational decision to jump, their lizard brain tells them to save themselves."

322

"What's a lizard brain?"

"The limbic cortex is the ancient part of the human brain that remains unevolved since we descended from the earliest life forms. It's there even in lizards to provide all animals with the basic drive to eat, sleep, seek shelter, procreate, and fight to survive. It's the part that makes us all seek life over death."

"You're saying the victim's lizard brain told him to get his feet under him in order to break his fall in an attempt to save his life."

I slid the file to Jack. "Yes. The other thing that influences my opinion is the cell phone picture of his feet. I think this guy was going to impress his buddies by showing how close his feet were to the edge before he took a selfie with his cell phone. I think he took the photo of his feet, then lost his footing before he snapped the selfie. The phone flew out of his hand when he tried to grab for the edge."

A hint of a smile crept onto Jack's lips. "How long were you a St. Paul cop before you joined the Park Service?"

"I'm sure you've read my file."

"Refresh my memory."

"I was with the SPPD for nearly twenty years before I took a medical pension."

Reacting to the sound of the sizzling meat, Jack checked his watch. "How do you like your steaks done?"

"Both Jill and I like them medium-rare."

Jack flipped all four of the steaks and closed the grill. "Would you take that file back inside and bring me a platter? Tell Carly the steaks will be done in four minutes."

I paused at the patio door with my hand on the handle. "Did I pass the test?"

Chuckling, Jack shook his head. "You should be teaching the course."

Carly was carrying plates and utensils into a small dining area when I walked into the kitchen. Jill balanced four bowls of salads in her hands. The smell of frying onions and potatoes filled the air. "Jack says the steaks will be done in four minutes. He needs a platter."

"There's a platter in the cupboard over the wine glasses," Carly said as she walked into the dining room.

On the patio, I handed the platter to Jack. "I take it you're not Mormons?"

"Always the detective, I see. What gave us away?"

"The wine."

"You don't think members of the Church of Latter-Day Saints sneak a glass of wine now and again?"

"I know Minnesota Baptists who have a beer after mowing the grass. But I thought Mormons are stricter than Baptists."

Jack shut off the gas burners and forked the four steaks onto the platter. "I grew up an Episcopalian and Carly was a

324

non-practicing Catholic. We don't flaunt or overdo our drinking around our Mormon neighbors, but we do enjoy a glass of wine with supper."

I held the door for Jack and followed him into the dining room. Carly set a bowl of fried potatoes on the table and gestured for me to take a chair at the head of the table, facing the kitchen. Jill sat next to me, spreading a napkin on her lap.

After Jack sat, Carly said, "Let's let the steaks rest for a minute while we eat salad." She paused while the rest of us poured dressing on our salads. "Thank you for finding Chris Jenkins' killer."

Jill glanced at me while chewing her first bite of lettuce. I nodded as I picked up the salad fork. "That's what Jack sent us to do."

Carly shook her head. "No, Jack sent you to investigate a disturbed grave at Little Bighorn Battlefield. You solved Chris' murder all on your own."

"The crimes were intertwined," Jill explained. She then provided a sanitized version of our previous week.

"I grew up in Colorado, on the Wyoming border," Carly said as she spread dressing on her salad. "My parents took me to a rodeo as a toddler and I was hooked. As a girl, I thought the barrel racers were the elite of female athletes. Then Chris Jenkins rose to the top. She was pretty, smart, articulate, and a top money-maker. She was the Simone Biles of the rodeo circuit, taking home more money than any other barrel racer."

Jill nodded. "She was a role model for a lot of ranch girls."

"More than that, she was a spokesperson for the rodeo circuit. She spoke out about social issues, sexism, and supported our western way of life. I saw her on a New York talk show, and she lambasted one of the hosts for her PETA activism. Chris pointed out that the PETA advocate had no more right to dictate what people who lived on farms and ranches did, than someone like Chris had to criticize the directing of a Broadway musical."

I nodded. "Sadly, her social conscience is what got her killed."

Carly stopped with a forkful of lettuce halfway to her mouth. "How so?"

"Chris overheard a conversation about cattle rustling. She confronted the rustlers during the Black Hills Roundup, and they killed her."

Carly set her fork down and stared at Jill. "That was the motive for killing her?"

Jill nodded.

Jack set his salad aside and reached for the platter of meat. "I think the steaks have rested enough. We should eat them while they're hot."

Carly was obviously troubled by Jill's comments, but her hostess instinct took over. "We forgot to pour wine!"

Jack passed the steaks to Jill and whispered. "Carly considered Chris Jenkins a saint. Thanks for gently revealing the story to her without the gory details."

Carly came back into the room with the wine bottle and walked around the table pouring for each of us before taking her seat. She studied my face for a moment. "Doug, you really took a beating. I don't think anyone told Jack how bruised you were. Did that happen when you were chasing the killer?"

Jill couldn't stifle her chuckle. "Doug got into a scuffle with a drunk cowboy a couple days before the big chase."

Jack jumped in to clarify the comments. "Jill was arresting a suspect. Doug was assisting her when one of the suspect's friends decided to intervene."

"You certainly paid the price," Carly said as she scooped fried potatoes onto her plate.

"You should've seen him the day after the incident," Jill said. "His eyes were black, and his nose was a mess. He had a concussion, so the doctor wouldn't clear him for duty. He spent several days playing cribbage with my father to kill time."

Jack was focused on cutting his steak when he said, "About that. I wasn't aware that the doctor had cleared you for duty when the caravan of cops went out to arrest the suspect in Chris' murder."

"I rode along as an observer," I said, not looking up.

Jill covered her mouth with her napkin and whispered, "Bullshit."

Carly froze, but Jack broke into laughter. "Your reports were…ah…unclear about Doug's medical status and involvement in the ranch confrontation."

"I was just fine."

Jack wiped his mouth and took a sip of wine. "Just fine, but in need of additional treatment at the ER after the chase."

I sighed. "I rode in an ATV and the young trooper who was driving was excited about not missing the arrest. So excited that he bounced the ATV over every clump of sagebrush in the prairie."

"Just to be clear, I don't condone officers ignoring medical orders."

I leaned back. "I have standing orders from my mother to watch over Jill. If anything happened to Jill, there might've been a second murder—mine."

"Matt Mattson has already warned me about your…creative expense reports."

"I'm sorry Carly, but I'm feeling a little uninhibited by the pain and stress of the last week. Jack, our expense vouchers reflect our spending. I hope you understand that we were pursuing an active investigation with full vigor. Sometimes that means we may not have every receipt for every expense. I hope you can trust and support us."

Carly glared at her husband. "Jack, are you planning to be a paper pushing bureaucrat, or a law enforcement resource supporting his people?"

Jack lifted his hand. "You're covered."

Jill looked at him. "You understand, this won't be the last time our expense vouchers may…have gaps."

"I'm concerned about the results and you two deliver. The budget is my problem and as long as you're solving crimes, we'll figure out the other parts."

Carly smiled and looked at Jill. "Jack said you'll be moving into a new house when you get back to Texas. That's exciting."

"My friend Mandy found a house down the block from them in Port Aransas. We'll be on Mustang Island, a few blocks from the Gulf of Mexico. It's a two-bedroom rambler that had been owned by two elderly sisters, so it's been well-maintained."

"And it's close to your friends. That's nice."

"I've lived my whole adult life in either Park Service residences or rentals. I'm really excited about owning my…our own house. I'm looking forward to picking out the décor."

Jack nodded. "We've been all over the country. Our oldest son attended four different schools, and now lives in Mississippi, near Natchez Trace, where he graduated from high school. Our middle son and daughter graduated from high school here, in Utah. We also felt like vagabonds until I took this job and moved to Salt Lake City."

I looked at Jill for a moment, weighing my words carefully, aware that my verbal filter hadn't been functioning well since the concussion. "Mandy Mattson is a hoot. She's a Southern debutante who swears like a mule skinner when she's angry. She's initiated Jill into her circle of golf friends, and she's taken us under her wing. Mandy and Matt make Port Aransas feel like our home."

After finishing dinner, Jill wiped her mouth and took out her phone. "Mandy has been texting me pictures of the house and decorating ideas since we flew to South Dakota." Carly slid her chair next to Jill, watching and listening as Jill paged through the images she'd received.

Jack stood and nodded toward the patio. We stood on the patio, staring at the mountains. "I know you and Matt Mattson were close and reporting to me will be a transition. It's obvious that you and Jill are capable investigators and a good team."

"Thanks. I was hoping we'd be able to work together without too much friction."

Jack looked at me. "You two have friends in high places and they've made it clear to me that I should steer, but not control you. To be frank, I didn't appreciate that advice. Not knowing you, or your capabilities, I held the reins tight during this investigation." He blew out a breath, then looked at me. "That doesn't need to happen again."

"What's our relationship going to be?"

"I sent you a file of open investigations. Please look through them to determine if there's something that was missed by the rangers. If you find something intriguing or glaring, let me know how you'd like to address it. In addition to that, there are ongoing incidents that require a more seasoned investigative eye than the local rangers have. I assume you'll be willing to take on an active role if an investigation is more complicated than the local law enforcement rangers can handle."

"We can live with that."

Jack offered his hand. "Welcome to the National Park Service Investigative Services Branch."

Jill and Carly stepped onto the patio as Jack and I shook hands. Carly smiled and said, "It appears that you boys have figured out how to play nice together."

Jack smiled. "We have."

Carly crossed her arms and nodded at Jack. "That's good, because I really like Jill and I'd hate to think I'd have to listen to you whining about what the Fletchers were or weren't doing."

Jill looked at Carly. "Jack brings his work home?"

"Oh yes! I hear about every misstep taken by his investigators and what he'd have done differently if he'd been on the scene."

Jack looked like he'd been struck by a thought. "One thing that has to change, Doug; answer your damned phone when I call. I don't want to hear that you left it on the charger in the hotel or it's in your other pair of pants."

Jill's eyes sparkled and she smiled. "Yes Doug, answer your phone so the boss doesn't have to call me."

Knowing I'd pay later I said, "Yes, dear."

The End

Other BWL books by Dean Hovey

Doug Fletcher Mysteries
Stolen Past
Washed Away
Dead in the Water
Death in Shifting Sands
Devils Fall
Prairie Menace
Down River
Burnt Evidence
Gator Bait
Grave Survey
Dead End Trail

Pine County Mysteries
Killer Secrets
Deadly Mixture
Fatal Business

Whistling Pines Cozies
Whistling up a Ghost
Whistling Pirates
Whistling Bake-Off
Whistling Artist

2021 Bestselling Author
Dean L. Hovey

Dean Hovey is the award-winning and best-selling author of three mystery series. He uses his scientific background, extensive research, and a number of consultants to add reality and depth to his stories. One reader said his characters are like people he'd like to invite over for a beer and discussion.

Hovey's Fletcher mysteries follow US National Park Service investigators Doug and Jill Fletcher as they solve crimes in a series of parks and monuments, sometimes with a bit of humor and often with their evolving relationship. The Whistling Pines mysteries are humorous cozies set in a northern Minnesota senior residence, following Peter Rogers, the Whistling Pines recreation director, as he stumbles through murder investigations in his small town. The Pine County mystery series follows sheriff's deputies C.J. Jensen, Pam Ryan, and Floyd Swenson as they investigate murders in east-central Minnesota, dealing with small-town crimes, criminals and their own personal dilemmas.

Dean and his wife split their year between northern Minnesota and Arizona.

BWL Publishing

bwlpublishing.ca